Praise

"Zingy and madcap and unexpectedly tender, *The Odds of Getting Even* is full of surprises from start to finish."
—Katie Cotugno, *New York Times* bestselling author of *Meet the Benedettos*

"Witty, charming, and highly romantic, *The Odds of Getting Even* is a delightful romp with a hint of slapstick and the obligatory snake in the grass—I loved every page."
—Abbi Waxman, *USA Today* bestselling author of *The Bookish Life of Nina Hill*

"Equally hysterical and heart-stirring, *The Odds of Getting Even* is a delightful ride through awkward meet-cutes, wild miscommunications, vulnerable secrets, and fist-pumping redemption. . . . An irresistible swoon-fest!"
—Julian Winters, award-winning author of *I Think They Love You*

"My love for Jean and Charlie is infinite. I could swim in the charm and wit and sweet, tender emotion of this book forever. And the humor! Amanda Sellet makes me cackle like no other, and *The Odds of Getting Even* proves once again that she is a wordsmith par excellence."   —Megan Bannen, author of *The Undertaking of Hart and Mercy*

"An entertaining and fast-paced tribute to classic screwball comedy, full of breezy banter, quirky characters, madcap misadventures, and a smile on every page."
—Jacqueline Firkins, author of *Marlowe Banks, Redesigned*

"Sweet and fizzy, like a champagne cocktail—*The Odds of Getting Even* takes misunderstood snake-lover Charlie and jaded-artist Jean on a bouncing adventure through the far corners of America. I had so much fun!"
—Katie Shepard, author of *Sweeten the Deal*

"Sellet's witty voice sparkles in this hilarious romp—seriously, she could teach a master class in the art of misunderstandings gone awry!" —KJ Micciche, author of *The Book Proposal* and *A Storybook Wedding*

"*The Odds of Getting Even* froths with whip-smart, voice-y humor and over-the-top fun. 10/10 snakes agree that this rom-com is hiss-terically funny." —Jen Comfort, author of *What Is Love?*

Praise for *Hate to Fake It to You*

"A perfect beach read." —*Library Journal* (starred review)

"Inspired by the screwball comedies of Hollywood's golden age, this madcap rom-com offers plenty of hijinks. . . . The Hawaiian setting and light-hearted tone may appeal to readers looking for a beachy romance." —*Booklist*

"Amanda Sellet's adult romance debut *Hate to Fake It to You* hit every single comedic note for me. Perfect for fans of Sophie Kinsella." —Alicia Thompson, bestselling author of *Love in the Time of Serial Killers*

"I absolutely LOVE this screwball romantic comedy and cannot wait to read Sellet's next book in the series!" —Sarah Hogle, author of *Just Like Magic*

"A delightfully hilarious read, *Hate to Fake It to You* is the perfect book companion for readers seeking a rom-com with heart and wit." —Lily Chu, author of *The Stand-In*

"Quirky, original, and laugh-out-loud funny . . . To sum it up in three words: WHAT A HOOT!" —Suzanne Park, author of *So We Meet Again*

ALSO BY AMANDA SELLET

Hate to Fake It to You

Belittled Women

By the Book

The ODDS of GETTING EVEN

Amanda Sellet

ST. MARTIN'S
GRIFFIN
NEW YORK

First published in the United States by St. Martin's Griffin, an imprint of St. Martin's Publishing Group

EU Representative: Macmillan Publishers Ireland Ltd, 1st Floor, The Liffey Trust Centre, 117–126 Sheriff Street Upper, Dublin 1, DO1 YC43

www.stmartins.com

Design by Meryl Sussman Levavi

Art: apple © archivector/Shutterstock;
snake silhouette © Oleg7799/Shutterstock;
four aces playing cards © Roman Kybus/Shutterstock;
palm tree © Andy Vinnikov/Shutterstock;
pine tree © imranhridoy/Shutterstock

Library of Congress Cataloging-in-Publication Data

Names: Sellet, Amanda, author.
Title: The odds of getting even / Amanda Sellet.
Description: First edition. | New York : St. Martin's Griffin, 2025.
Identifiers: LCCN 2025006865 | ISBN 9781250906274 (trade paperback) |
    ISBN 9781250906281 (ebook)
Subjects: LCGFT: Romance fiction. | Novels.
Classification: LCC PS3619.E4673 O33 2025 | DDC 813/.6—dc23/eng/20250303
LC record available at https://lccn.loc.gov/2025006865

Our books may be purchased in bulk for specialty retail/wholesale, literacy, corporate/premium, educational, and subscription box use. Please contact MacmillanSpecialMarkets@macmillan.com.

First Edition: 2025

10   9   8   7   6   5   4   3   2   1

For my beloved "little" brothers, who enriched my childhood with their niche interests.

Even when I didn't ask.

Dan, Luke, and Joe, this one's for you! But please don't read past this page.

PART I

In the Garden

Chapter 1

The upside of working the graveyard shift on the concierge desk was that most of the guests were asleep by two in the morning, which meant Jean could do her own thing without anyone breathing down her neck. Unless she was scheduled with Pauline, in which case she was treated to a private concert, because Pauline was physically incapable of not singing along with the soft background music that piped through the lobby's hidden speakers. Even though they were instrumental tracks, and Pauline wasn't known for her sense of melody—or her memory.

"Be the raft in the storm of my heart, na na na na," Pauline warbled, butchering the chorus of an Adriana Asebedo song so popular there were probably babies all over the world who'd absorbed the lyrics into their DNA while being conceived to that tune. She paused to look over Jean's shoulder. "What's that?"

"A logo. For a client." Who was also one of Jean's best friends, but "I'm jazzing up my buddy's food truck menu" sounded less impressive.

Pauline studied the ballpoint figure Jean was doodling on a piece of hotel stationery. "That's pretty good. The little pineapple guy, on the surfboard. You should be an artist or something."

Jean opened her mouth to explain that she already was an artist, thank you very much, but the resort-issue polo she was wearing didn't exactly scream "future Frida Kahlo."

"Yeah." She thought about leaving it at that, but then Pauline would start singing again. "I almost got a job as an illustrator. For a magazine."

"Cartoons and stuff?"

"No." Jean spoke with conviction, although she wasn't totally sure this was true. "Like the front cover."

Pauline frowned. "Isn't that usually a real picture? With a camera?"

"Reality is overrated." Jean scowled at the surfing pineapple, adding a dripping whisk.

The song changed, but before Pauline could join in, the phone rang.

"Dolphin Bay, how can I make your dreams come true?" Pauline half sang into the receiver. The standard greeting landed a little differently at this time of night. Less luxury, more brothel.

Jean set down her pen, swiveling her chair to face her coworker. The other benefit of the late shift was that if something did come up in the middle of the night, it was more likely to be weird. And in Jean's experience, nothing made time fly like an infusion of freakiness.

"I'm very sorry to hear that, sir. Of course we'll send someone right over. It's no trouble at all. Have a great day at Dolphin Bay."

It was a little late for that unless she was talking about tomorrow, but Jean didn't care about the semantics. "What is it this time—a live tiger? Somebody wants to store their pile of raw diamonds in the main safe? Smuggling in a team of acrobats? Pancake emergency?"

"What's a pancake emergency?"

It was typical of Pauline to seize on the least interesting question. "Somebody who wants a big stack of pancakes delivered to their room five minutes ago, still warm."

"Oh. No, nothing like that. Sunset Cottage needs more towels."

Towels! Talk about the beige of problems.

It was a good thing Jean hadn't taken the call. There was no guarantee she would have won the struggle not to comment. *Is that the best you can do, Richie Rich? Extra* towels?

The sad truth was that money couldn't buy flair, Jean reflected as she grabbed a stack of fluffy white bath sheets from the supply room. Hence the swarms of trust funders desperate to carry the same bag or wear identical shoes. If Jean had that kind of cash, she'd go bold. Distinctive. Eyeball-searing. None of this clean-cut, party-line, herd mentality.

There was a slim chance he wanted the towels for something like mopping up a pool of blood. That would be unexpected. But if there was a body to dispose of, surely Sir First World Problems would have asked for a tarp and ropes, or a shovel? Dolphin Bay did advertise itself as a full-service guest experience, especially if you were loaded enough to afford one of the private cottages. The promise was right there in the blandly luxurious, allergic-to-color marketing materials. *Where Dreams Come True: Find Your Paradise at Dolphin Bay, an Exceptional Holiday Experience on Oahu's North Shore.*

It was only a matter of time before someone called the front desk asking for hookers and blow.

Expecting an underpaid stranger to help you clean up a crime scene wasn't that big of a leap from some of the entitled behavior Jean had witnessed at her parents' restaurant, back in the day. Although there was only so far you could push it at a golf course snack bar. *Ooh, you're so daring, making your teenage waitress bring you more maraschino cherries!*

The island breeze shifted the palm fronds overhead, reminding her that she wasn't in Wisconsin anymore. At least Mr. Oops I Took My Bath Towels to the Beach had given her an excuse to stretch her legs. Maybe there was a business opportunity here. A lot of Jean's skills were tough to monetize, but setting up shop as a Doula of Bad Ideas had potential. The voiceover for an imaginary infomercial played in her head:

Do people's eyes glaze over when you tell "funny" stories?
Are you the human equivalent of a pair of pleated khakis?
Is your one life neither wild nor precious?
I can help you shake things up!

Rich people got plenty of ass-kissing. Some of them secretly enjoyed when you gave it to them straight—and not only with top-shelf liquor.

Leaving the main walkway that during the day carried droves of sunburned guests between the hotel's main building and the private beach, she turned down a narrower path. Past the koi pond and a row of two-person loungers Jean never wanted to look at with a black light, then through the trees until a series of slate pavers ended at the porch of a modest two-thousand-dollar-a-night holiday cottage, tailor-made for those who wanted to enjoy the amenities of a big resort without sharing an elevator with ordinary mortals.

There were half a dozen of these "cottages" scattered around the grounds. Jean's coworkers liked to speculate about celebrity guests registering under false names, but she doubted Dolphin Bay was pulling starlets and chart-topping musicians. The young and hot would be hiding out at an eco-resort in Brazil or Vietnam or someone's private Swedish island. Dolphin Bay was a little too old school. This was a place your rich parents could hang. Or *their* parents. Paddleboarding was an option, but people mostly stuck with golf. And no one was going to shame you for ordering a daiquiri instead of some obscure artisanal alcohol tarted up with twelve plant essences and a culturally appropriative name, served by a twenty-three-year-old with a Rip Van Winkle beard.

The Dolphin Bay clientele tended to be well preserved and

tastefully dressed but not exactly tantalizing, because another regrettable fact about money was that it did not automatically turn people sexy. In Jean's experience, rich people often married hotness, first because they could, and second to give their offspring a fighting chance at having hair after thirty. Even then they tended to stick with a very specific "my other car is the *Mayflower*" style of attractiveness. Young billionaires with gleaming abs might be thick on the ground in fiction, but in real life they mostly had the vaguely amphibious look of career politicians.

In other words, the odds of intrigue were not in her favor, even at this time of night.

Jean knocked on the door of Sunset Cottage. "Towel delivery!"

No one answered. There was a puddle on the outdoor table from the recent rain, and she couldn't exactly leave clean towels on the ground, so Jean keyed the door open with her employee badge.

"I have your towels," she said. "I'll just leave them—*oh*."

It turned out Jean was going to see a body this evening, only this one was very much not dead. She'd heard of guests who got their kicks from exposing themselves to staff, but it was clear this guy wasn't turned on by Jean's presence—and not just because she could see the relaxed state of his man parts. It was the yelp of panic that tipped her off. And then the flush that traveled up his chest like a lava flow in reverse as he tripped over his feet, bumbling for something that turned out to be a pair of glasses with heavy black frames.

Only when he had them on did he think to cover himself with both hands.

"Nice snake," Jean said after a silence so thick you could have spread it on toast. Someone had to break the ice. Or maybe not ice since the temperature in the room wasn't exactly frosty. More like warm—and getting hotter by the second.

He looked down at the place where his hands met. "Are you referring to my . . . sexual organ?"

"No, the other one." She circled a hand to indicate the rear view. "Your ink."

As comprehension dawned, he looked profoundly relieved. Go figure, Jean thought, adding that tidbit to her mental sketch of Naked Guest. A guy who doesn't want to discuss his junk.

"I like the color," she added.

He glanced over his shoulder, as if to remind himself what was tattooed on the smooth round cheek. "It's a green snake."

"Uh-huh." Somewhere between chartreuse and olive, Jean would have called it, but not everyone cared about those distinctions.

"That's the name, I mean. *Opheodrys vernalis.* Also known as the smooth green snake. Although some refer to them as grass snakes." He paused, and Jean got the feeling he was wondering whether he'd said too much. She gave him her undivided attention, hoping he could see that she was fully engaged in the snake trivia. That seemed to be the encouragement he needed to venture one more fact. "Green is my favorite color."

"I like it too." She couldn't help letting her eyes wander then, down the long legs and back up again, past the stomach (a classic one-pack that looked delectably squishable) to the hunched shoulders and shaggy dark hair. He looked like someone from a time before gyms were invented. Not big or chiseled but with nice lines. Turn him to stone and he could easily stand in an Italian grotto with a flute in his hand, dingdong on display. Except for the glasses and farmer tan. "I'd ask if you have any other tats, but you know." Jean raised her chin in the direction of his nakedness.

"Oh. Yes. I'm sorry." His black brows drew together behind the Clark Kent frames, shoulders jerking as if he wanted to rub a hand over his face before he remembered why that wasn't a good idea.

It was a remarkably handsome face. Had he not been standing there buck naked, Jean would have spent more time studying the contours of his cheekbones, the well-shaped lips and large, dark-lashed eyes. Without the beginnings of a beard to roughen his appearance, he would almost have been too perfect.

"Let me just—" He broke off, gaze bouncing around the room before he reached for something on the desk to his right, leaving one hand in place like a five-fingered fig leaf. Halfway there he decided to switch hands, briefly flashing Jean as a result, like an amateur magician who can't figure out how to disappear his rabbit.

Panic turned his movements even jerkier. His outflung arm made contact with a glass of water, knocking it onto its side.

"Shoot," he said, biting his lip in dismay as the contents dripped onto the floor.

A polite person would have excused herself to let him get dressed, but Jean had no such scruples. The more he blushed and twitched, the more comfortable she felt. She'd always had a thing for awkward people. Plus, she was curious about this gawky stranger with the butt tattoo and the beautiful face who seemed so ill at ease in his expensive cottage. What turnip truck had he fallen off?

Instead of leaving, she threw a towel at him, hurling it like a Frisbee. "Think fast," she said, as it hit him in the chest.

Rather than using it to cover himself, he crouched and started sopping up the spill. Jean took the opportunity to get another look at the snake coiled across his hindquarters. It was good work: sharp lines, vivid color. She would have asked about the artist but didn't want to fluster him even more, so she chucked another towel at his head.

"Put that on."

More bumbling ensued. Even with her eyes averted, Jean had the impression a scarecrow in roller skates was trying to dress himself with one hand.

"Thank you," he said when he managed to work himself upright, the towel tied around his waist.

She nodded, like it was all part of the job. *You, sir, are but one of the many charmingly flustered nudists I have assisted in the wee hours of the night.*

"So," she said, now that they'd achieved a socially acceptable level of exposed flesh. "What happened?" Jean felt like a coast guard captain who'd just pulled someone from the wreckage of their kayak.

"I was out on the patio." He rubbed his chin and jaw with one hand. (She suspected this was the gesture he'd started to make earlier; it had the look of a habitual motion.) The other hand remained at his hip, anchoring the towel. "It's been a while since I slept indoors."

Jean nodded at him to continue, filing that information away for later.

"And then I got up." He hesitated, another wave of color spreading across his face. "To do something inside."

Her theories, in no particular order: 1. Drugs; 2. Jerking off; 3. The shits. Jean was proud of herself for not asking a hotel guest if he had intestinal issues. And her friends thought she had no filter.

"I got distracted," he continued, and this time she couldn't help herself.

"By what?" She knew in her bones it was going to be something weirder than scrolling Instagram.

"*Journal of Herpetology*?" His voice lifted at the end, turning it into a question.

Bingo, Jean thought. This guy was a gold mine.

"You probably haven't heard of it." The wistful glance he shot her suggested he hoped otherwise.

She tried to let him down gently. "No, but I think I can guess. It's a journal, and it's about herpetology. Am I close?"

"The study of snakes. And other reptiles. If it was just snakes it would be the *Journal of Ophiology*."

Jean nodded as if she'd known that all along. In her defense, the study of STDs was not a completely unreasonable guess. "*Journal of Snakeology* doesn't have the same ring. Or just *SNAKES!* All caps, exclamation point."

"It's a very reputable publication. One of the top scientific publications in the field." Not the kind of place to give itself a funny name, in other words. She liked that he sounded apologetic rather than offended.

"Okay. So you grab your journal. Hot off the presses, a real page-turner, and . . . ?"

"I have an article," he admitted. "I like looking at it."

It took Jean a few seconds to decipher the mumbled bit at the end. "In the *Journal of Herpetology*?"

"Yes. I mean, I'm second author."

"Congratulations." She considered throwing him another towel to celebrate, like a dolphin trainer flinging fish.

The hand holding his makeshift white kilt twisted, drawing Jean's attention to his narrow hips. "It probably seems like a small thing to you."

Me as in the person whose job is delivering towels in the middle of the night? His sense of social hierarchy seemed to be broken. "No, I totally get it. My best friend is always trying to get articles published, so I know it's a big deal to have a byline."

"What's her field?"

Rather than selling her roommate down the river by admitting that Libby's writing career was still in its fledgling state (in the barely hatched sense), Jean kept it broad. "Human psychology."

"Very competitive."

"No kidding. I keep telling her to look for back doors. You have to be willing to do whatever it takes to make a space for yourself. If that's what you really want."

He nodded, but it looked a little sad.

"Can I see it?" she asked, to distract him from whatever thoughts were bringing him down. "The article."

It seemed like an unnecessary clarification, considering she'd already gotten a good look at everything else, but a lot of things sounded dirty under the right circumstances. Late at night, in a luxury vacation cottage, with a handsome man wearing only a towel, for example. And a king-size bed clearly visible through the doorway behind him.

He glanced that way now, and Jean wondered if he was about to bust out some previously unseen moves. She tried to imagine him in seduction mode, blushing as he stammered out a *hey, girl,* or *come here often?*

"Do you really want to?" he asked, in a confidential murmur that sent a surprising shiver up her spine. Nerd flirting for the win. Maybe shyness was her kink.

Coming back into the moment, Jean realized he was looking not at the bed but the table beside it—and more specifically, the *Journal of Slithery Things.*

"I wouldn't have asked if I didn't." If they'd been acquainted for more than five minutes, he would know that about her, but Jean didn't mind giving him the CliffsNotes version of her personality.

Another quick glance at the bedroom and then back at Jean. "It might be a little boring."

"You haven't bored me yet."

"Really?" He looked like she'd given him a dozen roses. "That's nice of you to say."

"Nah, I'm not a sweet talker. I'll pretty much always either straight up tell you the truth or go so far rogue that reality is a distant planet." She meant it to be reassuring, like pointing out a guardrail, but he looked a little spooked. "Option A in this case," Jean said, before quickly changing the subject. "Speaking of your article, does it have illustrations? I did some technical drawing for a dissertation once, and I'm thinking snakes must be a lot easier to draw than horseshoe crabs." She paused, considering her audience. "No offense to snakes. I'm sure they're very complex."

"Oh, they are." It looked like he had plenty more to say, but he stopped himself cold. Jean wondered who had taught him not to go off on his pet subject, as if there was something wrong with having unusual passions. The odder the better, as far as she was concerned. There were few things more disappointing than people who oozed through life with no intriguing quirks. No thank you, sheeple.

"I suppose I'd know more about them . . . if I'd read your article." She let that sink in, softening him up. "Must be pretty cool to see your name in print. It's probably in the table of contents and everything."

It was an obvious cue to introduce himself, but it flew right over his head. He was in his feelings again, a sideways S taking shape between those inky brows as he studied the floor. He raised his eyes to her face, full of earnest interest. "What's *your* name?"

"Jean. As in, a pair of, but singular." She gestured at her lower body, though she was wearing the regulation white shorts, not jeans. "I could tell you it was short for Eugenia but then I'd have to kill you. Which seems like an unfortunate end to a promising friendship."

"Oh." He blushed at the last word, looking equal parts pleased and startled. "I'll call you Jean then."

"I have a name tag, but I never remember to put it on." Leaning toward him, she lowered her voice. "Kind of like you with pants."

More jaw rubbing, though it couldn't hide the redness of his cheeks. Jean took a step toward the bedroom, sensing he needed a push. Otherwise, he might still be dithering when the sun came up.

"Where were we? You came inside, you started reading, and . . . ?"

"It rained. A lot. We never get rain like that where I'm from."

"Death Valley?"

"No, though I've always wanted to go. They have sidewinders!"

"I . . . did not know that." She waited for him to go on, but he seemed to have forgotten the original question. It was hard to tell whether he was easily distracted or didn't like talking about himself. "So where are you from?"

He ducked his head. "Um, South Dakota."

"Deadwood?"

"Not far from there. Do you know Bear Butte?"

"I do now." She gave his towel a significant look.

"Oh, well. It's not that type of bare. More of the claws and teeth kind." He cleared his throat, glancing at her from under lashes so thick they were like windshield wipers inside his glasses. "Usually people ask about Mount Rushmore."

"I'm unique."

"Yes," he agreed, a smile breaking free.

"Don't try to butter me up, Dakota. What happened with the rain? Did you leave all your clothes outside? Or is this a lifestyle choice?" She gestured at his bare torso. He placed his free hand there, covering a few inches of skin and hair between his pecs.

"I left the sliding glass doors open. The rain came flooding in. There was so much of it." He looked troubled at the memory. "I tried to clean it up, but the floor is still pretty soggy."

Somewhere along the line he seemed to have missed Rich People 101. They tended to be quick on the trigger when it came to blaming the resort for the most minor of inconveniences, even if it was their own fault. He could have demanded a new room or a cleanup crew or a spa gift certificate for his troubles instead of a few measly towels.

She briefly entertained the idea that he was not, in fact, a paying guest. But if he was a squatter who'd broken into one of their most exclusive lodgings, it seemed unlikely he'd call the front desk with a request.

"It took all the towels I had to wipe up the floor, and then I tried to wring them out so I could use them again, since everything was still damp, but it didn't really work. And then I was sweating from all the running back and forth, so I decided to take a shower."

Jean waggled her brows. "Nice."

"Oh." He bit his lip, obviously dismayed. "I didn't mean to sound . . . suggestive." As if mentioning a shower was more indiscreet than flashing her.

"Then you shouldn't have talked about cleaning. There's a whole genre of men-doing-chores erotica. The dishwashing ones are my favorite."

"I had no idea." He blinked at Jean as if she'd thrown his whole world out of focus.

"That's because I just made it up. But it could be true. Back to the shower." She mimed scrubbing herself, mostly to see him blush again.

"I forgot there weren't any towels to dry off with afterward."

"So there you were, naked and dripping?" she prompted.

"I tried using a kitchen towel, but it's not really the same. Drying off a plate and drying off . . . you know."

"Human flesh?"

"Er, yes. And it was very humid, so it felt like the air needed its own towel. I hated to bother anyone, but I didn't want to get the furniture wet, and I wasn't sure how long I'd have to stand up before I stopped being damp, so I called the number on the phone and then you came." He paused, wincing a little. "I didn't expect anyone to get here so quickly."

"I'm known for my land speed. In the water, not so much. I'm originally from the mainland too. Though I've been here long enough to get used to the weather."

"How did you—" He broke off, shaking his head. "I'm keeping you from your work. Sorry. And I'm also sorry for, ah, you know—"

"The anatomy lesson?"

He nodded, flushing again. Jean watched him swipe a hand across his forehead with a quick jerk, like she might not notice if he was fast enough.

"Sweating again?" she asked, checking the parts of him she could see for evidence. There was some definite dewiness at the base of his throat.

"Sorry. I'm a little nervous."

"You're not afraid of me, are you?" Jean made her eyes big and innocent, letting her lips take on just a hint of a pout, like a ceramic figurine at the Hallmark store: Little Girl Who Dropped Her Ice Cream.

"No," he said, after thinking about it for a few seconds. "I suppose I'm not. Afraid, that is." The discovery seemed to surprise him. He stood a little straighter, shoving his glasses back up the bridge of his nose. "You're the first person I've talked to today," he confided. "Or yesterday."

"On purpose?"

"Sort of. I don't mind being alone. It's easier than a crowd."

"You're not like the boy in the bubble or something? Or on a silent, naked retreat?"

"Do you get many of those?"

"You would've been my first." She added a wink because the innuendo amused her. Had she crossed the line between joking and coming on to someone? Maybe, but Jean preferred to operate on instinct, and right now she was having fun. That was her definition of a green light. Her gaze landed on the neat rows of cards spread across the duvet. "You play?"

He nodded. "Solitaire, mostly."

Talk about a cry for help. "When are you checking out?"

"Why?" Of all the invasive questions she'd asked since barging into his space, that was the one that seemed to put his back up.

"Maybe I should come back. To keep you from going full Wolf Boy."

"Really? That's—I mean, I wouldn't want to impose—"

Jean held up a hand before he could stammer himself into a knot. "Don't get any funny ideas. I'm not going to touch your snake."

"I don't have any snakes with me, Jean." His tone was deadly serious. "It's illegal to bring them into Hawaii. They would decimate the bird population. I'm sure you know what happened in Guam—oh." Something in her expression must have clued him in. "You weren't talking about that kind of snake."

She shook her head. "But I wouldn't mind hearing more. Since you're clearly an expert."

"I don't know about *that*. I don't even have a PhD." If he'd been wearing something more substantial than a towel, he would undoubtedly have stuck his hands in his pockets and rocked back on his heels.

"If you say so." Jean set the remaining towels on the teak credenza that served no purpose other than filling half the wall and turned to go. "Maybe I'll teach you a real game." She tipped her head at his abandoned cards. "If you're still here."

"Jean," he said, as she started for the door. "You won't tell anyone, will you?"

"That you play naked solitaire?"

He shook his head. "That I'm staying here."

That dialed her interest up several notches. "Secrets are my favorite food group." Also, it would be hard to expose the presence of someone whose name she still didn't know, though she suspected it wouldn't take much to tease the information out of him. For now, she preferred to maintain the air of mystery, so she mimed locking her lips and throwing away the key.

"Jean?" he said again, when she was at the door.

She glanced over her shoulder, watching him scramble for an excuse to keep her there a little longer.

"Thanks for the towels."

"My pleasure," she replied, with extra sauciness.

"It was nice meeting you," he mumbled, blushing some more. Talk about an open book.

"It was, wasn't it?"

Snake Boy bit his lower lip, fighting a smile. "So tomorrow, maybe?" He looked around the living room with a frown. "I should straighten up."

Jean pictured him fussing with a feather duster, then arranging bowls of mixed nuts—preferably still in the towel. It was an undeniably appealing image, but she didn't want to make it too easy on him.

His eyes locked on her as she took several slow steps in his direction. She watched his nostrils flare, pretty sure he was sneaking a hit of her perfume.

"No promises, Mr. Clean. I might get a better offer. Maybe there's an even more naked spider scientist behind one of these doors."

"Arachnologist," he murmured, frowning. Jean thought he must be jealous of his imaginary rival, until he went on. "How could someone be more naked? Oh!" Letting go of the towel, he scraped his hair back from his forehead. "If they were bald."

Jean dragged her eyes from the hip bones exposed by his sagging towel, nodding as if she'd had the exact same thought. Of course a bald spiderologist would be even more nude. That was just logic.

"If you do come back," he started to say, before breaking off.

She raised an eyebrow.

"I'll be here." He pressed his lips together as though afraid of what might slip out. "That's all."

Another step brought her within touching range. He tensed as she raised a hand, slowly drawing a finger over the left side of his chest, one short line bisected by another in the opposite direction. The pounding under his skin suggested she'd found the right spot, the rapid beat mirroring the spike in her pulse at the moment of contact.

"You forgot to cross your heart." Spinning on her heel, Jean left him to his thoughts. She had a hunch a lot of them would be about her.

That and snakes, obviously.

"The Lost Weekend"

by ADRIANA ASEBEDO

Like salt to the sea
You came for me
Damp skin and tangled sheets
My silent storm
Bring me to my knees

"The Lost Weekend"

PAULINE'S VERSION

Salty salty cheese
Don't get on the sheets
It's getting warm
When you bring the storm
I'm begging for your knees—Ooh yeah

Chapter 2

Disaster.

That's what Charlie expected when he made the reckless decision not to board his connecting flight. What was he thinking, missing a plane on purpose? The answer was that he wasn't, beyond a low chorus of *uh-oh uh-oh uh-oh* that he managed to drown out long enough to make his way here. His parents used to talk about this place, from an anniversary trip they took when he was a kid. The illogical part of his brain hoped the sentimental memories might soften their disappointment when they realized he wasn't coming home.

Yet.

Of course he'd have to go back. Eventually. This was more of a blip. Another in the long line of normal, expected things Charlie hadn't quite been able to get right.

But if running away was such a bad idea, an inner voice argued, would he have found a free taxi the second he stepped outside the terminal? Or managed to book a private cottage online, no human interaction necessary? And would a beautiful whirlwind of a girl have knocked on his door tonight? Surely those were signs from the universe saying, *walk this way!*

Charlie pushed away from the wall he was leaning against, in case she changed her mind and came back. (A person could hope.) He was still reeling from the impact of seeing her in focus for the first time. The shining dark hair and snapping eyes. Her little rosebud of a mouth, always in motion except when she smiled at him and everything stopped. How one person could fill an entire cottage with her presence.

He shook his hands out as he wandered into the living room, nerve endings still tingling with residual Jean energy. She was his complete opposite: quick and confident, instead of clumsy and one step behind. Not to mention the prettiness. Was this what it felt like to be an echidna, sensing electric currents as they passed over your skin? The feeling was so strong he could almost *hear* the buzzing.

The noise stopped for a few seconds before starting again, an insistent hum that . . . seemed to be coming from his phone.

Ah. Charlie had known this moment was inevitable, but he wouldn't have minded a little more time to think about Jean before the real world came calling.

He took a deep breath before answering. "Hello, Mugsy." There. That sounded rational and calm. Unfortunately, his even tone failed to kick things off on a positive note. There was a groan of exasperation so loud he had to hold the phone away from his face.

"Don't you 'Hello, Mugsy' me! What the hell is going on? Why aren't you answering your phone?"

Charlie could picture his oldest friend pacing around her workroom, trying to stomp out her frustration like a human Godzilla. "There was someone at the door. Well, not at the door exactly but *near* it," he started to explain, but Mugsy's sharp intake of breath cut him off.

"You didn't open it, did you?"

"It's fine, Mugsy."

"None of this is fine! I'm losing my chill."

"Yes, I can hear that—"

"Your parents are freaking out!"

Charlie didn't have an immediate answer for that one. He cleared his throat. "She was very nice."

"*She?* She who?"

"The person at the door." It was a definite role reversal, Charlie needing to explain things to Mugsy. She really was rattled. He felt a pang of guilt, but it wasn't strong enough to make him regret his choice. "It was because I needed towels."

There was a long silence, during which he suspected Mugsy was counting to ten. "What?"

"That's why she was here. Because of the towels. It's a long story," he added, guessing Mugsy would be less receptive to the details than Jean.

"Charlie."

He winced. Only Mugsy could infuse his name with that exact blend of care and worry. It was almost like hearing her say, *I don't think you can handle this.* Charlie braced for her to tell him he was making a mistake. Usually this was the point where he would cave and ask her what she thought he should do, but this time, he stayed quiet. It would be hard to explain that he needed to stay in case Jean came back. It was practically a date.

Hopefully.

The pause stretched between them, until finally Mugsy sighed. "I don't know how long I can cover for you."

The wave of relief was so strong his knees gave out, sending him crashing onto the edge of the mattress. "Please, Mugsy. I'll take anything I can get."

I Like Snakes

by CHARLIE, AGE 8

Snakes are very smooth. They move fast.
Snakes are good at hiding.
They like to be left alone.

Chapter 3

Jean didn't usually bother making excuses to herself. Most choices boiled down to "because I wanted to." You could dress it up in noble intentions, but that was the underlying truth.

And yet she found herself running through a list of reasons it made sense to go back to Sunset Cottage when her shift ended the next night:

Loneliness was a documented social problem, so it was basically a mission of mercy.

Her lucky deck of cards was right there, in her bag.

Maybe he'd let her draw him like one of her French girls, and live models were hard to come by.

She was actually showing restraint by waiting this long, considering how close she'd come to turning around last night and finishing what they'd started.

Not that this was a booty call, necessarily. There was plenty of fun to be had with her naked snakeologist beyond the physical. It was also true that there was such a thing as being too honest with yourself. You had to leave room for surprises, even within the confines of your own brain.

Bottom line: If she waited too long, he might be gone. If he was even still here, Jean told herself as she raised a hand to knock.

The sound of running footsteps was followed by a soft thud of impact that rattled the door before it cracked open. Snake Boy lit up at the sight of her, like Jean was the Easter Bunny driving an ice cream truck that was also full of puppies.

"You came back." He glanced behind her, squinting into the darkness on either side of the path, before returning his attention to Jean with another shy grin.

"I forgot to pick up your wet towels."

"Oh—"

"That was a joke, Dakota." She kicked off her shoes before slipping past him.

"I thought you might forget," he said, closing the door behind her.

"Mind like a steel trap." She held up the small blue box. "I brought cards. Are you ready for some poker?"

"Oh! I . . . um." Frowning slightly, he glanced over his shoulder. "Do you mind waiting here a second?"

With a shrug, she settled onto the couch as he hustled into the bedroom and shut the door. What was he hiding in there? Besides his article in *Snakearama*. Jean didn't have long to wonder. The door flew open again a moment later and he zoomed into the kitchen before detouring back to the living room to set a sloshing glass of water on the coffee table in front of Jean.

"Would you like anything else?" he asked, a little breathless. "I have granola bars."

Jean indicated the bag she'd set on the floor. "I brought snacks."

"That was nice of you." He leaned against the arm of the couch, smiling as if she'd wheeled in a three-tiered dessert cart instead of hitting the vending machines in the staff lounge. They stayed like that until he suddenly jerked upright, remembering his secret mission.

"I'll be just a minute." He held up a finger before dashing into his bedroom.

So far Jean gave him top marks for entertainment, and they hadn't even started playing cards.

The muffled noise of drawers opening and closing, a heavy object being dragged across the floor, and hopping on one leg ensued, followed by a loud thud and some G-rated cursing. Did he have a pogo stick, or was there a pony on the loose?

"Everything okay in there?" Jean called.

"Almost done," he assured her, sounding winded.

She sipped her room-temperature water, enjoying a pleasant sense of anticipation. Coming back here had definitely been the right call.

"Okay," he panted, throwing the door open. "I'm ready."

It took a few seconds to process what she was seeing. "Is it opposite day?"

"Why do you say that?" He looked down at his newly bulked-up torso.

"Because you went from zero to dressing like a sixty-year-old man." She frowned at the rain poncho he'd draped over himself like a tent. It couldn't fully conceal the layers of padding beneath. Jean thought there might be a sport coat under that cardigan, and she spotted the collars of at least three different shirts. It looked like a suitcase worth of clothes. "Did you catch a cold from running around naked, Dakota?"

He tugged at one of his shirttails. "It's Charlie, actually."

"Okay, Dakota Charlie." She turned around, trying to decide where to set up. The bed looked comfortable, but even Jean recognized that as a bad idea, so she slid onto the carpet. "What's the story? With this look you're rocking. It's giving 'I didn't want to check any bags.'"

It took him a few attempts to fold his heavily padded legs, but eventually he managed to join her on the floor. "Just trying to even the odds."

"I hate to tell you this, but there are no weight classes in poker." She paused to give him a flirty glance. "Unless you want to throw in a wrestling component. Greco-Roman poker could be a thing."

His face flushed, though this time it might have been from the sauna effect of wearing so many outfits at once. "I know you're going to be really good."

Jean put a hand to her cheek, pretending to be scandalized. "Are you getting fresh with me, Charlie?"

"At poker," he said, blushing harder. "I'll probably have to take off everything and I didn't want the game to be over too soon."

Oh. He thought they were playing *strip* poker. Jean wanted to tease him, but one look at his face—slow-roasting atop his prison of many garments—told her that a) he was used to losing and b) he'd taken a lot of crap for his lack of gamesmanship.

"Good thinking," she said, shuffling the deck. "Okay if we use my cards?"

"Sure."

"*Bzzz.*" Jean made a game-show-buzzer sound effect. "Never let someone else choose the deck. There are scammers everywhere."

Wide-eyed, he started to get up. "I'll go get mine."

She put a hand on his knee to stop him. "It's okay. You can trust me—at least with cards. Beyond that, you're taking your chances."

"Oh." He laughed at himself. "I thought maybe it was a test."

"Call it your first lesson. The second is that I'm an exception to most rules. Now cut."

She tried to go easy on him, even though it went against her instincts. Jean had never thrown a game of cards in her life. Or anything else that could be gamified; once you made it a competition, she was all in. In this case, she also felt strongly that he needed to get out of those clothes before he overheated, so there was a humanitarian aspect to consider. Getting to see more of his skin as he gradually peeled away the layers was a bonus factor. Not just for ogling purposes, but because she enjoyed watching him relax as the barrier of too much clothing eroded. Divesting him of the final grandpa-style undershirt had been a favor to both of them. Probably she should finish the job and take it outside for burning later.

"Sorry I'm not better at this." He looked down at his stomach, brushing a few crumbs out of the light dusting of hair between his belly button and the waistband of his bathing suit.

Jean suspected he had at least one pair of underwear hidden beneath the trunks, which couldn't be comfortable. The trick was getting him to strip without crushing his spirit.

"You're a work in progress," she said. "Which is my favorite kind." That wasn't blowing smoke. Jean had always loved the exploratory phase of making art—letting instinct and imagination drive the bus.

He seemed pretty cheerful despite the whupping she'd administered, shaking his head in amazement every time she won another hand. Her snake guy had a childlike capacity for delight. Jean was thinking about trotting out her supply of knock-knock jokes next.

"You're so talented," he said as he set down his lackluster hand, folding yet again.

"Oh yeah?" She gathered the cards and started shuffling without looking, fancying it up a little to impress him. This had the advantage of allowing her to watch him shimmy out of those shorts. More like three pairs of underwear, Jean guesstimated now that she could see the outermost layer.

He nodded, settling back to a cross-legged position before thinking better of it and bending his knees in front of him. His eyes were glued to her hands, hypnotized by the rapid movements.

"Don't hold back, Doc." She knocked her knee against his thigh.

"Not a doctor yet." His smile dimmed. "I'm not like you."

"I am also not a doctor," Jean pointed out. "Though I have been known to role-play." Even when she wasn't trying to flirt, he kept teeing up opportunities no reasonable person could resist.

"You have incredible fine motor skills." He twirled his fingers, probably imitating her rapid-fire card shuffling, though it looked more like he was trying to solve an invisible Rubik's cube.

If that's what he'd noticed about her, it was time to up her game. She slapped the deck face down on the table. "Let's try something else."

"You won't get in trouble with your work?"

"What are you talking about?" She gave him her patented "sincere" look, widening her eyes and pursing her lips like a pinup. "This *is* work. I'm your personal hospitality consultant. It's part of the service we provide. Your pleasure is our privilege." The eyebrow waggle was unnecessary, but enjoyable. Predictably, he blushed.

Jumping to her feet, Jean hurried into the kitchen as if this were her luxury bungalow, rejecting various condiments before grabbing the pepper grinder and carrying it back to the coffee table, where she set it on its side. Poking one end, she sent it into a wobbling spin.

"What game is this?"

"You've never played spin the bottle?"

He shook his head. "I guess I didn't get invited to the right parties."

"Imagine truth or dare, only it's all dares. Your secrets are safe."

Charlie exhaled in relief. An amateur would have chosen that moment to press for information, but Jean knew when to use a nail file instead of a sledgehammer.

"We'll choose our own dares, so you can stay in your comfort zone." Boundaries had never been Jean's strong suit, either on the "noticing" or "respecting" side of the equation, so this seemed like a necessary precaution. "I'll go first."

The pepper grinder rattled to a stop pointing slightly more toward Jean. "I challenge myself to walk across the room with this magazine on my head."

After she failed to keep the glossy resort guide from hitting the floor, Charlie attempted to stand on one leg for a minute while Jean timed him.

"Nice try, Karate Kid."

They went back and forth, risking nothing spicier than downing a handful of wasabi peas, before Jean casually raised the stakes.

"I challenge myself to take off my shirt."

"Jean." He put a hand on her arm to stop her. "This isn't really part of your job, is it?"

Oh dear. He was the easiest mark she'd ever met, but in a strange way, his innocence was so complete it almost felt like a protective shield. Who would take advantage of someone so pure? Teasing didn't count; she suspected he needed more of that.

"I clocked out at ten, Captain Underpants." She smiled at his gusty exhale. It was as if she'd told him (and everyone else in Whoville) that Christmas wasn't canceled after all.

He tracked the movement of her hands as she raised the hem of her polo a couple of inches and then lowered it again, faking him out a few times before ripping it off in one quick motion and tossing it onto the sofa.

It was a fluke of the laundry cycle that she happened to be wearing her best bra, black and lacy with a little bow between the cups. Or so Jean chose to believe, even though there'd been another clean one in the drawer, a dingy cotton number. But that reveal wouldn't have left him looking like he'd been tased.

"Your turn." She nodded at the pepper grinder.

He seemed to have forgotten the game, along with basic functions such as breathing and the use of his arms, because when he finally spun the "bottle," it skidded across the table before thumping to the floor.

"Um," he said, without bothering to verify that it was pointing at him, "I challenge myself to recite a poem."

That was . . . unexpected.

Gripping the edge of the table with both hands, he closed his eyes before diving in. "Two paths diverged in a snowy wood and I, um, took the path less traveled by?"

It came out in a rush of overlapping syllables, his voice rising at the end as if he was asking instead of telling. "Those probably aren't the right words, but I hate public speaking more than anything."

"That was very brave." *And you are painfully adorable.* Jean kept that thought to herself, suppressing the urge to pinch his cheeks. Or dig her hands into his rumpled hair and kiss him senseless. One of those.

But she couldn't resist reaching past him to get to the pepper grinder, enjoying his sharp intake of breath as her side brushed his front, skin against skin. When the bottle spun to a stop facing her, Jean pretended to think it over, tapping her chin with one finger, even though she knew exactly what she wanted to do.

"I challenge myself," she said, slowly turning to face him, "to kiss you."

Rising to her knees, she started to edge toward him, stopping when he placed a hand on her bare shoulder. It rested there an instant before he jerked away as if stung.

"Jean." He pushed his glasses up his nose, giving her a better view of his solemn expression. "You don't have to do that. If you don't want to."

She leaned closer so she could whisper in his ear. "It was my idea."

"Good point."

Jean sat back. "Unless you'd rather I didn't?"

"No, no. Be my guest." He took off his glasses, waving a hand like he was gesturing her to precede him through a revolving door. "I'd hate to be a bad sport."

They grinned at each other, small and fleeting in his case, but Jean still felt the trace of it as she pressed her lips against his.

It was a good mouth, smooth and warm and welcoming. She took her time exploring, keeping it lips only. For now. When she pulled away, his eyes stayed closed, giving her a chance to study the planes of his face at close range, the inky hair and pale hollows of his cheekbones and jaw. "Heartbreaker" was the word that came to mind—like an old-time movie star.

He blinked at her, slowly resurfacing. "I think that might have been more than one."

Jean tapped her lower lip with the pad of her index finger. "Do I get a penalty? Maybe I should go again."

"That would be cheating. It's my turn now."

As it turned out, he wasn't only talking about spinning the bottle. He leaned forward with his eyes closed, pressing the slowest, sweetest sigh of a kiss to her lips, leaving Jean no choice but to up the ante by daring herself to climb onto his lap.

"Comfortable?" he asked, when she finished wiggling herself into place, using his shoulders as handholds.

"Very." She tightened her legs around his waist, watching his breath stutter as she rocked her hips. "What's your move, cowboy?"

His eyes tracked down her body to the lacy triangles of her bra. "I . . ."

"Go for it," she told him when he trailed off. "It's easier than poetry. And it's practically see-through anyway."

"That's true." He swallowed. "You're good at logic too."

"I like to think so." Despite the fact that no one else in her life appreciated Jean's problem-solving skills.

His hands moved from her waist to the bottom of her bra, fingers brushing the clasp in back.

"I challenge myself to do this," he said in a rush, undoing the strap and peeling it off. He started to fold it, but Jean yanked it out of his hand and threw it against the far wall.

At first, he could only blink, eyes wide and fixed on a point below her chin. "So pretty," he finally whispered.

"Are you talking about my boobs?" Jean glanced down, in case they'd gotten a glow-up without her noticing.

"And this," he said, tracing a finger along the dark edges of the tattoo she'd designed for herself, climbing up her bicep and around the curve of her shoulder until it almost touched her collarbone. "What kind of flowers are these?"

"Plumeria. They have the most incredible scent."

He bent to press his nose to her upper arm. "It makes me dizzy how good you smell."

She thought about letting him believe that was her natural fragrance but didn't want him to get the wrong idea. "That's gardenia. It's my perfume."

"It's the best smell I ever smelled."

"Better than baking bread?"

"Mmm." Charlie rubbed his face along her arm. "Or fresh-cut grass. And . . . fruit." He trailed off like he couldn't remember the names of any specific varieties just then.

"Strawberry?" Jean suggested, thinking he might be looking at her chest.

"Peaches." His voice was thick, like she'd drugged him. "And cream."

"You still with me, Dakota?"

He breathed a noise of assent against the inside of her elbow. "I like the birds too."

"Ravens. They remind me of me."

"Because of your shiny black hair, or being so smart?"

"Let's go with that." Although she would have said cunning, and occasionally obnoxious. His version sounded better.

You really like me, don't you, Charlie? She kept the words on the inside, not wanting to freak either of them out.

Jean wasn't a stranger to making a strong first impression. People might be dazzled initially (or possibly shocked), but the shine wore off once they realized she wasn't interested in being their party monkey—wacky fun, on command!—or watering herself down to be more socially acceptable. It was different with Charlie. His admiration felt too sincere to second-guess. She was still processing the compliment when he wrapped his arms around her ribs and yanked her against him, chest to chest. His face pressed to the side of her neck.

"You feel incredible too," he said on a ragged inhale.

Jean didn't answer right away, due in part to how tightly he was squeezing her, but also because she had not seen the hug coming. "You didn't spin for that," she said, to cover her surprise.

"Hugs are free." He gave her another squeeze before loosening his grip slightly. "Did you know a python can feel the heartbeat of its prey as it constricts?"

"I did not."

"They tighten their coils every time they breathe out, until the blood can't move around anymore."

"Just to be clear, that's not your endgame?"

His laugh rumbled against her stomach. "I promise not to constrict you to death." He ran a hand up her back, fingers spanning the space between her shoulder blades, and then down her side. The pressure was right on the line between ticklish and not. "I can't stop touching you."

"Do your worst." She licked the hollow of his throat, hoping it would give him ideas.

"Did you know they can smell with their tongues?"

"Snakes?" Jean didn't really need to ask, but it was part of the fun of being with him. *Here we are, talking about reptiles. As one does.*

"They use them to pick up odor particles and deposit them in there." He pointed at the roof of his mouth. "They have a special organ."

That's what she said. Jean didn't crack the joke, because she didn't want Charlie to think she was laughing at him.

"I have a theory." She paused to make sure she had his full attention. "About why you're here."

He stiffened beneath her, and not in the interesting way; he'd been in that state since Jean took off her shirt.

"Don't worry. I'm not asking you to confirm or deny. This is about my powers of deduction. Okay?"

His nod was reluctant.

"So you're a scientist, right? One of those orciologists?"

"O*phi*ologist."

"I guess the other one is probably killer whales."

Charlie frowned. "I'm not sure—"

"The point remains," Jean interrupted. "You're a sexy science guy."

"Well now, I don't know about that," he started to quibble, until she shushed him with a finger to his lips.

"A scientist who studies snakes—and yet Hawaii doesn't have snakes." She wiggled back and forth, torturing them both. Maybe she had a future in witness interrogation. "Where was I?"

"Snakes," he supplied, a little breathless.

"Right. I knew that. My hunch is that you're on the way back from somewhere. Possibly Asia."

"They have lots of snakes," he agreed, like he was considering it alongside her. "Especially Indonesia. Komodo dragons too."

"But do they have Caramello Koalas? Because I saw a pile of wrappers in your kitchen." Her first thought had been that a mess like that in her apartment would have been a summoning circle for bugs, but the resort was vigilant about pest control. Jean's second observation was that her snaky friend had recently been in Australia.

He started to nod, but she grabbed his chin to keep it still.

"On the other hand, you don't seem like a resort person. I mean that as a compliment. So that tells me you're not here on vacation. Am I getting warmer?" She rocked forward on his lap, provoking a strangled gasp of agreement.

"Are you ready to hear my brilliant conclusion?"

"*Yes*," he sighed, hands tightening at her waist.

She tweaked his nipple to make sure he was listening. "Witness protection. That's what I think is going on."

"Um," he said, which could be interpreted a lot of different ways.

"That's why you're hiding out. Charlie probably isn't even your real name." Of course she'd checked the booking system as soon as she got back to the desk last night, but while Adams was a reasonably normal last name, she really didn't think her guy was a Samuel, much less a Samuel Adams. He might as well have registered as Bud Light. Then again, not everyone had Jean's knack for subterfuge.

"I'm thinking you saw something deep in the jungle," she continued. "Jewel mine, smugglers, a ruined temple with a doomsday cult practicing their weird death rituals—no!" This time she pressed her whole hand to his mouth. "Don't say a word.

It's better if I don't know. I like to think I'm the kind of person who could resist being tortured, but how can I be sure until they bring out the pliers, you know?"

He made a noise behind closed lips.

"You can answer that one," she said, removing her hand.

"Like a snake pit. Except I guess that's more execution than torture."

Jean bracketed his skull with her hands, thinking, *I might keep you*. She let her forehead come to rest against his, in the gentlest possible headbutt, before pulling away again. "I have experience getting caught up in circumstances beyond my control, so I can empathize. You set out with one agenda and the next thing you know, you're in the shit." She booped him on the nose. "How are you holding up?"

"Uh."

"That wasn't a dick joke. You can talk to me about your feelings. I'm a lot deeper than I look." Jean paused. "That was also not an innuendo."

"Well, I can't really complain about the current circumstances." He looked down to hide his grin.

Jean kissed him again, because she wanted to, and it was easier than admitting how strongly she agreed. "Do you know what?"

He shook his head.

She whispered the words against his lips, like a seductive promise. "I challenge myself to race you to the bed."

By the time he caught on, Jean was up and running. She had the advantage of agility, but once he got off the ground, Charlie's long stride quickly closed the gap. They collided in the doorway. Jean used the momentum to bounce herself at the bed, landing a millisecond before he crashed into her again, both of them face-planting on the mattress.

She didn't wait to catch her breath. Wedging her shoulder under his side, Jean tipped him onto his back, pinning him to the mattress before he returned the favor, cradling the back of her head with his hand as if she were made of blown glass.

They were laughing but also going all out, which was one of Jean's favorite moods. Charlie tickled her, she bit him on the shoulder. When Jean went for the wedgie, the double layer of underwear proved to be an insurmountable obstacle.

Defeated, she let him settle on top of her, bracing his weight on his elbows. "Do you surrender?" he asked, breathing hard.

Jean wriggled a little, careful not to dislodge him. "I win, actually."

"How do you figure?"

"Maybe this is what I wanted all along."

He looked down at the place where their bodies met. From the waist up, they were naked, in his bed. It didn't take a genius (as she suspected he was) to see the possibilities.

"Let's call it a draw." A hint of mischief softened the line of his mouth.

It was only a spark of devilishness, but Jean felt confident she could coax it into flame, given enough time. "Can I see it now?" she asked, tracing the sharp line of his jaw with her fingertip.

His glasses were still in the living room, giving her an unobstructed view of his glossy black brows drawing together in confusion. "My article?"

"Your snake."

"You mean the tattoo?"

"That too." Jean slid her hand down his back, working her fingers under the elastic of his waistbands (both of them) until she could squeeze the delicious curve that marked the general vicinity of his inked-on snake.

He swallowed. "If you want."

And yet he seemed in no hurry to move while she had her hand in his pants. Yanking it free, she smacked his backside.

"Get along, little doggie." She was pretty sure that was how they talked where he was from. Jangling through the tumbleweeds in their spurs and big hats.

He rolled onto his side with an abashed expression, struggling to pull down both pairs at once. "I'm not very good at this," he apologized, locked in battle with his own knee.

"It's hard to do a quality striptease without the music," Jean sympathized. "Do you want me to hum for you, Houdini?"

Her a cappella bump-and-grind soundtrack wasn't technically helpful, since it made him laugh so hard he had to stop and catch his breath, but eventually he untangled his ankles and kicked free of his underwear. And since he looked a lot less self-conscious now that they'd taken a time-out for comedy, Jean counted that as a win.

"My turn." She gave him a sultry look while unzipping her shorts. Holding eye contact, she rose to her knees and started to push them down, only to stage a pratfall and sprawl across him. "A little help?"

Charlie scrambled to comply, pulling her out of the shorts like they were on fire. He paused with his thumb hooked under the lacy elastic at her hip, meeting her eyes.

"These too?"

"Don't you want to see my butt tattoo?"

"You have one?"

She shook her head. "It's just a ploy to get me naked."

"Am I crushing you?" he asked, when at last he was stretched out on top of her, skin-to-skin.

"Don't you dare move."

"Okay." He held perfectly still. "Jean?"

"Yes, Charlie?"

"I'm not very . . . fancy. In terms of my moves."

"You're doing fine."

He nodded, more out of politeness than because he actually

believed it, if the tightness around his eyes was any indication. "You'll let me know? If you want me to try something different."

"I'm a big believer in starting with the fundamentals. Like learning to cook. You don't go straight to lobster thermidor." Whatever that was. "You have to master the basics first."

"Like macaroni and cheese?"

"Don't sell yourself short, Dakota." She added an eyebrow wiggle in case bumping him with her hips didn't get the point across. "You're at least a manicotti."

The blush looked more like a sunburn. Jean felt another twinge inside her rib cage at his innocence, and the fact that he had admitted it to her, rather than trying to bluff. What was that story, about the shard of ice getting stuck in someone's heart so they couldn't feel? Only this was the opposite: a melting. She sensed a big messy scrum of emotions waiting to break free. "Think about it. It's a lot easier than poker. Or public speaking."

"Okay." He was a billion percent too trusting, batting those obscenely long lashes at her like Bambi in man form.

"I'm waiting for my sexy snake facts." The pads of her fingers traced the slightly different texture of his tattoo.

"Like what?"

"I don't know. I figured you'd say something about anacondas."

"Well, they're cannibalistic. I mean, they'll eat other anacondas," he added when Jean didn't respond.

"I know what cannibalistic means. You just went a different direction than I was expecting."

"Oh." He looked down at her with a worried expression. "What should I have said?"

"Hey, babe, wanna ride my anaconda?"

"An anaconda can weigh up to two hundred and fifty pounds. I wouldn't want to get your hopes up."

Jean snorted at that, reaching up to tug a piece of hair at his temple. "What else have you got in that big brain of yours?"

He gave the question serious consideration, like he wanted to impress her with the best possible answer. "Did you know some snakes reproduce parthenogenetically?"

"Depends what it means."

"The females don't need a male to fertilize their eggs. They do the whole thing by themselves."

She rolled Charlie onto his back before climbing on top of him and pinning his arms above his head. "Where's the fun in that?"

Proceedings of the Society for the Study of Herpetology

Social Patterns in Semi-Arboreal Ambush Predators

Elinor Thompson and C. Poncefort Pike, under the direction of Dr. L. Sterrett, Herpetology

ABSTRACT

Is the ball python (*Python regius*) a more solitary breed than its terrestrial forager counterparts, or are its social patterns merely more elusive and misunderstood? Comparisons to species such as Butler's garter snake (*Thamnophis butleri*), well-known for its intricate, female-driven social networks and tendency to gather in large groups, may have created the false impression that the ball python rejects the company of its own kind.

However, new evidence suggests that putatively solitary species such as the timber rattlesnake (*Crotalus horridus*) may choose to aggregate with kin under certain conditions.

In this paper, we will explore the subtle sociality of nonvenomous constrictors.

Chapter 4

Charlie tried very hard to pay attention to the sound of Mugsy's voice, but it was like having a conversation with someone on the ground when you were standing at the top of a mountain. He was lying on a pillow that still smelled like Jean, half-drunk on the memory of her touch.

Should he have asked her to stay? He assumed Jean knew she was welcome to spend the night—that in fact he would be desperately grateful for even another hour of her company—but it wouldn't be unusual for Charlie to guess wrong about something like that. Was it pushy to ask for more of someone's time, especially from a person who everyone must want to be around, since she was like a human campfire, all warmth and light and dancing sparks? He was about to ask Mugsy's opinion, when he realized she was already saying something.

"—leaving at eight thirty tonight. Can you make that?"

"No!" he said without thinking. "It's much too soon."

Mugsy's sigh was a typhoon, wafting across the ocean to hit him in the face. "That's like six hours from now."

"Yes, but traffic."

"Then leave now."

"I don't want to get stuck waiting at the airport. With all the people."

Mugsy was quiet for a moment. "Can't you wear a baseball cap and sunglasses?"

"Like that ever works."

"Listen, Charlie. I get that it's a tough readjustment, but you can't hide forever."

"I know."

"It'll be easier once you're home. You just need to get here, and people will leave you alone."

He wasn't sure which of them she was trying to convince. "Maybe I don't want to be alone." Or at least, not totally alone.

"Well, you won't be. You'll be with your family. And me."

"But what about seizing the day? Following your bliss—"

"That's fine for a graduation card, Charlie. This is real life. Your parents are counting on you. You got to go away and do your thing, and now you need to come home. That was the deal."

"This isn't about snakes, Mugsy." There was silence on the other end of the phone. "Mugsy?"

"I never thought I'd hear you say that."

Charlie sensed an opening. "My parents don't really need me, Mugsy, they only think they do. I'm terrible at business. And people. Parties too. It's a trifecta of my worst qualities."

She was too honest to argue the point. Charlie rolled over, feeling a lump under the rumpled bedding. He dug his arm under the sheet, half listening while Mugsy said something about caterers.

It was Jean's lucky deck. They'd played a game in bed, later. Jean said it was called Go Snake, but the rules bore a suspicious resemblance to Go Fish. He held the box to his chest. "I have to go, Mugsy."

"So should I make the reservation? I can book the car service from here."

"You know how you're always telling me to stand up for myself?"

"Yes," she said, with obvious reluctance. "But Charlie—"

"That's what I'm doing."

"You want to find your own way to the airport?"

"No." That would be the opposite of brave, doing what other

people wanted instead of following his gut. "There's something I have to take care of first."

"What am I going to tell your mom and dad?"

"Tell them not to worry. I'll be fine."

Maybe even better than that.

Jean's search history

biggest snake ever
most dangerous snakes
unusual snakes
weird facts about snakes
funny looking snakes
snake puns
are snakeskin boots made with real snakes

Chapter 5

Jean watched the pen's rotation slow, waiting until the last possible second to flick it again. This game sucked, but she was too fidgety to sit still and couldn't leave the concierge desk until Pauline got back from break.

Was there such a thing as a two-night stand? Jean couldn't shake the feeling that it would look pathetic to show up at Charlie's cottage again. She was debating an ironic towel delivery (was it too soon for inside jokes?) when the phone rang.

"It's an amazing day at Dolphin Bay, even in the middle of the night," she said, trusting that whoever it was would pay more attention to the faux cheery tone than the actual words.

"Jean?"

She slammed a hand over the pen. "Who wants to know?"

"It's me." There was a long pause. "Charlie."

"Refresh my memory."

"Well, I'm tall and I have glasses—"

"Charlie," she chided. "I'm kidding."

"Oh." He sighed in relief.

"You're still around, huh?" Jean already knew the answer, because the fancy phone system had lit up to show it was a guest call, not an outside number. This way she sounded nonchalant, which was essential to maintaining the correct power dynamic. Jean refused to be one of those chumps who lets herself fall for a tourist, especially after watching her roommate go gaga over a short-timer who (shocker!) ghosted her after returning to the mainland. That was Dating While Living in a Vacation Hotspot 101. Know the score going in or live to regret it.

"Would you maybe want to come over after work?" Charlie asked, all shy and uncertain. Before she could answer, there was a surprising addendum. "I'll make it worth your while."

"Are we talking money or sexual favors?"

"Not money. I have something of yours."

"You stole my panties?"

"No! It's your cards." He lowered his voice to a whisper, even though Jean was the one in a public building. "I'm holding them hostage."

"How devious of you, Dakota. Perhaps I'll swing by." She could kiss him for making it so easy to do what she wanted.

"That would be—great. Wonderful. Perfect."

"But don't hold your breath," she cut in, before he tangled himself in a thicket of synonyms.

"Of course not."

"I'm an unpredictable person."

"A wild card," he suggested.

Jean wondered if he could hear the smile in her voice. "Exactly."

Charlie opened the door before she could knock, not even pretending he hadn't been waiting.

She handed him the beers she'd wheedled out of one of the bartenders.

"Would you like to watch a movie?" he asked, as if this was a real date. "Or I could order food?"

"I had something different in mind." It was important to establish up front that she was calling the shots.

Jean considered the couch, quickly deciding that her supervisor would lose it if they stained the upholstery. She headed straight for the bedroom instead.

"How do you feel about art?" she asked, yanking the duvet off the mattress and throwing it onto a nearby chair.

"Uh, positively? I mean, I'm in favor. Though not all art is good . . . or so I'm told. I'm not sure I always know the difference." He trailed off with a worried frown, on the verge of working himself into a state.

Dropping her supplies on the bed, Jean walked the few steps back to where he was standing, grabbed hold of his shoulders, and pulled herself onto her tiptoes. When his mouth was in range, she silenced him with a kiss.

"How do you feel about me painting *you*?" she clarified, when he was still and settled, holding her at the waist.

"You want to paint me?"

Jean nodded.

"Uh, sure." He bit his lip. "I wouldn't know how to say no to you anyway."

The power! The responsibility! Jean took a second to let the thrill wash over her. "Good. After you take off your clothes, you can lie down on the bed while I get set up."

When she returned from the bathroom with a glass of water, he was stretched out on his side with his head propped on one hand, like a naked woman in an eighteenth-century oil painting.

"Is this okay?" he asked, bending one leg at the knee. "If you want me to hold a piece of fruit or something, I have bananas in the kitchen."

"Just out of curiosity, where are you imagining I'd put the banana?"

He started to give a serious response before noticing her barely suppressed laughter. "I don't know much about art," Charlie confessed.

"And I don't know much about snakes, so we're even. Glasses off." She held out her hand for them, placing them on the bedside table.

"Don't you need something to paint on?"

"Nope. Roll over."

Charlie blinked in confusion. "Over where?"

"Onto your stomach."

"You're painting my back?"

"Exactly."

She knelt on the bed beside him. "Are you ticklish?"

"Just a normal amount."

"Good. This might feel a little cold. And wet."

Despite the warning, he flinched at the first stroke of the brush. "You're painting *me*?"

"Like I said. Now relax. I have big plans for your backside."

An hour later, Jean cracked open a beer. "Drink," she said, holding it to his lips.

"I can use my arms," he protested, starting to lift himself at the waist.

She pressed him down with a finger to the shoulder blade. "It needs to dry." A tilt of the can cut off whatever else he might have said. Jean used the sheet to wipe off a few droplets that spilled from the corner of his mouth. "What do you think?"

"It's a pale ale. Light, refreshing, not fruity exactly but there's something different. An herb, maybe?"

"I was talking about your modeling career, but okay. Somebody knows his booze." She must have stumbled onto his secondary passion, right after things that slither. A stray thought wormed its way to the front of Jean's brain: Would *she* ever land on Charlie's list of obsessions?

"It was hard to avoid, growing up." He sounded so gloomy about it that Jean braced for a story worthy of a country song. "My family loves their beer." There was a pause, during which he seemed to realize how that must sound. "I mean—in a normal way. There was beer around. For the adults. Not that they were drunk all the time or neglecting me."

"I won't report them," she promised, giving him another sip. "It's a flower, by the way. Hibiscus. The big red flowers with the thing"—she wiggled her finger—"in the middle."

"The pistil?"

She shrugged. "Sure." Setting down the can, Jean crawled across the bed to kneel next to his hips.

"How does it look?"

"Not to toot my own horn, but if Hieronymus Bosch wasn't such a downer, he could have painted this." She'd started with the snake, adding in a tree that stretched upward to follow the line of his spine and then slowly filling in the garden around it. Two naked human figures were waiting for faces. Jean hadn't decided whether the Adam in her Eden should be wearing his glasses.

"Can I see it?"

"Not yet." She picked up one of the tubes of paint, squeezing a blob of carmine onto his skin before shaping it into an apple with her brush. "Are you sick of me poking you?"

"I could stay like this forever."

Total sincerity, no hint of cheesy self-consciousness, like he was trying to wow her with a line. It knocked her for a loop hearing him say things like that. She wanted to ask the universe, *where did you find this one?* But she already knew the answer: right here, in this cottage, hidden away from the world. Hopefully this wasn't one of those tragic timeslip situations where he was stuck in a parallel dimension fifty years in the past.

"Maybe they should add body painting to the spa menu." She fanned the bristles over his shoulder blade, adding a peacock to the scene. Lush foliage climbed the walls, like something from *Where the Wild Things Are*, only sexier, because no one was wearing a wolf suit (or anything else). "Do you think people would pay for this?"

"From a stranger?"

"That's generally how it works."

"And—you'd both be naked?"

"Just the customer, usually. Like when you get a massage."

He was conspicuously silent.

"You've never had a massage? You should book one while you're here. Make the feds pay." She felt his back rise as he sighed.

"I'm not actually a government witness," he admitted. "I hope you're not too disappointed."

"You have other qualities. Like your big, thick . . . back." She poked him. "No laughing."

"It's hard."

"Already?"

"Jean."

She trailed the brush lower. "So you didn't stumble onto a gang of thieves."

"Snake smugglers would be more likely," he pointed out.

"Is that a thing?"

"I'm afraid so. A man once transported three Burmese pythons across the border in his pants."

Jean's hand stilled. "On a plane?"

"A bus."

"That's messed up. On so many levels."

"I think geckos would be more uncomfortable. Because of the legs."

"Like if you had to rank what kind of reptiles you'd least want in your pants, that would be the top one?"

"No, a Gila monster would be worse."

"I'll try to remember that next time I'm packing for a trip." She waited until the vibrations of his laughter settled to add teal spots to the peacock's tail.

"I told my friend about you."

Jean ignored the rush of pleasure. "Did you?" The plan was to leave it at that—cool and neutral—but curiosity got the better of her. "What kind of friend?"

"An old friend. Since I was a kid. She's a woman."

The brush swished in the glass, further muddying the water. "But not *your* woman?"

"No." He huffed at that, the sound muffled by the pillow under his cheek. "The other way around, maybe. Mugsy definitely thinks she's the boss of me. Probably because she used to be my babysitter."

"Ah." Once the initial relief passed, Jean replayed the rest of his statement. "So was this 'Mugsy' your sexual awakening?"

"No." His face went up in flames. "But I thought her girlfriend was pretty cute." His shoulders twitched, followed by a guilty sideways glance. "Sorry. I didn't mean to move."

"It's okay. I'll add a bolt of lightning to cover the crack. You were saying?"

"I think Mugsy's group tolerated me because she made them, even though I was a few years younger. I didn't really have many friends of my own."

"Nothing wrong with being selective."

"When I say I didn't have many friends, I really mean any. Except Mugsy. And my parents paid her to hang out with me."

It almost sounded like a joke, but Jean could hear him frowning. Setting down her brush, she walked around the bed and crouched in front of him until they were at eye level.

"That sounds difficult," she said, patting his forearm. "And I know childhood wounds can cast a long shadow. But there's something important I want you to remember."

"What's that?"

She lowered her voice to a tender whisper. "We were talking about *my art*, Charlie. Way to hijack the conversation."

Jean watched him go from startled to amused. After kissing

the last trace of worry from between his brows, she returned to her spot on the bed and picked up her brush.

"I assume they're not still paying her?" Although a lot of grown men would probably benefit from hiring a professional sitter, instead of outsourcing those tasks to their wives or girl-friends.

"No." He paused to consider. "Not for that, anyway. She does work for them."

Before Jean could ask about the family business, he was back to running himself down.

"It doesn't really change the fact that I'm not good with people, like you. I bet you can talk to anyone."

"Eh. It's probably good there aren't more people like me. For the fate of the world." She worked a darker blue into the sky be-tween his shoulder blades, shading it toward evening. "So what did you tell your friend? That you met a rude hotel employee who barged in on you naked and now she won't leave you alone?"

"I said that I met someone interesting and smart and beau-tiful."

Jean waited for the punchline, but apparently that really was how Charlie saw her. She could have joked about getting his pre-scription checked but found she didn't mind having one person in the world who thought she was all that.

"And what did she say?"

"That I should run a background check."

Jean barked a laugh.

"She thinks I'm too trusting," Charlie confided.

"Well, she's not wrong. We barely know each other and you're letting me cover half your body in permanent ink. I hope you like My Little Ponies."

"It's permanent?"

"Got you." She tickled the inside of his thigh. It was like taking candy from a baby. Only not *her* baby. In the *ooh-baby* sense. Obviously.

Either he wasn't listening or didn't find it funny, because his only response was a thoughtful silence.

"Is it about the ponies? Because I made that up too." Taking hold of his calf, she wiggled his leg back and forth. "Still with me, Dakota?"

"You know how people say things that get stuck under your skin, and you can never get them out? It seeps into your veins, like venom." He slid her a doubtful look. "That probably doesn't happen to you."

"I too have experienced human emotions," she assured him. "Now, what is it?"

"Someone told me I was creepy for liking snakes. Because a normal person would be grossed out."

She white-knuckled the paintbrush. Where did these basement dwellers get off trying to bring a unicorn like Charlie down to their level? Jean liked her people the same way she liked her paintings: full of unexpected twists. A hot science nerd with a tender oddball core, for example. Charlie was a bonbon of a person.

"Screw the haters. Those are the same jerkwads who are all, 'I didn't even want to take a bite of that apple. It's that woman's fault. I'm more of a lean protein guy.' Like okay, bro. Who was your scapegoat last year?" Leaning forward, she kissed the side of his shoulder she had yet to paint. "For the record, you're not a snake, you're a snack."

"A snack," he repeated, bemused.

"*And* a living breathing work of art." She cocked her head, considering the long slope of his back and slender hips, not to mention the perfect peach of a rear end. He probably looked great in jeans. It was a little backwards that she'd mostly seen him pantsless, but Jean wasn't going to complain.

"Does it look cool? Can I see it?"

"What, the painting? Yeah, that isn't bad either."

He started to move, but Jean held him in place with a hand to the back of his thigh. "Let me take a picture so you can get the full effect." She brought him his phone, holding it to his face to unlock. "This way you don't have to worry about me posting nudes of you all over the internet."

His face paled. That was probably the ultimate nightmare for someone as reserved as Charlie.

"Which I would never do," she said. "Revenge, sure. Porn, not so much."

Standing on the mattress, she snapped a series of shots, first full-length and then close-up, so he could appreciate her detail work. He propped himself on his elbows to study the images, flicking through them so slowly Jean had to clench her fists to keep from shaking him and saying, *well? Is it awesome or what?*

"This is—" He broke off, staring at the screen.

"It's a garden," she explained. "But a jungly one, with extra snakes."

"Is that a bed?"

"Mm-hmm. Why should they only be for bedrooms? When you think about it, most spaces would be improved by adding a bed."

"That's true. Better than putting a bathtub in your yard." He zoomed in on the next pictures. "Is that you?"

"Yeah."

"And I'm there too."

She nodded.

"It's incredible." He twisted to look at her. "That's what I was going to say before."

"Oh."

"I could tell what it was. I just can't believe you painted all that—on *me*."

"You're like a mullet. Business in front, party in the back." She knelt beside him, looking over his shoulder at the image he was still studying. "Don't feel like you have to stop saying nice things."

"I wish it was permanent. Do you think I can just shower my front half, to make it last longer?"

"You'd probably need help. Okay fine, I'll give you a sponge bath."

"Should I sleep on my stomach, so it won't smudge?"

"I think you should enjoy it in the moment and not worry about tomorrow. That's part of the fun."

"So if I want to keep it there's no way to make it last?"

Jean figured the odds were about fifty-fifty they were still talking about his body art. "Did I mention the paint is edible? Maybe you should do me next."

His expression was torn. Sexy arts 'n' crafts or real talk? Jean knew which one she'd prefer. She had no problem speaking her mind; it was the heart she tried to avoid.

Climbing onto the low dresser, she made a V with her knees, crooking a finger at him. "Get over here, pretty boy." She gave him her best come-hither look. "I promise not to mess up your paint."

"Jean."

"I know. I'm a terrible influence. The formal apology is in the mail."

He moved toward her, fighting a losing battle against the smile that was trying to break free. The sweetness of his expression, with that lock of dark hair falling over his forehead, undid her almost as much as the grip of his hands on her thighs as he positioned himself in front of her. For all his gentleness, Charlie was the sharp end of a knife pointed directly at Jean's hidden weak spots.

She wasn't *scared* of him exactly, because Jean laughed in the face of danger. But it did feel like an opportune moment to test her deflector shields.

"Listen." Jean pressed a hand to his chest before he could get any closer. "We're just having fun, right?"

He looked like he wanted to argue.

"We don't have to talk about it. This is me telling you not to develop unrealistic expectations. Don't put too much faith in me, because I'm not the most reliable person in the world." *And I don't want to disappoint you.* She kept that part to herself.

His palms moved up and down her thighs. Jean wasn't sure which of them he was soothing. After a long, thinking silence, he presented his counterargument.

"Would an unreliable person tell me not to trust them?"

That took the wind out of her sails. Jean's mouth worked, her usual glibness failing. "Actually," she started to say, but he shook his head.

"I love that you don't treat me like a child. Or act like there's something wrong with me."

"There's nothing wrong with you." She pulled him closer, wrapping her arms around his neck. "Except that you have un-usually excellent taste in women."

He looked down, brow creased. "Do you think I like you too much? More than you like me."

"Little do you know, I'm only pretending not to be gaga for you." *Shit.* Where had that come from? "I mean, I don't put my art on just anyone. They have to be sexy as hell." Jean hadn't shifted gears that roughly since her first time driving a stick—no pun intended—but Charlie didn't call her on it.

"Jean," he said, shaking his head.

There was the blush she loved. *Liked.* She liked his blush. *Dammit.*

Jean's Rules of Poker, for Charlie:

-Listen to Jean.

-Unless she asks to see your cards. That is a trick!

-A "pocket pair" has nothing to do with your "nuts."

-Try not to say "shoot" every time you draw.

-When I say "runner runner," we have to race to the bedroom.

-Pants are always optional.

Chapter 6

"I can't help noticing you're still here," Jean said a few nights later.

Her cheek was resting against Charlie's chest, nestled in like a woodland creature in a bed of moss. It was better than any weighted blanket. He had never realized how intoxicating it would be to have someone trust him this much. Probably because no one else had ever thought of him as a soft place to land.

When he didn't respond beyond a contented *hmmm,* she lifted her head to look him in the eye. "That was your cue to tell me how much time is left on the clock."

Charlie threaded a strand of her hair through his fingers, feeling the silky glide. Everything about Jean was a treat for his senses. Well, maybe not the knuckle she was poking against his rib cage. That tickled.

"I don't want to leave." It was the most honest answer he could give.

"But that's not how life works. Especially for someone like you."

"What do you mean, someone like me?" He felt a flare of panic. It wasn't that he wanted to hide things from her; he just couldn't bear the thought of her looking at him differently. He wanted to stay the Charlie she knew. The real him. Her Charlie.

"Just passing through," she said, and he remembered to breathe. "Look what happened to my poor best friend."

"Libby?" Charlie was showing off a little, but only because he liked knowing things about Jean's life. And unlike some people, Jean appreciated his ability to recall random facts.

"Yeah." Jean laid her head back down on his chest. "She met someone and *kablam,* he broke her heart. Total shitshow."

"I thought you said she was disgustingly happy with her new boyfriend, and they were going at it like rabid giraffes?" Charlie had a stomach-churning vision of Jean finding someone lively and fun the second he was out of the picture. His hand came to rest on the back of her head, reassuring himself she was here now.

"It's the same guy. But for a while she thought he was gone forever."

"You mean . . . dead?"

"Back to the mainland," Jean corrected, putting an end to the tragic surfing accident Charlie was imagining.

"But then he came back," he prompted.

Jean sniffed like that was a minor detail.

"So the story has a happy ending."

"If you say so."

It was his turn to administer a teasing poke in the side, though as always when he touched Jean, it wound up more of a caress, wandering over the curve of her waist. "It won't be like that with us."

"Don't worry about me, Dakota. We're having a good time. Zero expectations and no pressure. Easy peasy, light and breezy."

He frowned. That was a lot of ways to say the same thing. It felt like she was trying to push things backward when Charlie wanted to go full steam ahead. Yes, they were having fun. And being around her made Charlie feel like *he* was fun, even though he was still terrible at poker. Luckily, Jean seemed just as happy to play war with her lucky deck, or pretend the floor was lava, or build a pillow fort in the living room.

Anything could be a game, according to Jean. But being playful didn't negate the fact that this was the best week of his life. Charlie would have described it as being like a kid again, except he'd never felt this carefree in his actual childhood. And he was very glad to be a grown man right now.

"I saw your grad school stuff," Jean said.

"I'm not going to grad school."

Charlie wasn't sure why he'd requested application materials he knew he wouldn't get to use, much less spent hours drafting a letter to one of the visiting professors he'd met in Australia, to see if she was taking on new PhD students. Was he delusional or torturing himself? Charlie's mom called him a daydreamer, but his father had accused him more than once of being out of touch with reality.

Which was probably why his impractical brain was spinning a whole new scenario in which Jean came back to South Dakota with him. Maybe just for a visit at first, because she wasn't going to move in with him this soon. Unless she wanted to, being a bold and decisive person. It might not sound like the greatest place compared to where she lived now, but Charlie could imagine Jean enjoying the wide-open spaces, red rocks and pine trees, the endless blue sky. And he knew she was fond of beer, so there was that. The other part of his past might not even be an issue, since Jean wasn't the type to let other people's opinions bother her.

Maybe Charlie could give his parents what they wanted—his entire future—if he had Jean in his life.

"I know you're smart enough," Jean said, reminding Charlie that while he was building a cozy dream life for the two of them, she was trying to talk to him in the present. "And it can't be about the money, because you could pay a semester's tuition for what a week in this cottage is costing you."

"I had some saved." His only expenses for the last six months had been bug spray and candy bars. There wasn't anything else to buy at the research station, unless you wanted to splurge on extra toilet paper. "Plus it was the first vacancy that came up on the website. I guess I didn't plan to stay this long."

Charlie felt her sudden stillness, even the fingers Jean had been stroking across his stomach freezing in place. "Is it because of me?"

"Partly," he admitted. "Among other things."

"Like what?"

"I'd rather blow all my money than feel like it's the most important thing in my life. It has a way of owning you, if you get too attached."

"I wouldn't know. But I respect the renegade spirit."

No one had ever called him a renegade before, probably because he wasn't one. That didn't stop Charlie from glowing at the praise. "The other reason is that I'm not looking forward to going home," he admitted.

"Why?" She propped her chin on her arm, dark eyes studying his face. "Tired of all the farm chores? Baling hay and shucking corn?"

"What?" Were those more sex jokes? He'd had no idea before meeting Jean that there were so many code words for making love.

"Forget it. Finish your thought."

That was easier said than done. "Have you ever run away from your responsibilities? Even when you know you shouldn't?"

"What do you think I'm doing right now? People have probably been ringing the bell at the concierge desk nonstop." She paused for a second before winking at him. In a flash, her expression turned serious again. "Wait, is this your way of telling me you're married?"

"Of course not! But it is a family thing."

"You have kids?"

He grabbed her hand before she could poke him again. "My parents are having a big party. For their anniversary. They want me to be there."

She waited for him to go on, clearly not seeing the problem. "Are you afraid you're going to have to make a speech?"

"It's the whole thing. Large groups of people are not my strong suit. And my parents' friends are not really interested in the same things I am."

"You can't just avoid talking about politics?"

Charlie shook his head. "I wish it was that simple."

"So you don't want to go, but you feel bad about it," Jean summarized. Her tone was hard to decipher. "When's the big day?"

"Next week." Charlie waited for her to say, *Don't go, I'll miss you too much.* But Jean was silent, turning her head so her other cheek was pillowed against his midsection.

"I'd rather stay here with you," he told her, in case there was any doubt.

She grumbled something against his stomach. It felt like she was blowing a raspberry, but Charlie could still make out the words, "For now."

He didn't think arguing with Jean was the best way to change her mind. He would have to show her how he felt with his actions. "Do you want to stay tonight? I could rub your feet."

"Nice try, perv." She pinched his thigh. "You just want to cop a feel."

"You do have very pretty feet."

"I could be persuaded to stay. If you make it worth my while, King Cobra."

"Jean." He tried to sound stern, but it was hard to focus when her hand was sliding down his hip, and then lower still. "Have you been reading about snakes just so you can tease me?"

"Wouldn't you like to know."

She was absolutely right. Charlie wanted a permanent front-row seat for the three-ring circus that was Jean's mind. But he didn't want to spook her, so for now he'd do it Jean's way, telling her with his body what he couldn't put into words.

Concierge Desk Report, Second Shift (Jean H.; Pauline P.):

Incident: Ice machine on third floor reportedly making "loud clunking sound."

Resolution: ~~Explained concept of "ice machine" to guest.~~ Referred to maintenance.

Incident: Emergency laundry request from the King Conch suite.

Resolution: Tide pen once again saves the day.

Incident: Two guests caught skinny-dipping in infinity pool.

Resolution: Staff may need professional counseling to unsee dangly old man bits.

No other incidents of any kind. Especially at the cottages.

Chapter 7

Up to now, Jean had made a point of leaving before sunrise, so spending the night felt like a milestone. Not necessarily the positive kind, considering how badly she'd jacked up her plan to let this situationship unspool on its own. Slow chaos, like one of her chef friend's sourdough starters.

With the same potential for mess.

She'd never hooked up with a hotel guest before, much less played slumber party at his cottage. But Charlie was exceptional in more ways than one.

At some point in the wee hours, she'd woken up chilled by the powerful resort AC, not having packed any pajamas. Charlie soothed her like she was a nervous pony, clicking his tongue and making little shushing sounds. It was probably a tactic he'd picked up in his farm-boy youth. The next thing she knew, he'd taken off his T-shirt and slipped the warm cotton over her head, smoothing it down her body.

"Finally," she grumbled, throwing herself back at the pillow.

Jean slept blissfully after that, even though it usually took her days to adjust to a strange bed in an unfamiliar room. It was the buzzing of Charlie's phone that finally woke her.

"Charlie," she groaned without opening her eyes. When that didn't get a response, she flung an arm toward his side of the bed, surprised to find it empty. Rolling over, she reached for his phone, intending to bury it under a pillow (or fling it across the room), when the bathroom door opened, and Charlie stepped out, buck naked.

His smile slipped when he saw her hand on his phone. "Did you—" he started to say, hurrying across the room.

"Make it stop," she ordered, pulling the sheet over her head.

"Sorry."

When he didn't immediately join her in bed, she peeked out to see him frowning at the screen.

"Everything okay?" she asked.

"I think so." He swiped out of the open tab before crossing to the dresser and setting his phone down.

"Do you want me to—"

"Stay for breakfast?" he interrupted, before she could offer to leave. The mattress dipped as he sat beside her, cupping her hip with one hand. His phone buzzed from the other side of the room. Their faces were close enough for Jean to spot his microscopic flinch.

"Do you want to check that?"

"No." He shook his head, in case one denial wasn't enough.

"I can let you get back to it." She kept her voice light. It was the most casual offer in the history of casualness. No one had ever been this casual before.

Charlie blinked at her, and Jean wondered how nearsighted he was without his glasses. Would he be able to tell if she crossed her eyes?

"Back to what?" he asked.

"Whatever you need to do. Snake stuff. Whoever's blowing up your phone."

"There's nothing in the whole world I'd rather do than drink a cup of coffee with you."

Jean held her breath, diving through the sweetness of his words like a wave that threatened to sweep her off her feet. The pounding of her heart was getting a little aggressive. Like excitement or . . . panic.

"Nothing?" she teased, wrestling him onto the mattress.

Jean had plenty of time during her evening shift to figure out how to even the cosmic balance. Charlie had brought her coffee in bed that morning, so she would spice up his night with a little treat of her own.

As soon as she clocked out, Jean crept to his front door, placing a rolled sheet of paper on the mat. She rang the bell before lunging off the patio to hide behind a trio of oversize ceramic planters.

The door opened with Charlie's typical hinge-straining enthusiasm. His smile fell when he realized there was no one there.

"Jean?" he said, uncertainly.

She watched him squint down the path, trying to see into the darkness beyond the trees.

"Is there someone there?" He was retreating into the cottage when he spotted the paper.

"What's this?" Charlie murmured, bending to pick it up. A grin broke out as he read the words painted across the top of the page. "A treasure map."

He took a step down, pausing when something crunched underfoot. Lifting his leg, he peered at the scraps clinging to his heel.

"The trail of breadcrumbs," Jean hissed. "You're supposed to follow it."

"Jean?"

"I'm a disembodied voice. Totally anonymous."

"Oh, right." Charlie glanced at the path. "They're very big breadcrumbs."

"I thought tortilla chips would be easier to see."

"Good point, anonymous voice. Am I supposed to eat them?"

"No. That would be gross. But I appreciate your commitment to the process."

He sidestepped the next chip before stopping again. Charlie's shoulders tensed as he looked back at the door of the cottage.

"Go on," she coaxed. "You haven't even gotten to the first prize."

"There are prizes?" he asked, perking up.

"What kind of punk-ass treasure map do you think this is?"

"Sorry." Charlie took another tentative step forward, and then another, at which point he spotted the fluorescent duct tape arrow pointing at the outdoor table. A brown paper bag sat on top, with the words OPEN ME on the front.

"Go ahead," she stage-directed when he hesitated. "It's just a present. Not something weird."

"But I don't have a gift for you." He turned back to the door, like he was thinking of running in to grab something for her. One of the lamps, maybe. Or a remote control.

"Just open it." This was not the kind of surprise that benefited from a big buildup.

"It's a shirt," he announced, like she might not know what was in the bag.

"Now we're even. Since you gave me a shirt."

"I'm not sure *gave* is the right word."

"The important thing is that it's mine now." It was soft and stretchy and smelled like Charlie. He'd have to pry it out of her cold dead hands.

"Is that the end of the treasure hunt?" he asked, examining his new Dolphin Bay polo. New-*ish*, anyway. In the borrowed-from-the-laundry-room sense. Jean refused to pay people who were supposed to be paying her.

"No, Mr. Low Expectations. You have to put it on."

He shrugged it on over the shirt he was already wearing. "What now?"

"Into the wild blue yonder."

"We're going flying?"

"No." Though it was touching that he thought she had access to a plane. "You have to follow the map. We're going out."

Charlie glanced down at the paper in his hands. "Out *there*?"

"Yes." Technically he was pointing at a parking lot, but that was beside the point.

"I probably shouldn't. I told Mugsy I'd . . ."

"You told Mugsy you'd what?" she prompted when he trailed off.

"Be available. In case she wanted to call." A shadow passed over his features.

Jean emerged from behind the planter, tired of trying to boss him around from a distance. "What if I said you could bring your phone with you on our excursion? Seeing as how it's highly portable?"

He watched her stalk closer. "That's nice of you—"

She silenced him with a finger to his lips. "Do you know why I brought you this shirt?"

"So we can match?"

"No. But also sort of. If someone sees you out there, wearing *this*," she drew a soft line from his mouth to his chest with the tip of her finger, "what do you think will happen?"

Charlie opened his mouth to guess, but she cut him off.

"You'll be invisible. Hidden in plain sight." Jean didn't know exactly why Charlie was avoiding the outside world, but she had ruled out a number of possibilities, including agoraphobia. Charlie had been out in the wild studying snakes, which would freak out plenty of people who weren't phobic about leaving home. And yet he'd told housekeeping he'd do his own cleaning. It was hard to imagine a more serious sign of your aversion to human contact than that.

"But—"

"Nobody cares about the resort staff," she said, cutting off his protest. "We're like elves. Magically getting shit done."

"Or the Kapuas mud snake."

"Absolutely." Jean reached up to slide both hands into his hair, gently massaging as though working shampoo into a lather. "In what sense?"

"Changing color to camouflage yourself from predators."

Jean smoothed his hair away from his face before taking a step back. "I could get into that."

"If you had the right kind of scales."

"Would you still like me if I did?"

"Of course."

She narrowed her eyes at him. "Would you like me *more* if I had scales?"

"I don't see how I could." His little shrug, like it was too obvious to be worth thinking about, hit Jean right in the feels.

It was tempting to go full Dr. Seuss on him: *Would you like me in a house? Would you like me in a blouse? Would you like me here or there? Would you like me anywhere?*

"Let's go," she growled instead, frustrated with the mushification of her brain.

Charlie's face fell. "I guess you must be sick of staying in."

"This is about *you,* not me."

"You're tired of me?" His sigh was resigned, like he'd known it was a matter of time.

"No, I just don't want you coming down with scurvy or rickets or whatever from not going outside. You need vitamin D."

"It's nighttime."

"So we'll go buy some chewable vitamins. Come on, Charlie." She handed him the treasure map. "The sooner you find the treasure, the sooner we can go back to playing our favorite game."

"Which one is that?"

"X-rated Swiss Family Robinson. Duh."

He found the next prize at the base of a palm tree, helpfully marked by another arrow. Jean followed at a distance, peeling off the tape after he passed and making helpful shooing gestures when he looked back.

Not much farther now, and then Charlie could relax. And set down the picnic hamper Jean *might* have overpacked, judging by the way he was listing to one side.

The good news was that they had yet to test Jean's theory about the effectiveness of a uniform shirt as camouflage. There was a tense moment when a flash startled Charlie into ducking behind a tree trunk, until Jean convinced him it was a random tourist taking a picture of the waxing moon, even though it would inevitably wind up looking like a watery tennis ball. Despite the near miss, Charlie was like a little kid hunting Easter eggs, breaking into a run when he spotted the final arrow pointing him toward a winding trail through the brush.

Jean ripped off the tape and wadded it up, shoving it in her pocket as she jogged around behind him to the main path, which was wide, direct, and well lit. By the time Charlie made it through the trees, she was waiting for him on the secluded beach, arms stretched wide.

"Ta-da!" she said, trying not to sound winded.

His face lit up. "I was hoping the treasure would be you."

"What? No. Look at your map."

"A river of silver," he read, eyes moving from the page to the ribbon of moonlight shimmering on the dark surface of the water. "I like that. It's very poetic."

She sketched a bow. "Thanks. But the actual prize is the picnic. Although I should have brought a blanket. Or one of your many towels."

"It's perfect like this." He set the basket at her feet, folding his long legs as he dropped to the ground.

During the day this spot would be full of snorkelers and sunbathers in tropical print swimwear purchased for the occasion, sucking in their stomachs as they posed for photographic proof of how much fun they were having. Jean liked that Charlie didn't act as if he were starring in his own reality TV show, beaming crucial updates to the world. And also that he had a little padding around the midsection, in contrast to his skinny limbs. It gave her something to hold on to.

"You'll be singing a different tune when you're trying to get the sand out of your butt crack." She handed him a sandwich and the thermos of wine. "Speaking of poetic."

"We could go in the water and swish around a little."

Jean swallowed a mouthful of bread. "I wouldn't."

"Too cold?" he guessed.

"Too sharky."

Charlie was quiet for several long moments. "I'm scared of sharks," he finally admitted.

"Yeah." She lightly thumped the side of his head. "As you should be. Even snakes are probably scared of sharks."

"A black mamba can kill an elephant."

"On land, sure."

He turned to her with a curious look. "You think an elephant could outswim a snake?"

Always interesting, the detours and off-ramps of his mind. "I was thinking the snake wouldn't be out there." She gestured at the gently breaking surf.

"Snakes are good swimmers. Not even speaking of the aquatic and semiaquatic breeds."

Jean shuddered. "Thanks for sharing. Like I need more nightmare fuel."

He placed his napkin and waxed paper in the basket, then patted the space in front of him. Jean happily settled between his knees as he wrapped his arms around her from behind.

"I didn't think you were scared of anything," he said.

"Eh. I put on a good front." She leaned back, resting her head against his shoulder.

He rubbed his cheek over her hair. "Were you ever not brave?"

Jean could hear him drawing a line between them, like they were sitting on opposite ends of a seesaw: Brave Jean on one end, Scared Charlie on the other.

"It's not that I'm not afraid," she said, swan diving off the pedestal he'd put her on. "I just don't care about a lot of things that bother other people. Not including water snakes."

"Isn't that what being brave means?"

"I don't think it should count unless you're doing something that scares *you*. Being rude comes naturally to me, so why would I get a gold star for telling people off?"

Charlie *hmm*ed in her ear, like he wasn't sure he agreed.

"Do you want to know how I know the difference between being brave and not giving a crap?"

"Yes," he said at once.

It was not a story Jean enjoyed telling, even to herself. But he'd exposed his vulnerable parts to her (in more ways than one), so maybe she could give him this in exchange.

"When I was in high school—"

"I bet you were cute."

"That's beside the point. But yes. I was freaking adorable. Kind of like now, minus the confidence. Which is where the problem started." She sat forward, picking up a piece of driftwood and dragging it through the sand. "There was a guy."

Behind her, Charlie grunted.

"Spoiler alert, we hate him now," she said, before he could get too jealous. Even though she kind of liked that he felt that way. "For context, my parents run a snack bar at a golf course."

"Here?"

"Back in Wisconsin. Beer and pop and fried things with a couple of homestyle entrées like chili or spaghetti—anything ground meat–based—for people who don't want to deal with a three-course meal up at the clubhouse restaurant. That was more of a linen tablecloth place. As opposed to picnic tables." Jean recognized that the furniture was not an essential part of the narrative but some things you had to ease into.

"What's the name of it? Their bar."

"Bogey's."

"Like it says on your box of cards?"

It must be a scientist thing, that attention to detail. "I still have a couple of decks. From back in the day." Or more accurately, she had *one* pack left from home, in a faded blue box. Which now lived on Charlie's bedside table.

"It's a golf term, but my parents also hung framed pictures of Humphrey Bogart. The actor, like from *Casablanca*."

"With the white jacket, and the bowtie? He was cool."

"Yeah, he doesn't really give 'loaded potato skins' vibes but I guess maybe my mom thought he'd class up the joint."

Charlie shifted behind her. "It sounds like you didn't like it."

"I didn't like the pressure. My mother was always after me to smile and be polite and not draw weird cartoons on people's bills or put hot sauce in the ketchup bottles. Basically, she wanted me to be less 'me.' Especially when I was working, which was most of the time."

"Even when you were a kid?"

"Pretty much from the time I could carry a tray. That's how I knew all the people my age whose families were club members, even though they went to the fancy private school. I guess even rich kids are impressed when you have unlimited access to a Coke machine."

"I'm sure they liked you," Charlie said. "With or without the soda."

"Maybe." She didn't say *but not enough* because that would have given away the ending. "It was fine until I got older, but eventually it started to turn weird, especially if I had to wait on them. Was it worse if they left me a tip and made me feel like a charity case, or straight-up stiffed me, like I was their bitch? It's hard enough to know where you stand at fifteen or sixteen without bringing capitalism into the mix. Plus I always worried I smelled like the fryer, from being there all the time. You know how when you're so steeped in something you can't even smell it anymore? I figured that was probably me and cheese fries."

Charlie's hand settled on her back, more warmth than weight. She thought of telling him that her perfume habit dated from that stage of life but couldn't bring herself to admit she hadn't always smelled like tropical flowers.

"There was one guy in particular who was sort of a ringleader." Jean forced out a laugh. "So of course that was who I decided I wanted to be with. If you're going to dream, dream big."

"What was his name?"

"You won't believe me."

"I always believe you. Even when you're making things up."

"Smithson Oliver Barrett. Smitty to his friends."

"Like you?" Charlie asked.

"I thought so. For a while." She shook her head. Or maybe it was a shudder. "His great-great-grandfather made a fortune selling cheap beer to the masses, but supposedly they'd transcended their blue-collar roots. Everything was all very hoity-toity. Golf and skiing and let's pretend we're on *Downton Abbey,* Midwestern edition. 'Our beverage of choice is champagne.' That kind of thing."

"Barrett as in Barrett's Best?"

"Yep. The famous blue can of BB. Or as we called it, PP. Because that's how it tasted. Although nobody said that in front of Smitty because he was rich and good-looking in that money way."

Charlie reached past her, burying the base of his plastic cup in the sand. "I don't know what that means."

"Tan, straight teeth, expensive haircut. Maybe the eyes are a little small and the forehead bulges out, but everyone pretends not to notice because he's young and cute-adjacent, in a generic way." She glanced back at Charlie, catching the tightness in his expression. "Your hotness is totally unique, like an El Greco saint. Smitty was just okay, but that didn't stop him from acting like his family was crafting luxury watches in a Swiss chateau instead of churning out the favored brewski of frat boys. His parents were even worse. They treated him like royalty. The heir apparent, on his aluminum throne."

She waited for Charlie to share her amusement, but his smile was strained. "Families," he finally said, like that covered it.

"They cut both ways, don't they? If I'd stopped to think, I would have realized that a girl with ties to the greasy appetizer business was never going to be good enough for the little prince. But I wasn't big on slowing down, so I totally blew off my parents when they tried to tell me I was 'getting too big for my britches.'"

Jean traded her driftwood stylus for raking her fingers through the sand. "I'm sure you can see where this is going." Maybe she could hand wave the rest, let him fill in the blanks.

"Well, I know you left there and came here, which is pretty far away from Wisconsin."

As often happened with Charlie, what seemed like a simple statement sliced right to the heart of the matter. It was true that Jean had put as much distance as possible between her adult life and the place where she grew up, and this experience was a big part of why. Steeling herself, she spewed out the rest.

"Fall of my junior year there was a big football game, and Smitty the Douchebag convinced me we should have a party after, at Bogey's. Just a couple of 'our' friends." Though maybe the air quotes should have been around "friends" instead, since he only seemed to notice Jean when no one else was around. Either way, they were not people who gave a shit about her.

"Like an idiot, I let him have the keys, supposedly so he could go in and start setting up if he got there first. He and his buddies left at halftime, and when I finally realized they were gone, and begged someone to give me a ride, the place was trashed. He'd invited half the school. It was like raccoons in a dumpster. They tore through everything. Food, beer, condiments. Not even eating and drinking it, just making a mess. I walked in and I knew, with total clarity, just like that." She snapped her fingers.

"That you were in big trouble?"

"No. Well, yes, but that came after. I knew I wasn't even a person to them. My feelings didn't matter, my family didn't matter, our business didn't matter, we were just background noise. You want to know the really sad part?"

"Not really," he admitted. "But you can tell me if you want."

"I thought it was going to be some big romantic night, like the party was an excuse to spend time with me and after that we were going to be together, officially boyfriend and girlfriend. Only instead of a rom-com it turned out I was starring in a sad cautionary tale. My little teen dream got taken out back and shot in the head and then run over."

He scooted closer, pressing his legs against hers. "What did your parents say?"

"Let's see." She counted off the answers on her fingers. "'You're grounded for the rest of the school year'—which was not really a hardship since my social life was dead in the water. And I had to work every day until I paid them back. Cleaning, repairs, everything those assholes ruined. Again, I could see their reasoning, even if I wouldn't admit it at the time. The part that burned me up was that they blamed me for all of it. That was Dickhead's story. It was her idea, she invited everyone, he was the real victim, because I was a femme fatale and an evil mastermind. But I guess it was easier to go along with that version of events than confront his wealthy parents about the sociopath they were raising."

"That's so unfair." His voice trembled, like this was Charlie's first encounter with injustice.

"Also it made no sense. I mean, hello, why would I trash *our* business? Where's the logic? It was all, 'You know Jean. She's always been wild.' Like there's a straight line from giving the dog a haircut or drawing on the wall to juvenile delinquency. Meanwhile Smithson is out there crashing his new Acura a day after he got it, and shattering his mom's crystal vase playing Nerf guns in the living room, and setting their outdoor kitchen on fire trying to reheat a Styrofoam container full of leftover Chinese in the freaking pizza oven, but I'm the asshole? Please."

Jean tried to exhale the residual frustration. She really should be over this by now, able to look back with the evolved perspective of a twenty-seven-year-old woman, and yet the embers were still there, smoldering. She made an effort to steady her voice.

"Long story short, I made it my life's goal to never be that big of an idiot again."

"You're not an idiot."

"That's because I wised up and realized it didn't matter what I said or did. They'd already decided what kind of person I was, and nothing I could do or say would change their minds. If you're going to do the time, might as well do the crime."

"Vandalism?" he whispered.

"Being myself. To everyone there—including my parents—I would always be *too much*. So I got out. Not the next day, because I was still in high school, but as soon as I could. And I found people who can handle the real me, at least most of the time. No more trying to impress jerks who don't deserve my unique brand of awesome."

She could feel Charlie thinking. Maybe he saw her differently now—the poor girl with bad judgment who came *this close* to having a criminal record.

"Did he break your heart?" he finally asked. Something tight inside Jean unclenched.

"What heart?" She thumped her chest. "It's pure titanium in here. And rusty chain saws. With a delicate lacing of barbed wire."

He smiled as if she'd said something funny. Maybe she had, maybe she hadn't.

"That guy was just a shark, cruising around all full of himself. 'Look at me, I'm an apex predator. Maybe I'll take a bite out of this surfboard, see how it tastes. Not a seal? Oh well, gotta jam.' And then you're left to bleed out because those big teeth took a chunk out of your thigh. But it's fine, because now I know I'm an acquired taste."

Charlie burrowed his face into her neck. "I acquired it right away."

It should have felt suffocating—not the physical hold he had on her, but the weight of someone liking her too much. There was so much room to fall from a height like that. And yet it filled her like sunlight, sinking into the cracks and warming her blood.

"Ugh, feelings," she groaned, fake gagging. "They're like water snakes inside you."

"I just wanted you to know, Jean. In case there was any doubt. You're my favorite flavor."

She hesitated, the need for reassurance warring with her general policy against sounding needy. "You're not freaked out by my dark past?"

"I get it."

"You do?" It was hard to imagine gentle Charlie getting bamboozled into a crime spree.

"I have some issues with my family," he clarified. "About their business. That's the other reason they want me to come home."

"Besides the anniversary party?"

He answered with a sigh. "My dad expects me to take over after he retires. But it's not the life I want."

Jean tried to picture Charlie riding a tractor, somewhere dusty and far away. "That wouldn't leave much time for doing snake science."

"No, it wouldn't. But we were talking about you."

"That's okay. I'm sick of that story." She hesitated. "You're sure you're not spooked?"

"I like it when you tell me things." He kissed the back of her neck.

"I like it when you tell me things too."

"Even if it's about snakes?"

"Especially then." She raised his arm to her mouth, pressing her lips to the pulse point at his wrist. "I didn't mean to get all heavy on you. Otherwise I would have written, 'unsolicited emotional vomit' on the treasure map. Right next to the X."

"The treasure was perfect." Charlie pressed a kiss to the top of her head. "Better than gold doubloons."

"The chocolate kind or real ones?"

"Both. Now I need to plan something special for you."

"Like what?"

"I can't tell you. It's a surprise."

"Charlie," she wheedled, turning to face him. "Please." In case the pleading eyes weren't powerful enough, she gave him a lingering kiss.

"I'm sorry, Jean. But no."

"Why not?"

"Because I haven't thought of it yet."

"Okay, but if you did know, you'd sing like a canary, right?"

"Anything for you."

She harrumphed like she doubted him, even though Jean was

perilously close to believing every word out of that beautiful mouth. "We'll see about that."

"Tomorrow?"

"If you're lucky."

"I don't need luck if I have you." He pulled her closer, a warm blanket of Charlie.

"Fine. You talked me into it."

"I'll be waiting," he promised, pressing his cheek to hers.

Note on the Back of a Candy Wrapper:

I owe Jean one (1) foot rub.
Signed,
Charlie

Chapter 8

"Just a second," Charlie yelled late the next evening, pausing to check his reflection in the hall mirror. He hadn't expected Jean for another hour at least, so it was lucky he was already dressed. The rest of him could have used more work. He shook his head as hard as he could, then roughed up the top with his fingers. For the first time, Charlie regretted not devoting more of his teen years to mastering his hair, instead of treating it as an independent entity with a will of its own.

The second knock was louder, clearly telegraphing impatience. Charlie was surprised Jean hadn't let herself in. She must not want to spoil the surprise.

"Coming," he called, hurrying through the cottage. After one last adjustment of his costume, he threw open the door, stepping back to assume what he hoped was a sexy yet funny pose, biceps flexing.

And then he jumped high enough to give himself a wedgie, because it wasn't Jean standing on his doorstep, and this costume wasn't really one size fits all.

"What the hell?" Mugsy threw up a hand to shield her eyes. "I do not need to see that."

"I'm not naked, Mugsy."

"There were nipples."

"Just the one." He glanced down to double-check.

She cautiously lowered her hand, looking only slightly less freaked out. "Please tell me you're not involved in some weird sex cult. I do not want to walk in there and see a caveman-themed orgy going on."

"Of course not," Charlie said as she squeezed past him. "I'm supposed to be Tarzan."

That was what the costume place said anyway, though now that Mugsy mentioned it, the furry one-shouldered bodysuit could pass for prehistoric. It was the black spots on the tawny background that did it. Charlie had a feeling that if he went back to the website and searched "Flintstones," the same outfit would pop up.

He'd been so sure Jean would laugh, and then they could eat the banana cream pie waiting in the refrigerator, and maybe she would dress up too (it was a couples costume), and so on.

"Please don't take this the wrong way, Mugsy. It's not that I'm not happy to see you, but I'm a bit busy at the moment."

"Ha," she said from the kitchen, where she was helping herself to a glass of water. "Tell me about it. We are out of time. The first guests are arriving in a matter of days."

"So soon?" It was easy to lose track of the calendar when you were mostly living at night. And also trying very hard not to think about anything beyond this cottage.

"It's a centennial. That should have been plenty of notice."

He put his hands on top of his head, which had the unfortunate effect of making his fur suit ride up. It was scratchy on the inside, to the point that he'd been tempted to put on an undershirt, but that would have spoiled the effect. Besides, he hadn't been planning to keep it on for long. "Is there any chance we could talk about this later? Tomorrow, for example."

Mugsy gave him her most Mugsy look. It was an expression that said, *Can you hear yourself right now?* "No, Charlie, we can't. There's no time for that."

"But it's so late, and you must be tired from traveling—"

"Exhausted. Especially since I didn't have 'last-minute trip to Hawaii' on my bingo card for this week. Seeing as how I'm already up to my eyeballs in prepping for the biggest event in the history of the company your great-great-grandfather built from the ground up. So if you could hurry and grab your stuff, we need to get this show on the road."

"I'm not a child, Mugsy. They can't just send you to fetch me." It was a slight improvement on *you're not the boss of me*.

"Nobody sent me, Charlie." She looked a little sad.

"Oh." That was . . . good. He wanted his parents to give him more space. "I told you they'd be fine without me." Charlie lifted his chin in a posture that allegedly communicated strength and confidence, according to one of the many books his dad had given him about how to be a Man in Business Who Succeeds at Manliness and Business.

Mugsy shook her head. "This is a rescue, Charlie."

"What?"

"How do you not have a Google alert set up for your name?"

"That seems a little egotistical—"

"Not when it's this important! You have to think. Take precautions. Be less trusting."

"I do plenty of thinking." The rest he couldn't speak to, but if Mugsy wanted a tsunami of thoughts, Charlie had a surplus. "Also, I can't leave. I have a previous engagement."

"With your mysterious lady friend, who just happened to stumble into your life?" Her voice was muffled by the closet door, but he still picked up a strong note of sarcasm.

"Why do you say it like that?"

Mugsy dragged his suitcase into the middle of the bedroom, throwing it open before straightening. "Because somebody sold you down the river."

He shook his head, but Mugsy didn't stop.

"Your cover is blown. In a couple of hours, this place is going to be crawling with reporters and photographers and screaming teenagers. We'll be lucky to get out before the swarm descends."

Charlie swallowed the reflexive surge of panic. There was something he needed to say first. "It wasn't Jean."

"Who else knows you're here?"

"You," he pointed out, but Mugsy only shook her head, pulling open a drawer and throwing an armful of clothes into his suitcase.

"I told you to be careful, Charlie."

"I was!"

"Not careful enough." She reached for the field journal on the dresser, but he grabbed it first.

"Will you please listen for a second?"

Sighing, Mugsy turned to face him.

"It can't have been Jean, because she doesn't know who I am!"

Dear Mom and Dad,

~~I'm sorry~~
~~I hope this postcard finds you well~~
~~Hello from Hawaii! The weather is~~
~~I know you must be upset~~
~~Guess what? I met someone~~
I will be home. At some point.
I'm sorry.
Love,
Charlie

Chapter 9

The soft *whoosh* of the revolving door dragged Jean's attention from the origami python she was folding as a surprise for Charlie. She hoped the person entering the lobby was another employee, because her shift was over in fifteen minutes, and the last thing she needed was to get stuck helping a needy guest. Not when Charlie had been texting her all day with hints about his plans for the evening like, *I hope you're ready to swing, my jungle queen.* Followed by an immediate, *From vines,* in case she thought he was proposing a threesome.

Readying her customer-service smile, Jean stood and faced the front entrance. And then blinked several times, certain her eyes were playing tricks.

"Surprise!" said the voice of someone who should have been on a different continent. The beaming young socialite and erstwhile acquaintance of Jean's roommate's boyfriend held both arms wide, her halo of dark curls dancing like they had their own wind machine. "Miss me?"

"Hildy?"

"I know!" She bounced up to the desk, setting down an overnight bag that probably cost as much as Jean's last car. "It's like old times."

That was not Jean's first thought. "What are you doing here?"

"It felt like you were all hanging out without me, so I decided to join the fun." Propping both arms on the counter, her unexpected visitor leaned in. "And I'm hot on the trail of a story, so two birds, one stone."

Hildy Johnson was many things: college student, niece to

one of the most powerful men in media, and an aspiring magazine editor who was hopefully one day going to permanently hire Jean's best friend Libby as her star reporter. And possibly send a steady stream of illustration work Jean's way. She was also a champion meddler, a quality Jean both recognized and respected, though she didn't necessarily want to get roped into one of Hildy's schemes at this precise moment in time.

"Should I book you a room?" Jean asked.

"That can wait." For someone who had just flown across an ocean, Hildy was buzzing with energy, her skin practically giving off sparks. "Don't you want to know what it is? My big lead?"

Jean surreptitiously checked the time. "Totally," she lied. "Although that's really more Libby's department."

"Which obviously I stopped there first, only apparently, she's off 'taking pictures of birds' with her lover man," Hildy said, adding index-finger air quotes.

"I don't think that's a euphemism. That is what they're doing. Since Jefferson is a wildlife photographer."

"Mmkay," Hildy said doubtfully. "Super inconvenient for me, but don't worry. I'm already working on Plan B."

Jean felt a prickle of foreboding. She thought of texting Charlie to tell him she'd be late, but there was still a chance she could make a quick exit. Quick-ish. "Good for you."

"Right? It hit me on the way here. Since I wasn't going to invite myself to stay at your apartment."

"Not if you aren't current on your tetanus shots."

"Plus this way I can be right here with you, in the thick of it. Honestly, you're in an even better position to help. Hashtag silver linings."

"Because you need an artist, or is this a hospitality emergency?" Jean would happily toss a pile of towels at Hildy on her way to Charlie's.

Hildy glanced over both shoulders before answering. "Is there somewhere more private we could talk? Ideally with a bar."

The revolving door spun, spitting Pauline into the lobby to take over for Jean on the concierge desk. Clearly the universe was bending itself to Hildy's will. Sighing, Jean sent a quick text to Charlie. *Need to take care of something. Be there as soon as I can. Sorry.*

She'd make it up to him later. Stepping around the desk, she grabbed Hildy's bag. "Right this way, mademoiselle."

"It's a missing person," Hildy confided when they were seated at a secluded two-top near the terrace bar. She glanced down at the menu. "Which as you know is totally in my wheelhouse."

"You're not talking about yourself, are you?" A few ratings cycles ago, Hildy had been the subject of a media firestorm after briefly getting lost in a snowy wilderness, an experience she'd managed to parlay into a choice internship with her uncle's company. Despite her general bias against nepo babies, Jean admired the gamesmanship.

"This is a way bigger story," Hildy assured her. "*Major* celebrity."

Jean racked her brain for someone famous who'd disappeared lately. She hadn't exactly been keeping track of the latest gossip, especially since Charlie came into her life. "I give up."

"Adriana. Asebedo." Hildy gave each of the pop star's names the weight of an asteroid crashing down from the sky.

"Adriana Asebedo is missing?" Jean really had been out of touch, living her sexy cottage era. "And you think she's staying *here*?"

"Uh, no. There's no way she could travel without a security detail. I'm talking about someone Adriana Asebedo–adjacent." Hildy danced her perfectly sculpted eyebrows up and down, like that should be a big enough hint.

"The Beatles?" Jean guessed.

"No, silly. Her ex. Who she wrote the song about."

"You're going to have to be more specific."

"'The Lost Weekend.' Her 'silent storm'?"

"No shit. Seriously?" That song was legendarily horny, with a hooky melody and tinge of melancholy that basically said, 'I had the best sex of my life but now my lover is gone, and I'll never stop yearning for their touch.' It wasn't just a hit; that song was a cultural phenomenon that had spawned its own catchphrase: the Lust Weekend.

Hildy took a moment to savor Jean's reaction before setting down her menu. "I think I'll have a Pike's Pale Ale. Seems appropriate, under the circumstances."

Jean had forgotten Adriana's ex was some kind of beer person. That was what passed for normal in celebrity land: not an actor or a Formula One driver or a record exec, like her other lovers, but still filthy rich and camera ready. The song about him spent longer at number one than the relationship had lasted, which only seemed to intrigue her fans more.

"You can see it, right?" Hildy pressed the fingertips of both hands to the tabletop, like it was a piano she was about to play. "The Bangin' Beer Baron drops off the face of the earth, only to resurface months later. Where has he been? Does he still love Adriana? Is there a chance they're getting back together? It's mystery, it's second-chance romance, it's sex. This story has everything." She sat back, staring at Jean as if she expected her to burst into applause.

"And you think he's staying here?"

"I'm like eighty percent positive. Which is why I need your help." Hildy batted her lashes.

"What are you picturing here, fake room service? Or the two of us hiding in a laundry cart, and then we burst out and say 'gotcha!' There are four hundred rooms at this place."

Hildy waved this off. "We'll be strategic. First, there's the timing. He would have checked in about a week ago, because that's when he was supposed to get on a connecting flight through the airport here, but according to my sources, he went AWOL instead. Second, he's notoriously press shy, which means he won't want to be recognized. Last time there was a probable sighting, it was a mob scene. Somebody tagged a guy who kind of looked like him on Insta and the next thing you know, they're shutting down a Trader Joe's because shit got real in the salsa aisle. Because he's allegedly a sex god," Hildy added, at Jean's perplexed look. "Everyone wants to throw their panties at him. Or gift wrap the guy and deliver him to Adriana so she can be eternally grateful."

"Alive or like . . . a hunting trophy?"

"Who can say? Parasocial relationships are a tricky beast. I could write a whole dissertation about it, if I wanted to stay in school that long. But obviously this is where I belong. In the heart of the action." Hildy sat back, her expression smug. "He's not going to be in the main building. Too risky. You must have a supersecret special place for VIPs. A private villa or the penthouse level or something right on the beach?"

"There are cottages," Jean admitted, following a silent internal battle. It wasn't like she could pretend they didn't exist. Hildy was more than capable of checking the website.

"Great. That's where we'll start the search."

"There's more than one." Somewhere in Jean's nervous system, an alert was chiming.

"We only care about the ones with a hot young guy staying alone. Unless he's not alone, which would be a whole other layer to the story. 'Prince of Pilsner Cheats on Adriana!' That kind of thing. Though obviously I'd make it way classier."

"I thought they broke up."

"The public will still have strong feelings about him bringing his 'silent storm' to a different harbor, if you feel me."

Jean was not in the mood to analyze Adriana Asebedo's sex metaphors. "If he's even here. Much less seeing someone new."

"Which is why we'll cross-reference with the check-in date, do a little recon, and then bingo, Charlie Pike."

Jean was pretty sure the blood that should have been animating her brain had all drained down to her gut. "His name is Charlie?"

"I know, right? They never call him that. It's always Sexy Sudsy. The Hottie of Hops. Besides, I'm sure he's registered under a fake name. But that's not going to stop us. You know why?"

Jean shook her head.

"We know how to ID him beyond a shadow of doubt."

"We do?" Jean asked faintly.

"One of my cousins plays tennis with a guy who was in the same dorm as Charlie Pike in college, long before the Adriana days. And as we all know, locker rooms can be a gold mine of information. Especially about certain unique physical characteristics." She cleared her throat suggestively. "The kind you can't disguise with a pair of glasses."

"Are we talking about dicks?"

"No." Hildy wrinkled her nose. "Tattoos."

"Does he have a full sleeve?" Jean wondered if Hildy could hear the edge of desperation in her voice.

"Like that would narrow it down. Do you want to guess? I'll give you three tries. Location or what it is."

This was one game Jean had no desire to win. On the other hand, the suspense was about to kill her. She crossed her fingers under the table. "Tramp stamp?"

Hildy stuck her thumb out as she shook her head. "That's one."

"Barbed wire around the bicep?"

Another finger went up. "Second strike."

Jean had a hard time swallowing around the bitterness in her throat. "Please tell me it's not a snake."

"Damn!" Hildy smacked the table with her hand. "I can't believe you got that. But you'll never guess where it is."

"You might be surprised."

Hildy's eyes narrowed in speculation. "Is there something you'd like to tell me?"

"No," Jean said honestly, standing up from the table. This was a time for action, not words.

"Where are you going?" Hildy reached for her bag. "Does this have something to do with Charlie Pike? Jean! Let me come with you."

"Not now, Hildy." Somebody was about to get his ass handed to him.

Snake and all.

Prince of Pilsner Disappears!

VIP Mystery of the Week, Page Seven

While Adriana Asebedo and seven of her closest pals enjoyed a girls' trip to Cabo in the wake of her latest breakup, the singer's ex is nowhere to be seen. Reports that the junior brewing magnate was spotted homesteading in Alaska were recently debunked, leaving the public to wonder: Where could he be hiding?

Chapter 10

Mugsy rubbed her temples. "What makes you think this girl doesn't know you're beer royalty?"

"There's no such thing, Mugsy. Beer is a fundamentally democratic beverage."

She held up a hand. "Your name is on billboards and neon signs."

"I'm just Charlie to her. And she's Jean to me. That's all we need." He didn't want to say more than that, because it was nobody else's business.

"Did she ever have access to your phone?"

"No." It was a reflexive denial, followed by a carousel of inconvenient memories. Jean taking pictures of the painting on his back. The time he'd come out of the bathroom to find her reaching for his phone to silence it. Totally normal and reasonable moments that it was not cool of Mugsy to make him question.

"Do you know *her* last name?" Mugsy challenged.

"I know she's from Wisconsin." Though maybe mentioning her family wasn't the best move, after what Jean had revealed about her history. Mugsy could be a little quick to judge. "And she's a very talented artist."

"It's Harrington. Her last name." Mugsy barely paused to let that settle. "How about her roommate? Do you know what *she* does?"

His hand almost shot up. This one he could answer. "She's in the sciences."

"Oh really? Then why does she have a byline on a travel story that lists her as a Johnson Media freelancer?"

Charlie frowned, trying to remember Jean's exact words. "How do you know all this?"

"Because I spent five minutes on the internet, Charlie. And you know what I found? Two Jeans work at this resort, one of whom is a French guy. It was a couple of clicks. Everything I needed to know about this woman you were shacking up with. And then some."

Not everything. He couldn't bring himself to voice the protest with Mugsy looking at him like he'd just given a scammer his bank account number. "I must have misunderstood."

"Or you were lied to." Mugsy tossed a book into his suitcase.

"It doesn't mean anything bad."

"Then why was Hildy Johnson—also of Johnson Media— spotted checking into this resort half an hour ago, according to one of her many Instagram fans?"

"I don't know."

"Charlie."

"What?"

She pressed her lips together, like she was debating how much to tell him. It was a look he knew well, the same *will Charlie be able to handle this* calculation she'd been making since he was a kid. "I'm sorry," she said at last. "You deserve better."

The worst part was that Mugsy sounded so sure, not a shadow of a doubt in her mind. Compared to that kind of certainty, Charlie's confidence had more holes than a colander. All those years of taking Mugsy's word for it, of trusting that she knew better, that his perceptions were never quite right, pressed down on him.

"Charlie—"

"I know we're in a hurry." There was no need to prolong a conversation that was painful for both of them. Mugsy had never liked talking about emotional things, and right now he was nothing but feelings. It was as if he'd been holding a winning lottery ticket that turned out to be Monopoly money. He used the excuse of grabbing a handful of clothes to turn his back. "I need to change."

Closing the bathroom door, he leaned his back against the wall, slowly sinking to the floor. He felt like a shriveled balloon, abandoned in a corner days after the party.

Why would someone like Jean want to be with him? She was the most vivid person he'd ever met, a scarlet macaw of a girl, when he was a plain house sparrow. Of course she was only interested in him as a story to tell her friend, who could sell it to the world.

One of the towels slipped off the rack, landing on Charlie's head. He pulled it lower, covering his face. Was it from the stack Jean had brought him, that first night? Maybe Mugsy would let him take it home, as a memento. He pictured himself trying to explain that he wanted to steal one of the resort's towels, against all sense of personal honor or hotel guest ethics.

Why do you want to remember her? Mugsy would ask. (Even in his imagination, the words were in her voice.)

Because . . . this was the happiest he'd ever been in his life. Even if it wasn't real.

Charlie sucked in a shaky breath, thinking he might catch a hint of Jean's scent, but all he got was a mouthful of cotton. Choking, he pulled the towel away from his face, dabbing at his eyes before wiping his nose.

Oh great. Now he'd ruined the first thing she ever gave him with tears and snot. How typical of him, making a mess of everything.

A loud clunk sounded from the other side of the wall, followed by something heavy rolling across the floor. He needed to get out there before Mugsy tried to carry all his luggage herself. Not that she wasn't strong and capable, but because it would be rude not to help.

The problem was that Charlie didn't trust himself to hold it together, and he hated for anyone—even Mugsy—to watch him fall apart. It felt like that would confirm all the worst things people had ever thought about him.

Crawling on his knees across the tile floor, Charlie reached the walk-in shower. He turned on the spray full blast. A trick he'd learned years ago was that the noise of the water drowned out the sound of crying, washing away tears as fast as they could fall.

The showerhead was the fancy kind that released a gentle rain of droplets. Lowering his head, Charlie waited. Rivulets ran down his shoulder blades, but for some reason, the tears wouldn't come. He was a block of ice, the warmth of the water unable to melt his frozen core.

I don't want to cry in the bathroom alone. It felt backwards and wrong, like putting on a pair of shoes he'd outgrown. He'd truly believed sad and lonely Charlie was behind him. New Charlie wanted to tell Jean what he was feeling, because she unlocked something that made it easier to talk instead of keeping everything inside.

But Jean wasn't here. She would never be with him again.

Okay, that did it. The tears were flowing now.

Adriana's New Man Is an Aquarius!

The Stars in Our Stars: Celebrity Horoscopes

What does that mean for our girl? He's creative, smart, a free thinker, but hopefully not too wishy-washy. Aquarius lovers are fresh and fun, but it can be a struggle to pin them down. Sometimes they get a little too in their head, and who wants distance when you're in l-o-v-e?

Sound off in the comments: Is he a keeper or water under the bridge?

Chapter 11

"I am so mad," Jean informed the empty darkness as she hurried across the grounds. Not that she needed to hype herself up. If she were a kettle, Jean would be seconds from a full rolling boil.

How dare Charlie deceive her? How dare he ruin what they had by not being who he said he was? Or being who he didn't say he was. Same difference.

"Oh, I'm sorry. Did I say Charlie? I meant Charlie *Pike*. Beer Bachelor. Dater of pop stars. Snake scientist, my ass." *The Silent Freaking Storm*—she cut off that thought before it could take root. Jean had no desire to contemplate another woman's lyrical ode to Charlie's tongue.

And to think she'd been worried about going easy on him.

He is kind of quiet, an unhelpful part of her brain pointed out. *When he's not talking about snakes. That's probably where the "silent" thing comes from—*

"Shut up." She smacked herself in the forehead to drive home the message. "We don't care."

When Jean reached the cottage, the porch light was off, like he was trying to hide from her wrath. *Joke's on you*, she thought, pounding the door with the side of her fist. Playful knocks were for yesterday's Jean. What a freaking patsy!

The vision in Jean's mind had been crystal clear. The door opens. Before Charlie can get a word out, Jean plants both palms on his chest and shoves. And then: the yelling!

But it wasn't Charlie who opened the door. In a flash, Jean's entire plan skidded off track.

There was a woman in Charlie's cottage.

In that first feverish instant, Jean half expected to see Adriana Asebedo in full makeup and spangly stage costume, here to reclaim her man. But this was a face Jean had never watched in news clips or music videos. Her long dark hair was pulled back in a low, normal-person ponytail (not to be confused with the kind that required professional styling), and she was wearing jeans and a faded T-shirt that looked like regular clothes, as opposed to the designer boutique version.

Which made it even worse. This girl was so comfortable with Charlie, she didn't feel the need to dress up. Not that her big dark eyes and wide mouth required makeup to be striking. Was she another guest? Had Charlie been seeing her this whole time? Did she use gel or were her eyebrows like that naturally?

The angle of those covetable brows grew more dramatic as she stared Jean down.

"Turndown service," Jean blurted, when what she really wanted to say was, *you're holding his pajamas.* Jean loved the faded blue paisley of those old man drawstring pants.

Used to love. Past tense. Had been tricked into sort of liking. Against her better judgment.

"We don't need it," the other woman said, polite yet firm. She started to close the door.

"Are you sure?" Jean tried to smile, while also surreptitiously peeking into the cottage. Was that the shower running? Charlie was showering, and this person was here, answering his door? Jean's hands and feet were ice cold, probably because her blood had stopped circulating. Your heart had to be pumping for that.

Charlie's lady friend didn't return Jean's strained half grin. Possibly she was wondering why a deranged resort employee was trying to force her services on them.

Because I'm too stunned to move. Jean's pride saved her from the humiliation of admitting it.

"I don't have any change," the other woman said, frowning at Jean's continued presence. "We'll leave some cash on the dresser."

The door closed, followed by the sound of the dead bolt sliding into place.

Hildy found her on a lounge chair next to the infinity pool. Time had passed; Jean couldn't have said how much.

"You and the Silent Storm, huh?"

Jean flinched, less at being found out than the nickname. At least it wasn't the kind of question that required an answer. What would she even say? *Not anymore* implied that she and Charlie had been together at some point in the past. That seemed questionable at best, considering her "Charlie" didn't exist.

It wasn't until the cottage door slammed in Jean's face that she realized how big a part of her had expected Charlie to make it all better.

Charlie who? he was supposed to say, his face glowy with happiness like she was the best thing that had ever happened to him. *Jean, it's just me. Same as always.*

It didn't have to be a long speech. Actions spoke louder than words. Like inviting someone over for a "special surprise" and then letting your other girlfriend answer the door. Classy!

"I guess he was in Australia, doing some kind of research?"

"Snakes." Jean roused herself long enough to glance at Hildy, who had claimed the lounger next to hers. "Is that news?"

"The default assumption is always cult, rehab, or plastic surgery. Not that his face needs work." Hildy tried to pass her huff of amusement off as a cough when Jean glared at her. "Which obviously we hate his stupid face." She pretended to gag. "Last week there was a rumor he'd been spotted driving a UPS truck in Kentucky. Does he even have the legs to pull off those shorts?"

Hildy paused in case Jean wanted to weigh in. "But I guess we know where he really was." Her voice trailed off, another hopeful ellipsis. "You really had no idea?"

"Nope." The word tasted like fish oil. There were few things Jean hated more than not knowing the score. "He told me his name was Charlie."

"Just Charlie?"

"We mostly talked about other stuff." Snakes. Poker. Sex. The big-ticket items. It had been a game to her, trying to guess why he was there. *Way to ignore the clues, Jean-ius!* Charlie wasn't just shy or antisocial, any more than he'd grown up on a freaking family farm. He was hiding from the world. Deliberately incognito.

"It would be weird if he went around introducing himself as the Silent Storm," Hildy said, as if that were an excuse.

"Can we not?" Jean wanted to scream every time the chorus started up in her head. That entire (irresistible, inescapable, incredibly sultry) song was about longing for the one who got away, who spent the titular "Lost Weekend" taking you places your lady parts had never seen and then leaving you high and dry. Everyone who heard it came away hot and bothered. It was an anthem to sex—a banger about banging.

And apparently also a playbook for the guy she never would have pegged as being a player. This was the same Charlie who had strongly implied he needed Jean to show him the ropes in the bedroom. Only not actual ropes, because she hadn't wanted to throw him in at the deep end.

"Sorry! I just have so many questions." Hildy mimed shoving something back into her mouth.

"You and me both." Had he taken up with Jean because she was so very available, the human equivalent of extra towels? Did he always ghost the people he slept with, or was she not exciting enough for a guy who'd dated one of the most famous women in the world? Maybe it was because she'd fessed up to her less-than-glamorous past. Recreational slumming was one thing, but a semidelinquent with a family legacy of fried snacks? No thank you!

"Listen." Leaning forward, Hildy put a hand on Jean's knee. "I know it hurts, but I promise you won't always feel this way. Is it your fault you fell for someone who turned out to be a dirtbag? No. So you pick up the pieces and move on."

Easy for someone with a trust fund to say. "Move on where? My waitstaff gigs have fully dried up, my two best friends are busy with their own lives, I can barely afford my shithole apartment as it is."

"I'm talking *emotionally*."

"If you tell me my heart is a forge and that forge is on fire, I can't be responsible for my actions." They'd be shoveling sidewalks in hell before Jean was ready to take advice from an Adriana Asebedo lyric.

"Please. I'm talking about stepping past the sads into an exciting new phase."

"I know I seem vulnerable right now, but I'm not in the market for nutritional supplements or a life coach. See 'my ass is broke,' above."

"Ha! Why should you change? He's the one who did you wrong."

Jean managed to lift one shoulder in a half-hearted shrug. This was true, but not particularly useful information.

"I'm talking about real satisfaction."

"I don't have money for sex toys, either."

Hildy shook her head. "TMI. But also, take it from me. The best medicine is revenge."

The overcooked noodle that was Jean's spine snapped back into a semblance of its former shape. No wonder she felt so terrible, sitting there like roadkill. Jean was not that person. She didn't let anyone walk all over her. If Charlie thought he could play her for a fool, he'd picked the wrong woman to use and then cast aside like . . . a damp towel.

A flickering heat started low in her chest. "Are we talking Saran Wrap on the toilet? Swap his cold brew for soy sauce? Dead fish under the bed?"

"Hold that thought. I'm getting a notification." Hildy extracted a phone from the pocket of her linen pants. Her face fell. "Duck on a stick! Those bastards."

"What?"

"Someone beat us to the punch."

"Sabotaging his room?"

"Breaking the story." She turned the screen so Jean could read the headline *Beer Baron Goes Beach Bum* in acid green on a black backdrop. "I need to make a quick call. This was so much easier when I had my own photographer." Hildy skimmed through her contacts, holding the phone to her ear as she waited for it to connect.

"Who can we get to the Honolulu airport right away? No, not tomorrow. Listen to the words coming out of my mouth. We don't have time to run it up the chain, but that's okay because I know what I'm doing—oh great." She lowered the phone, rolling her eyes at Jean. "They put me on hold. And *click*." Hildy ended the call. "Screw that. We'll go ourselves."

"Go . . . to the airport?" Jean had a feeling she'd still be lost even if she'd heard both sides of the conversation. Weren't they going to confront Charlie? Or at least make it very hard for him to ignore Jean's existence?

"Oh yeah," Hildy said, as if it were obvious. "He'll make his escape ASAP, if he isn't already gone."

"Gone as in checked out?"

"For sure. My money says he'll get off the island before shit really hits the fan. The question is where he's going to ground." She narrowed her eyes at Jean. "You have insider knowledge. Where do you think he'll hole up?"

Jean could only shrug. She knew Charlie exclusively within

the context of his cottage—a fact that had been made abundantly clear tonight.

"That's okay." Hildy couldn't hide the pity in her eyes—or the disappointment. "Good riddance, right?"

She was clearly trying not to rub Jean's nose in her own uselessness. How much more pathetic could Jean get? It wasn't like her to have zero ideas. Surely there was something she could . . .

"Hildy."

"Hmm?"

"A story would still be worth something, wouldn't it? A real exposé, not just a quick sighting before he disappears again."

She looked up from her phone. "Are you saying what I think you're saying?"

Jean gave a slow nod. "I bet he'll go home. To South Dakota."

"You think?" That was more like it: Hildy staring at her with unmistakable interest. No more of this "poor Jean" nonsense.

"His parents are having some kind of party. He felt guilty about missing it. Allegedly." Who knew if any of that had been true?

She told herself it wasn't a betrayal, even after Hildy started "hitting up her network," which was apparently business speak for texting your sorority sisters.

Charlie had done her wrong. The lying was bad, and the cheating was worse, but walking away without a word? That hit like a harpoon to her heart.

Tell me you don't give a shit about me without telling me you don't give a shit about me.

Two could play that game.

The tables were about to be turned.

Watch your back, Charlie Pike.

PART II

Exile

Chapter 12

Charlie was grateful for the darkness blanketing the world outside the airplane window. That was the best he could say about the current situation: it was late at night, which meant he hadn't been forced to watch the island grow smaller and smaller before finally disappearing, along with his dreams of happiness.

In a few hours, ocean would give way to solid ground. They'd catch a connecting flight, cross a mountain range, and finally land in the vast flatness of the Plains. Or at least, that was how it looked from above, a patchwork of big grassy squares and reddish dirt that plenty of people lumped in with the rest of the Midwest as one unbroken stretch of emptiness, dotted with the occasional barn. It was easy to make those mistakes if you only glanced at the surface. People saw what they expected to be there, making assumptions like "it's all farmland" (when the nearest fields of corn and soybeans were hundreds of miles away) or "you'll become a beer executive" (when he dreamed of studying snakes instead of sales). Or how about "a beautiful girl could like you for yourself" (and not sell your whereabouts to the tabloids)?

The truth was a moving target.

He tried to picture home as a place he wanted to go. Visualizing a safe space was one of the calming exercises he'd been taught as a kid, often using the creek behind his house as a focal point. It felt sheltered there, shaded by canyon walls and cottonwoods, with a hush that reminded him of the inside of a library. Charlie loved the landscape he'd grown up in—and yet he hated the fact that he was going back. Defeated and humiliated, with his tail between his legs. Hard to believe this was the same night he'd planned to spend with Jean, laughing and eating pie and . . .

Closing his eyes, he took a four-count breath in through his nostrils, holding it for three seconds before exhaling. For now, he was in a state of suspended animation, neither here nor there. Maybe he could pretend it wasn't real, being in this tin can in the sky—a can that felt like a coffin. Charlie's scalp was sweating. He wanted to scratch it, but the hat was in the way, and he couldn't lift his arms without elbowing Mugsy.

Don't think all the dark thoughts at once. Pace yourself. That was another lesson he'd learned in therapy. Usually he had a hard time filtering, but today it was easy enough to pick one and stick to it.

Jean.

Had she gone to the cottage? What would she think when she realized he wasn't there? He flashed back to the text claiming she was running late, with that uncharacteristic "sorry" at the end. Maybe Jean had never intended to show up, if she really did what Mugsy claimed.

I hope she misses me even a millionth of a percent as much as I miss her. It was a childish thought, followed by an even less rational one. *I wonder what will happen to the pie?* It would be a shame to throw it away untouched.

He shook his head. Maybe there really was something wrong with him. Because even though Charlie knew he should be angry, all he felt was loss, like an announcement had just come over the PA system that the sun wasn't coming up tomorrow. For a few shining days, his world had seemed big and bright and exciting, as if Jean had opened the door to a magical dimension beyond the boring reality he'd always known and then held his hand as he took in the sights.

But that was wrong, wasn't it? He needed to stop thinking of

Jean as the best thing that had ever happened to him. Tomorrow, he decided. Or possibly the day after.

"I guess I'll never see her again." He was trying to sound brave, but the look on Mugsy's face was a close cousin to her familiar *you're giving me heartburn* expression. Charlie's mother liked to say that Mugsy was the oldest young person in the world. "What?"

She shook her head.

"Go on, Mugs. I can take it." At least, he *wanted* to be someone who could handle bad news. Or was it that he wanted other people to see him that way? Sometimes it was hard to tell the difference.

"I know it's too soon to tell you it's for the best, so I'm holding it inside."

Before he could thank her for sparing his feelings, she kept going.

"But it really is better this way, Charlie. You need to go home and face your responsibilities. It was never going to last, even if she wasn't . . . you know."

Did he know? It still felt impossible he'd imagined the whole thing. How Jean made him feel, the thrill of her company. He would have sworn she was at least entertained, if not smitten like him. Then again, he'd been told more than once he wasn't good at judging other people's intentions. Mostly by Mugsy, who seemed to be taking this episode as confirmation of her worst fears.

"This way you can feel good about doing your duty." She paused, apparently realizing it wasn't the most enticing prospect. "And make your parents happy."

That might have been an incentive, if Charlie believed it was within his power to please his father, short of becoming a different person. "I wasn't shirking. I just . . . thought they might be better off without me." And he didn't want to leave Jean, but Charlie kept that part to himself. It wasn't making excuses when two facts existed independently of each other.

"Why would you say that?"

He wasn't sure if Mugsy was objecting to the feeling or the fact that he'd admitted to it. One of the tricks she'd tried unsuccessfully to teach him as a kid was how to hide his weak spots, but there was a difference between giving ammunition to bullies and being honest with your oldest friend. "You've seen me at parties."

"Maybe you've grown out of it."

"My personality?"

Mugsy gave a long-suffering sigh. "I don't like people either, Charlie. But you can't let them get under your skin. You shake hands, you nod, you smile." She brushed her palms against each other. Piece of cake.

"Are you going to smile?"

She bared her teeth. It was an expression guaranteed to maintain a five-foot radius around Mugsy at all times. Maybe he could stand behind her.

"Your dad will do most of the talking."

It would have been more reassuring if his father didn't expect Charlie to stick close and laugh at all his jokes, pretending to have a great time. "It's too bad I can't buy a lifelike robot to take my place. It could hold up a sign that says, '*Good one, Dad!*' every thirty seconds."

Mugsy gave a grunt of agreement. "My robot's sign would say, '*No, I'm not related to Pocahontas.*'"

"I'm sorry, Mugsy. You have it much worse than I do."

"Yes and no. At least I don't get the backslapping."

"It is hard to keep a drink down."

She bumped her shoulder against his. "It's not going to be a huge crowd. Just a carefully selected group of beverage moguls who will hopefully decide to invest in your company. And assorted others," she added, like it was an afterthought. Charlie assumed she was talking about caterers and cleaners and florists—typical event staff.

"It's not my company." He frowned. "That sounded ungrateful, didn't it? I'm sorry."

Her eyes softened with understanding. "I know it's not what you want."

"That makes one of you."

"I'm not the only one who cares about you, Charlie."

His breath hitched. "You think she did have feelings for me?"

"Your parents." The words dropped like cement blocks. "Since that's who we're talking about right now. Not anyone else."

Right. He knew that. Except thoughts of Jean were like a fidget spinner in his brain, so easy to keep turning and turning. "If they love me, why can't they understand that I don't want to run Pike's?"

Mugsy held a finger to her lips, looking around to make sure he hadn't blown their cover. "Are you having some kind of delayed adolescence?"

"I went through puberty, Mugsy. You remember my voice."

"Everyone has an awkward phase."

"And for some of us, it lasts our whole lives."

"I'm just trying to figure out what's going on with you. There's something different, and it's not just the scruff." She flicked her fingers at his chin.

"Isn't it obvious?"

Mugsy didn't answer, probably hoping he'd drop it.

Charlie said the word to himself anyway. *Love.* With a capital L. At least on his side. "So she was just using me to get the story? You're positive?"

"Talking about it isn't going to help. You need to go cold turkey. Starting now. Flip the off switch." She snapped her fingers, like it should be that easy.

That must be another mechanism that hadn't been installed when they were making Charlie, because he had no idea how to turn off his feelings.

"If you have to think about her, focus on the part where she did you dirty."

The blush hit hard and fast.

"Not like that. Yuck." It was the same tone she'd used to scold him when he tried to turn the pages of a book while eating something sticky.

"What if she had a reason?" Charlie persisted.

"Like what?"

"Someone in her family needed emergency surgery and Jean had to get the money fast? It might have been a matter of life and death." Although she could have just asked him. He would have given her anything.

Mugsy responded with a skeptical brow lift. She was difficult to impress under the best of circumstances, which this was not.

"It just felt like she knew me. The real me." He needed Mugsy to understand that much at least. At first, he'd kept his identity under wraps because Jean was a stranger, and he didn't want anyone to find out where he was. And then he'd gone on not saying anything because it felt so good being plain old Charlie with her. The parts of his history he didn't mention were the parts he didn't want to claim. The public things: beer, business, being looked at, running away.

"Does she know your middle name?"

That was a low blow. "I was trying to impress her. Announcing that my middle name is Poncefort wasn't going to help." Or maybe she would have pretended to like that too. "I got it all wrong, didn't I?"

"It's not your fault she's awful."

Except it was his fault for being the kind of person no one

genuinely wanted to get close to. Hard to blame that on anyone else. "It's Adriana Asebedo all over again."

"No." Mugsy spoke too quickly, like she was trying to convince herself. "It's nothing like that."

"It's a little like that." In the not-really-caring-about-Charlie sense.

"I won't let it get that bad." Mugsy held up her hand like she was swearing an oath. "I'm going to help you handle the situation before it gets out of hand."

Did "the situation" mean being hounded by reporters for months, or Charlie's less-than-impressive reaction to the rabid tabloid attention? He didn't have the heart to ask.

"Sorry about the tight squeeze," Mugsy said, changing the subject with the subtlety of a rockslide.

Charlie would have shrugged, but there wasn't enough space. "I've been sleeping in a hammock for six months. Well, until last week." Memories tugged at him: fancy sheets, Jean's skin, the floral scent of her perfume—

Fingers snapped inches from his nose. "Stay with me," Mugsy hissed. "I was *trying* to say that I figured it would be easier to go incognito in coach. No one will be looking for you here."

A flight attendant bent to address them. "Cookies?"

Charlie tugged the brim of his baseball cap lower. "No thank you. I'm too sad to eat."

"I know exactly what you mean, hon." The uniformed attendant patted his arm, and Charlie's eyes pricked at her kindness. "It's always hard when the vacation is over."

Mugsy reached across Charlie, probably sensing he was about to start blubbering about lost love. "I'll have his cookies."

When they were alone again, Mugsy chewed with a thoughtful expression.

"Are they good?" he asked, wondering if he'd once again made the wrong choice.

"We're going to figure this out," she replied, before shoving the next cookie in her mouth. "Once we get past the centennial."

Charlie felt a barely-there stirring of hope. "Are you sure you don't want to take over instead, Mugsy? You're so good at running things."

"Wrong last name." She brushed crumbs off her shirt. "Besides, I have my own thing going."

"That's true." For almost as long as he'd known her, Mugsy's free time had been spent foraging for native plants and brewing them into teas. Her recipes were a blend of traditional knowledge picked up on visits to her maternal grandmother—Mugsy's main connection to the Lakota side of her heritage—and her own experiments. Some of the early results tasted like hot lawn shavings, but she'd improved a lot since then, to the point that she was serious about turning it into a business. She'd done a few seasonal ales for Pike's and had her own workroom in one of the outbuildings, but beer wasn't Mugsy's first love either.

Charlie tried to muster a smile. "At least one of us will get to do what they want. You should find love too. The real kind, that lasts. Not a brief doomed affair with someone too good to be true who leaves you more miserable than you were before." He tried to swallow past the lump in his throat. "What am I talking about? You're too smart to get caught up in something like that."

Mugsy choked on a mouthful of cookie. Charlie passed her his water.

"Nobody's perfect," she croaked, wiping her chin with the back of her hand.

"She did have a lot of great qualities. You should have seen the painting she did—" He broke off when Mugsy flicked the brim of his hat.

"Not her. She's the worst."

Charlie let that go without arguing. Just as well he hadn't gotten to the part about what she'd been painting. Or where. He wished it was still there, a tangible reminder of their time together, but the marks Jean had left were on the inside.

"Did you pack everything?" he asked.

"I think so. It was kind of a rush. We barely got out in time."

"What about the cards?"

She looked at him blankly.

"Playing cards. In a blue box."

"Does it matter? We have plenty of cards at home."

It mattered to Jean. And that meant it mattered to him, even though he knew it shouldn't.

Unless that part wasn't true either, and there was no snack bar and no Wisconsin—well, obviously Wisconsin was real, but the rest could have been a fabrication. Charlie didn't know the Barretts personally, much less whether they had a son with a destructive streak, but maybe Jean didn't either. Everyone had heard of Barrett's Best, the same way they knew about Pike's Pale Ale. She could have invented the whole story to make Charlie feel sorry for her, choosing the name Barrett at random. "Smithson" certainly sounded fake.

If her goal was to rouse his protective instincts, it had worked beautifully. Then again, Jean hadn't needed to go to nearly that much trouble to get Charlie on her side. He wasn't wired for deception, as evidenced by how bad he'd always been at lying—or knowing when someone was lying to him.

"It's just a party, right?" He glanced at Mugsy, who had developed a sudden preoccupation with rearranging the items in the seat-back pocket.

"Basically."

"I should be able to handle that." He tried not to make it sound like a question. How long could a party last—three hours? Four? Charlie had to be strong enough to get through one evening.

It would be a cakewalk compared to the pain of losing Jean.

A Hot Clips Sneak Peek

Adriana Asebedo, who rocketed to stardom at 15 after recording a demo in her dining room, wanted a completely new style for her upcoming album, *Heart Forged*.

"This is about taking ownership of my career, and my sound. I'm ready to push myself in a new direction. I've been writing my own music for ten years, but people still talk about my songs like I'm a teenager who loves bubblegum and sparkles. I want my fans to see another side of me."

Asebedo and her team partnered with in-demand commercial director V9 to create an edgier, more adult aesthetic for the video celebrating the album's first single, "Steel Eyes." Through an interpreter, V9 said they chose the desolate setting of the American West to symbolize the woman as artist, wild and free.

Chapter 13

A week of access to Hildy's deep pockets confirmed one of Jean's long-standing suspicions: the only thing standing between her present circumstances and total world domination was an influx of cash.

Short on rent? Hildy covered the next month on the grounds that Jean was on assignment for Johnson Media, so it was basically an advance on salary. New wardrobe and travel expenses? Ditto. Which meant Jean could pretend it didn't matter when the manager at Dolphin Bay let her go on the grounds that her work didn't meet their standards of discretion and guest satisfaction.

As if! She'd provided plenty of satisfaction—way more than Charlie deserved. But whatever. Jean had no desire to stick around to witness the Charlie Pike frenzy.

She wondered how long it would take the hordes of reporters and fangirls to realize he was gone and slink back to their subterranean lairs. If Jean didn't have bigger fish to fry, she would have stood out there with a megaphone:

Let me save you some trouble! He's not as good as he looks!

On the inside, anyway.

But there was no time for that, because the wheels of vengeance were in motion. Forget the sting of betrayal; Jean was pure action and forward momentum now. It was lucky her best friend was still trekking around Kauai, because Libby would have asked how she was feeling, and tried to get her to process the emotional fallout from trusting the wrong guy. But Jean had no interest in reliving the past, and sympathy could only slow her down.

A change of scenery and some risky behavior was the medicine she needed now.

Once Hildy ferreted out the information that the Pike family was holding a private centennial celebration at their estate in the Black Hills, the plan quickly coalesced over mai tais and coconut shrimp.

"It's Fyre Fest if it wasn't Fyre Fest," Hildy reported, having checked in with the cousin of one of her sorority sisters. "A smaller, more exclusive Coachella, with a select group of influential invitees. Well, influential in the beverage industry, which is not as glam as they'd like us to think, but whatever. You'll dazzle them with your wit and charm. They'll be eating out of your hand."

Jean grunted, ruthlessly suppressing an image of feeding Charlie dark chocolate and mango in bed.

"You're the perfect inside woman," Hildy assured her, mistaking the grumbling for self-doubt. "Charlie Pike is notoriously press shy, yet you managed to get past his defenses." She raised her glass to Jean. "Which means you could do it again."

"Hell yes, I can. I'll blow up his life. See how he likes them apples. The world needs to know who he really is." Not a shy, snake-loving future farmer enjoying his last taste of freedom but a spoiled little rich boy with a dubious relationship to the truth. Never trust a trust-funder. Jean chugged her drink, enjoying the warmth spreading under her skin. Who needed a lover's embrace when there was so much rum in the world? "If I'd known who he was, I would have had my guard up, since this is clearly his MO."

"First Adriana, now you," Hildy agreed, with a flattering lack of irony. "He loves 'em and leaves 'em."

It took Jean a beat to realize she meant "love" in the sense of making love. Hildy wasn't implying that Charlie had been *in* love with her. Since obviously he wasn't. "They must have been planning this for a long time. The party." As opposed to Charlie's side hustle scamming the ladies with his fake naivete.

"At least a year," Hildy confirmed. "For an event of this scale. Any time you want to get a bunch of bigwigs together, the scheduling is a nightmare. Worse than a wedding."

Which meant that Charlie—Mr. I Hate Crowds and Have No Plans for the Future—knew all along that he was about to skip town. Because according to Hildy's intel, his name was right there on the invite: *Charles Pike IV and parents Charles III and Sandy Pike request the pleasure of your company as they celebrate 100 years of Pike's Pale Ale . . .*

A far cry from, *Can you come over tonight, I have a surprise for you.*

Ha!

Though you could argue Jean had gotten a very big surprise. Several, if you counted the discovery of Charlie's other woman.

"You see what they're doing with the 'Special Performance by a Mystery Guest' bit?" Hildy waved a shrimp at her. "Dangling the possibility that Adriana Asebedo will be there, which obviously there's no way, but it gets people talking. 'Ooh, their son knows her, I wonder if that's who they mean?' And then they'll get some tribute band or one-hit wonder to play the actual concert, but it won't matter because by then they'll have a captive audience of drunk CEOs. Pay a few C-list celebrities to mingle with the suits, call the caterer, and voilà! Corporate nirvana. They'll be pushing the Prince of Pilsner schtick hard. Probably have a big blowup of his picture in *People* magazine."

Charlie would hate that, Jean thought, before giving herself a mental slap. What did she really know about him? Nothing true.

"I didn't think you were into this gossipy stuff. Sex lives of celebrities. Or people who used to have sex with celebrities." Jean felt the lower half of her face twist and had to pretend she'd swallowed a piece of shrimp cartilage, thumping her chest to sell it.

"I'm into *winning*," Hildy corrected, politely ignoring Jean's drowning-on-dry-land bit.

"Same." Their eyes met, and Jean saw the same mix of steely determination and a light buzz reflected back at her.

"To the sisterhood of scorned women." Hildy tried to clink glasses, but Jean slid hers out of reach.

"Except I'm nobody's victim."

"Preach!"

"The way I see it—" Jean stuck out her arm, fingers bracketing a point in the middle distance like it was a movie screen—"I was too easy on him before. Now the gloves are off. This is about showing him what he's missing." With a little help from a provocative new wardrobe. Good luck ignoring that, Charlie.

Hildy poked at the ice in her glass with a hot-pink straw. "I get that. You want payback, but without admitting he hurt you in the first place."

"Exactly! It was supposed to be two sexy strangers having a good time and then going their separate ways. But no, he had to ruin everything, so now he's going to pay." Probably. If she went all the way. In the not sexy sense. Jean scowled into her drink. "Why are men the way they are?"

"If I knew that, I'd write a bestselling book and then franchise it into a podcast and series of self-healing workshops and branded yoga apparel."

That was something Jean appreciated about Hildy: she had an eye for opportunity. It didn't matter that her agenda wasn't identical to Jean's. There was enough overlap to make the partnership work. Hildy would get her in the door, and Jean would teach Charlie a lesson he'd never forget. Everything Charlie had done to her—lying, seducing, and then leaving—was about to get served right back to him. Doubling down on the deception and dicking around with someone's feelings.

And then she'd one-up him by letting the press (aka Hildy)

have a field day with his secrets. Jean kept imagining tabloid headlines like "Charlie Pike Is the Father of My Alien Baby" or "I Saw Bigfoot Kissing Charlie Pike," but she'd leave the details to her co-conspirator.

"This is going to be epic," Jean said, ripping the tail off another shrimp.

"If we're talking about my story, then hell yes. There is dirt to be dug." Hildy tapped the side of her nose. "I can smell it."

"That's definitely part of it," Jean agreed.

The same way a fuse was part of a bomb.

Pike's Spike! Beer Sales Soar After Pike Heir Spotted with Adriana Asebedo

Bottle & Barrel Quarterly

Your dad's favorite beer is cool again. With reliable sources reporting a brewing (ha!) relationship between the youngest member of the Pike dynasty and the musical superstar, everyone wants a taste of one of America's oldest microbrews.

Does Adriana drink Pike's Pale Ale? We'll have to wait and see if she adds an "I Like Pike" sticker to her guitar case.

Chapter 14

The most boring week of Charlie's life did not help him forget Jean, contrary to Mugsy's assurances. That was the problem with falling for someone so distinctive. You couldn't pretend you'd ever meet a person like that again. She was the good kind of different—unlike him.

His parents made a fuss when he first arrived, telling him how happy they were he'd finally come home, even though he was late and "looked a little pale." Love with a side of judgment (and chewable multivitamins) was the standard script at the Pike household.

After that, Charlie did his best to fly under the radar, standing where they told him and blinking blindly into the flash for a new family portrait. He promised to try on the clothes hanging in garment bags in his closet and nodded at the party-planning details blasting him like a rogue sprinkler. It felt like being one of those cardboard cutouts they prop up in movie theater lobbies: resembles a real person from the front, but it's flat and empty inside. A stiff wind could have knocked Charlie over, and he wasn't sure he'd get up again. Lying on the ground seemed like a reasonable response to his current predicament.

More reasonable than pretending to care whether pigs in a blanket "set the right tone." The only tone Charlie could hear was a constant whine.

Why didn't she want me?

That was what it boiled down to, when everything was said and done. If she'd felt for Charlie a fraction of what he felt for her, Jean wouldn't have traded information about him for money.

And yet how could he blame her for not loving him? That wasn't something you could force on another person, because what was love worth if not freely chosen?

Maybe if he'd been brave enough to level with her, she would have made a different call. He tried to picture himself saying, "Jean, here's the situation. Can you take me as I am?"

Unless she hadn't felt anything for him at all. But that possibility was too upsetting to look at head-on.

Not for the first time, he thought of texting Jean, even knowing how pathetic that would seem. *Remember me? I can't forget you.*

Unfortunately—or maybe fortunately, for his dignity—Mugsy had confiscated his phone for a forty-eight-hour post-breakup digital detox, a concept Charlie suspected she'd invented on the spot. By the time he got it back, all traces of Jean were gone.

Charlie stared morosely at his phone, lying beside him on the bed like a useless hunk of junk. Mugsy might as well have kept it, for all the good it was doing him now.

The screen lit up, firing his nervous system with a burst of electricity. He nearly sent the phone skidding across the floor as he scrambled to pick it up.

An email!

If a person couldn't text you because someone else had rudely blocked their number without your permission, she might try to get in touch the old-fashioned way.

But no. It was from one of the professors he'd worked with in Australia. Under other circumstances, Charlie would have been thrilled to hear from a leading researcher in his field, but Dr. Dillingham had the disadvantage of not being Jean.

The message was brief.

A friend of yours was looking for you, Charles. I said I would pass along the information. And now I have.

He emailed like he talked: staccato bursts of information that circled back on themselves unexpectedly. It took Charlie a few reads to make sense of it, and even then there were lingering questions. What friend had emailed? When?

Although he tried not to sound too frantic in his reply, the urgency must have come through because Dr. D answered right away—an unheard-of reaction for a man who forgot there was such a thing as voicemail for months at a time.

As quickly as his spirits had soared, they came crashing back to earth when Charlie realized it was a form message, letting the world know the recipient was currently out of office.

Charlie didn't have time to play phone tag with Dr. Dillingham's graduate assistant. What if it was Jean trying to contact him? She could be in trouble and need his help. Or just want to talk, for whatever reason. If only he'd memorized her number. Or found out where she lived. If Charlie hadn't been afraid to leave his cottage, they could have hung out at her place—

The resort! Why didn't he think of that sooner? Charlie's hands trembled as he looked up the number. He let part of himself—maybe a pinkie's worth—hope that Jean would be the one to answer.

The familiar greeting hit him like a stomach cramp. They really did make dreams come true, at least until they turned into a nightmare. That probably wasn't the kind of customer-service testimonial they could put in their brochures.

He shook himself, swallowing the disappointment of not hearing Jean's voice. Time to focus on the task at hand.

"Yes, Polly—"

"Pauline," she interrupted. "But I guess you can call me Polly. The customer is always right."

"Right," he echoed, uncertainly.

"I know. That's what I said."

Charlie stopped himself from saying *right* again. Clearing his throat, he tried to explain that he was looking for an employee named Jean for reasons that were not at all nefarious or creepy. Probably he shouldn't have mentioned that part.

Pauline stopped humming long enough to say, "Nah. I don't know any Jean."

"Are you sure?" Charlie gave up trying to sound normal. He'd come *so close* to making contact. "Dark hair, smart as a whip, incredibly artistic?"

There was a lot more he could have said, but Pauline's laughter cut off his Ode to Jean.

"Just messing with you. Jean's my girl."

"Really?" Charlie hugged the phone to his chest, until it occurred to him that Pauline might be able to hear his heart pounding. "Could I talk to her?"

"No can do," Pauline replied.

There was a long silence.

"Why?" Charlie finally asked, when no further explanation appeared to be forthcoming.

"I'm not supposed to say." She barely paused. "But between you and me, she doesn't work here anymore."

He sat up in bed. "She doesn't?"

"We're heading into the slow season. They always cut back staff. And then that whole business with you-know-who."

Charlie had a sinking feeling he did know. "What happened?" he asked, already wincing.

"Oh man, you didn't hear about it? We had one huge celebrity staying with us. The Silent Storm, baby. Adriana Asebedo's ex," she added, when he failed to react.

"I don't know that I'd call him a celebrity—"

"Ha! Shows what you know. Anyway, that's why the boss was pissed. Jean never introduced him to Hot Stuff. He probably wanted to ask for some pointers." She laughed again, loud enough to cover Charlie's stricken silence.

"Your boss was mad? At Jean?"

"Big-time. Told her to pack her things and not come back. Major stink."

His hand tightened around the phone. Jean had lost her job— because of him?

"Oops, gotta go," Pauline sang. "Sorry I couldn't tell you anything. What did you say your name was? In case I run into her."

With a mumbled "thanks" he ended the call, pretending he hadn't heard her question.

Charlie tossed the phone aside so he could rub his face with both hands. What had he done? He should have put his foot down with Mugsy as soon as she showed up at the resort, instead of being a pushover.

So what if she sold me out to the tabloids? he could have said. *I still prefer her to every other girl I've ever met.*

No one was perfect—least of all Charlie. He'd been lying in bed feeling sorry for himself, when Jean was the one who'd suffered.

Part of him had been clinging to the idea that she was still there at Dolphin Bay, where he could imagine her going about her day. Only now the final tie between them had snapped.

The one thing he felt certain about was that Jean would never forgive him.

And he would never forget her.

Top 10 Reasons Charlie Pike Is Boyfriend Goals

The Hot Sauce, Celebrity Shag of the Week

1. He's hot. That face, am I right?
2. Tall. Wear those heels, girl. He's not going to mind.
3. Old-fashioned. Did you see him hold that door for her?
4. Free beer. He'll bring the party, thanks to a lifetime supply of Pike's Pale Ale.
5. Don't have to worry about his ex calling you out. No socials = no baggage.
6. Smart. Those glasses say "if there's a zombie apocalypse, I know what to do."
7. Not an actor. Finally, someone who isn't worried about his angles.
8. Country house. Sometimes you need to get away and pet some cute animals.
9. Has his own money. Is there anything worse than a freeloader?
10. Silent storm. Enough said.

Chapter 15

After a trio of first-class flights (which Jean was annoyed with herself for being too stressed to appreciate) and a fortune in extra luggage fees, they finally made it to Charlie's home state.

Hildy returned from the rental-car counter in high spirits.

"I got us a Jeep," she announced, dangling the key ring from her index finger.

The postage-stamp-size regional airport was still a two-hour drive from the Pike estate on the far western edge of South Dakota, hence the need for a vehicle.

"Are we going off-roading?" Jean had pictured more of a country estate, maybe a hedge maze and some topiaries, but the view out the window of the terminal was all tall grass waving in the wind. It was giving major *Little House on the Prairie* vibes.

"If a thing is worth doing, it's worth doing *in style,* as my second-to-last stepaunt used to say" was Hildy's ambiguous reply.

"She died?"

"They sent her to a farm upstate." Hildy snickered at her own joke. "Kidding. It was one of my uncle's semiannual divorces. Slightly more common than a leap year."

"Ah."

"Everybody needs a hobby." Hildy turned around like she might need to consult the signage for directions, but there was only one exit. "Ready to hit the road?"

"Among other things." Putting her back into it, Jean managed to roll their heavy luggage cart out the door.

Hildy insisted on driving, to help Jean get into the pampered-guest mindset.

Jean rolled down her window as Hildy threw the Jeep into reverse. "We might as well enjoy ourselves while we're here. My sources tell me the Pikes are going all out. Get Piked!" She lifted one hand from the steering wheel to shoot a finger gun at Jean.

"What?"

"That's the theme of the weekend. A little crass for what they're trying to do but—" She broke off, wincing at Jean's expression. "Sorry. I didn't mean to be insensitive. Since you've already been Piked. As it were." There was a hopeful pause, on the off chance Jean wanted to provide graphic details.

"Anyway," Hildy continued, raising her voice as they merged onto the highway, wind rattling through the vehicle, "as I was saying, this smells like a major image overhaul. The Pike's brewing brand is all about selling traditional middle Americana, right? It's been around forever, it doesn't taste like ass, but it's not too uppity either. Only with the way the industry's trending the last five or ten years, it's all about consolidation. The big companies eating up the little guys, and then they have a stranglehold on distribution, which means you're SOL trying to go it alone. Same thing that's been happening in the media world. On top of which, beer sales are down across the board. You've got your hard seltzers, your mocktails, all the vodka-drinking keto warriors." Hildy shook her head. "Not a good time to be peddling what is essentially a bottle of carbs. Makes sense they're looking for a sugar daddy. Or mama."

Jean stared at her.

"What?" Hildy self-consciously tucked a flyaway curl behind her ear.

"How do you know this stuff?"

"I have like seven-eighths of a business degree. Not to mention the ungodly number of executive dinners I had to sit through in my childhood. They thought I was there for the Shirley Temples, but no. I was soaking that shit up."

"What's the sugar mama part?"

"Based on the guest list, either they're looking to sell outright or take on a silent partner. Very different optics, obviously. And the price point is going to depend on how much the Pike's name is worth, as a legacy brand, so they're going to push the 'we've been around for a century' narrative hard. Ideal scenario for Charlie boy is a bidding war. If they have interest from Toho, they can use that to leverage a higher offer from Koskinen, and so on." She slid Jean an assessing look. "Those are beverage companies."

"I got that from the context."

"Toho is Japanese and Koskinen is Finnish. Whiskey and vodka, respectively. Though I guess it's not essential that you know that. You can always play the bored little rich girl card." Hildy pressed a palm to her cheek, eyes going wide and doll-like. "I don't know where the money comes from," she cooed. "I just like spending it."

Jean considered whether vapid was within her dramatic range. She'd been planning to skew a little closer to type: hard-bitten and surly young woman with a past. Hildy hadn't shared a lot of details about Jean's borrowed identity, but then again, Jean hadn't asked. A red haze had settled over her brain, like when you come home from a long shift so hungry you inhale everything in your path, not thinking beyond the urgency of the moment. Olives and off-brand Nutella? Why not!

"Just get me in the door," she'd told Hildy, like she was ordering at a drive-through. Fetch me an opportunity, an identity, and all the necessary accoutrements. And make it snappy!

All Jean knew was that an invite had been arranged for a distant acquaintance of Hildy's around Jean's age who happened to be related to a booze magnate with a silly nickname. Abracadabra, instant cover story.

"Am I supposed to be an airhead?" Jean asked.

"Does it matter? People love feeling superior, so playing down to expectations is a safe bet. You show them youth and attitude, they'll swallow the story."

"I have attitude."

"In spades," Hildy agreed.

"And you're sure I don't need a wig?"

"I doubt anybody there could pick Sockless Tommy's niece out of a lineup. She's just another ornamental female." Hildy glanced in the rearview mirror before changing lanes. "You're not losing your nerve, are you?"

"Who, me? No way. I've got this. It's classic sleight of hand. I make them see what I want them to see." It was way more punk rock waltzing in there looking exactly the same, minus the resort uniform. She cracked her knuckles. "I dare him to tell them who I am."

"And if he does?"

"I have something planned. Don't worry."

It was clear from the twist of Hildy's lips that she was, in fact, worrying. "It's not an accent though, right?"

Jean opted to overlook the lack of confidence. Some of her earlier accent work had relied more on vibes than technique, but surely that was the point. Creating an atmosphere, setting the mood, etcetera. "It's not *only* an accent."

The hum of the tires grew louder. Either they'd hit a rough stretch of asphalt or the silence from the driver's seat was intensifying.

"What?" Jean finally asked.

"I'm thinking about your narrative. It would be odd if Sockless Tommy's niece sounded like a Swiss goatherd or whatever you have in mind."

"She could have studied abroad."

"Simpler is better," Hildy countered. "Eyes on the prize."

Jean couldn't argue with that. She hadn't come all this way to do anything but win. "If he calls me out, I'll tell them Jean was my fake alter ego, and I was actually this Eve person all along."

"Huh." Hildy tapped the steering wheel with the tip of a petal-pink fingernail. "Okay."

Part of Jean had hoped for at least a little pushback. *How could anyone think for a second you weren't the original?* Maybe Jean wasn't as iconic as she liked to believe.

Turning her face to the window, she let the wind buffet her. The air felt eighty percent drier than she was used to, and the local colors looked similarly parched, like all the juice had been sucked out. Even the sky had a sun-bleached quality that matched the brittle brown and faded green of the grass. It was not unlike the way Jean felt on the inside, withered and desolate.

Despite its lack of lushness, there was an austere beauty that spoke to her artist's eye. How hard would it be to capture the clarity of the light, pale and golden as it washed over the soft hillsides? The shadows were lengthening into late afternoon, the line of pine trees black in the distance. It was a landscape she'd only seen in the kind of movies where everyone was on horseback.

"I feel like any second there's going to be a stagecoach robbery," she mused. "Or a cancan line of saloon girls. Hey, barkeep, give me a whiskey in a dirty glass." She squeezed the words out of the side of her mouth, like she had a toothpick between her teeth. Or a cigarillo. Something cowboy-ish.

"This won't be like that," Hildy assured her. "It'll be super posh. While also trying to pull the younger demographic with some hipster frills."

It seemed like a stretch for a beer company, until Jean remembered Smithson's family, with their luxury cars and general attitude of slumming in their own hometown. "I can be *fahncy*," Jean drawled, with the merest hint of BBC. "What if I'm Lady Eve Sidgwick, who is terribly proper?"

"Sockless Tommy is from Detroit. He made his fortune in

cinnamon schnapps." Hildy's nose wrinkled. "Anyway, you don't need any of that. You've got this in the bag."

"I know." Although the closer they got to their destination, the more Jean wished she'd lacquered on a few more layers of protection between her soft underbelly and seeing Charlie again.

Hildy rummaged in her tote, handing Jean a pack of gum.

"Thanks." Jean glanced at the chunky cocktail ring Hildy had insisted she borrow, as that finger tap, tap, tapped the raw hem of the three-hundred-dollar denim shorts and twice-as-pricey lace-up espadrilles that were allegedly "music festival basics." And that was just what she had on at the moment, not even speaking of the scads of outfits in the trunk. Hildy would undoubtedly make bank on whatever scoop Jean managed to score, but none of this would have been possible without the upfront investment. "It's really nice of you."

"Uh, you're welcome? You can Venmo me the five cents or just, you know, pay it forward. Preferably sugar-free."

"I'm not talking about the gum. It's all of it." Jean gestured at her clothes, the car, and the unfamiliar setting beyond the windshield, stretching to the horizon in a wash of sage green and toasted tan. "Were you always this nice?"

How well did she really know Hildy? They'd met, what, a month ago? Under weird circumstances? It happened that way sometimes when you lived in a travel destination. People waltzed into your life for a dazzling cameo before disappearing again. Though they didn't usually vanish in the night. Or use a false identity.

Maybe that was another thing to lay at Charlie's door. He'd given her trust issues. Emotional chlamydia.

"You know what they say about money?"

The lyrics of a dozen pop songs flashed through Jean's head before she settled on "Can't Buy Me Love." "No," she said, kicking that thought into the gutter.

"Easy come, easy go. Besides, it's cathartic."

"Buying stuff?"

"Teaching a man he can't get away with treating you like that." Hildy held out a hand, and Jean unwrapped a piece of gum and dropped it in her palm.

If only the rest of this adventure could be that easy.

Chapter 16

"Charlie!" His mother hurried across the foyer. "Why aren't you wearing the outfit I picked out for you? I put a sticky note on it and everything. It says 'Night One.'"

"I must have gotten sidetracked. Should I go change?" He looked hopefully at the stairs. Maybe he could forget to come back down while he was at it.

"That'll have to wait," his father said, taking Charlie by the elbow and turning him to face a man in a denim shirt with a handlebar mustache that didn't quite match the reddish-orange of his hair. "Charlie, I'd like you to meet Haggard Jones."

"H-Haggard?" Charlie stumbled a little over the name, not convinced he'd heard right.

"Of Haggard's Red Hots," his dad supplied.

"Ah." Charlie gave what he hoped was a knowledgeable nod. "Pleased to meet you."

"Likewise," the other man said, twisting the end of his mustache. "I guess you know all about getting scorched. You like it spicy, eh? Too hot to handle?"

"That's my boy," Mr. Pike chimed in, not exactly illuminating the subject matter. He looked expectantly at Charlie.

"Well, uh, sometimes you need special gloves." He was thinking of a cooking show he'd watched at the resort, about dicing hot peppers.

"Oh ho," Haggard said, with another belly laugh. "So that's how the kids are doing it these days. Teaching this old dog new tricks." He leaned closer, nudging Charlie with his elbow. "She is a *muy caliente* lady."

"She? Oh." He was talking about Adriana, not kitchen safety. Before Charlie could think of a polite way to tell the older man to get his mind out of the gutter, he was dragged away like a puppy on a leash.

"He's a seven-day wonder," Charlie's father informed him. "Canned cocktails that burn your taste buds off. Plenty of buzz, which is why we invited him, but I doubt he makes a go of it once the novelty of drinking carbonated hot sauce fades. Anyway, he's not the most important person here."

His father gave an exaggerated *ahem,* as if his son must know exactly who he was talking about. That added an extra layer of tension to the interval that followed, during which Charlie met a woman with silver-streaked hair and a nose ring who'd recently taken over her father's bourbon business ("Isn't that wonderful, Charlie? Keeping it in the family!"); a vodka producer from Iceland who invited Charlie to visit the hot springs there, which was confusing on multiple levels; and an aggressively fit couple from Canada who (when not playing pairs tennis on the over-65 circuit) were launching a new line of low-calorie brandy-and-wine spritzers.

"Do not use the word 'sangria,'" Charlie's dad warned as they left the husband-and-wife team. "It's a sore spot."

That much at least seemed within Charlie's capabilities. Unless he'd jinxed himself by thinking that? He tugged at the neckline of his shirt. Either it was too warm in here or anxiety was making him sweat.

"Don't fidget," Mr. Pike said through a toothy smile. "Everything is wonderful. We should get you a drink!"

"That's o—" he started to say, when Mugsy appeared at his side.

"Here you go." She held out a bottle of Pike's Pale Ale.

"Good girl," Mr. Pike said, beaming at her. "Still taking care of our Charlie."

"Dad, Mugsy does a lot more than that." Even though he felt slightly betrayed by the beer delivery, it bothered him more that his father still saw her as Charlie's handler, as opposed to an independent businesswoman.

"Of course," Mr. Pike agreed, scanning the room for other conversational opportunities. His gaze lingered on the patio doors, beyond which Charlie could see a cluster of younger guests. They were all laughing as a blond guy with slicked-back hair told a story, gesturing with the hand holding his beer. It looked like Charlie's worst nightmare—the loudness, plus all the competitive social undercurrents he'd never understand, not having studied primates—so he was surprised his father hadn't urged him to go out there yet. It was a script he knew well. *Go mingle with the other young people, Charlie.* Translation: why can't you be more like them?

No one had been more thrilled than Mr. Pike when Adriana Asebedo invited Charlie to visit her in L.A. His mom and Mugsy worried, but Charlie had been swept along by his father's encouragement. *Good to see you coming out of your shell, son.* Which was not a reference to oviparity, because when Charlie pointed out that some reptiles have live births, his father only frowned.

Dating, on the other hand, Mr. Pike understood. What could be more normal than boy meets girl? Even if the girl happened to be a global superstar and the boy couldn't handle the glare of the spotlight.

The bitter taste at the back of Charlie's throat was even more unpleasant than beer, so he took a cautious sip, choking when it hit his tongue.

Mr. Pike sighed at his son's lack of smoothness, but the truth was that Charlie had nearly done a spit take because it *wasn't* beer, despite the label on the bottle.

"Nettle and goldenrod," Mugsy whispered, covering her

mouth like she was about to sneeze. She must have poured out the beer and replaced it with one of her teas, a light floral blend with a hint of sweetness that was far more soothing to his jangled nerves than a bottle of bitter bubbles.

"Delicious," Charlie said, feeling only slightly guilty when his father perked up.

"That's right, son. Guess you couldn't get an ice-cold Pike's out there in the jungle."

"They call it the bush—" Charlie started to explain, but his father was already locked on to his next target, tugging his belt loops and smoothing his hair before beelining across the room. Mrs. Pike waved at Mugsy, who hurried to her side, leaving Charlie alone in the sea of people.

He'd asked a therapist once why crowds felt lonelier than being on his own. She quoted an old poem about a sailor that said something like, *water everywhere but not a drop to drink.* Because you couldn't drink salt water but seeing it all around made your thirst worse, like it was rubbing your face in what you couldn't have. Only Charlie wasn't desperate to talk to all these people, "working the crowd" like his father. If it was a question of longing, a deep and pressing desire, there was only one person Charlie wanted.

He wondered if it would always be like this, the hollow ache in his chest Jean had left behind. Maybe he didn't want it to hurt less, if this was all he had to remember her by.

A metallic clank disrupted his train of thought. It was the gin distributor from Scotland, easy to spot with his plaid bomber jacket, though you'd hear him coming first, thanks to the spurs he was clanking across the floor.

"Charlie!" His father circled an arm. "Come over here."

Here we go, Charlie thought. His dad was standing by the sliding-glass doors, no doubt about to throw Charlie to the wolves. He had a vivid memory of his father's voice yelling, "Sink or swim, son!" after chucking him into the deep end of the community pool. Like it was a question of willpower, and if Charlie didn't want to drown, he'd figure it out. Luckily, Mugsy had been there to grab him by the rash guard and haul him to the ladder.

"There he is," his dad said.

"Who?"

"The brains behind this entire operation." He clearly expected Charlie to be bowled over with amazement, as if turning their home into a fairground was a good thing. "Smithson is a natural leader."

That must mean Smithson was the one Charlie had noticed before, still doing all the talking . . . wait. "Did you say *Smithson*?"

"Yes." His father's chin lifted, indicating the mouthy blond outside. "Smithson Barrett."

"Smithson Barrett," Charlie repeated.

"Do you have an ear infection? Smithson Barrett, like I said." He checked to be sure no one was in hearing range before gesturing at Charlie to bend down. "Our rebranding consultant."

Charlie squeezed his eyes shut and counted to three before opening them again, but the mirage didn't dissolve. Smithson Barrett, Jean's high school nemesis. The jerk who let her take the rap for his crimes. *She was right about the hair,* he thought, squinting at the back of Smithson's head. It was hard to be certain with all the gel, but Charlie strongly suspected it was thinning, just as Jean had predicted.

Hard to believe *Smithson* was standing in Charlie's backyard. "What are the odds?"

"It was more about persistence. I gave him the full-court press."

As usual, Charlie and his father were speaking at cross-purposes. "Why?"

"Because we needed his magic touch." His eyes took on a faraway look. You would have thought he was bragging to a casual acquaintance about his son, instead of the reverse.

"Did you check his references?"

His father huffed at the ridiculousness of the question. "Smithson has done wonders for his family's business."

"If he's that great, don't they need him back at Barrett's?"

"He works with a very limited outside clientele. This is a real W for us, convincing Smithson to come on board. You could learn a lot from him, Charles. Take a page from his book."

"No thanks." He wasn't looking for lessons on how to be a weasel. No offense to weasels.

His father glanced at his watch. "We'll table that for later. I've got another surprise for you."

"That's nice," Charlie said, unconvincingly.

"Don't frown, son. It looks like you're worried." He hitched up his pants, elbows and toes angled outward in a stance that was probably supposed to telegraph confidence, even though it looked to Charlie like his dad's underwear might be riding up.

"You'll like this," his father promised. "It's a girl. Your kind of person."

It was anyone's guess what that meant. Glasses, most likely. Limited athletic ability. Not good at schmoozing.

"Can't wait," Charlie lied.

Chapter 17

As the cloud of dust kicked up by the Jeep's tires faded to a haze, Jean studied the scene in front of them. The iron gates and fully staffed security booth at the end of the private drive had set the expected hoity-toity tone, but between here and there, they seemed to have teleported to a different world.

"What the fuck, Hildy? I'm getting major dude-ranch vibes." It would be hard not to, what with the hay bales and hats, not to mention the red bandanas tied around every other neck.

Hildy pressed her lips together, *hmm*ing thoughtfully as a man in a checked shirt and painted-on Wranglers twirled his lasso for an older couple, who clapped when he finished the trick. "It is a bit frontiercore. Possibly my intel was a teensy bit faulty, regarding the theme."

"You think?" Jean glanced down at her midriff-baring bustier, barely covered by the fringe of her vest. "This ensemble does not say cattle drive. I look like a total imposter."

"You're from Wisconsin. They have lots of cows there."

"Gentle cheese cows. This feels more like angry steak cow country."

"Probably best not to call them that to their faces," Hildy cautioned, reaching across to unbuckle Jean's seat belt.

"I'm not planning to get that close to big scary cows." Jean braced her wedge heels under the glove compartment, resisting Hildy's attempt to push her out the door.

"Are we really talking about cows, or are you scared of seeing a certain playboy beer millionaire with soulful eyes?"

"I'm not scared. He should be scared of me." She crossed her arms, scowling at what looked like a troupe of square dancers. There were exactly zero crinolines in Jean's luggage. Sexy mesh bodycon dresses? Sure. Wholesome gingham? Not so much.

"Great. Hold on to that confidence. You said you want to be so luscious he felt personally attacked. Mission accomplished."

"But maybe I should be a different kind of thirst trap. To blend in." You'd have to come at Jean with a hot poker (which for all she knew might be part of the evening's entertainment) to make her admit it, but she'd been counting on at least *looking* like she belonged here with the Snooty McSnootersons. It hadn't occurred to her that they'd all be playing cowboy.

"We could go back to town and get some flannel shirts," Jean suggested.

Hildy rolled her eyes. "Because nothing says SEX like a plaid button-down. Also, what town? The last sign of civilization was half an hour ago. Over gravel roads. And that was a rest stop."

She had a point. Jean had asked more than once if they were there yet, especially after losing cell reception. The Pike family estate was nestled in a secluded canyon a stone's throw from the Wyoming border. It was picturesque, if you liked that kind of thing, but not exactly a retail hotbed.

"There's a trout stream too," Hildy had explained as they bumped over the rutted roads leading into the surprisingly green valley. The grassy slopes gave way to steep rocky walls topped with spiny red ridges that towered high above. "Really good fly-fishing."

"How do you know all this?" Jean asked.

"Research, babe."

That sounded more productive than getting sucked down the rabbit hole of gossip sites dissecting Charlie's relationship with Adriana Asebedo.

It was too late for regrets. They were here in the wilderness, cut off from the internet or the hope of a quick mall run. And Hildy was trying to physically eject her from the passenger seat.

Jean shoved back. "Quit it."

"Time to hop along. Go on, git."

"How come you get to do an accent?"

"Because I'm behind the scenes. You're the face of this operation." Hildy ducked down, hiding behind the steering wheel. "Now go out there and do your thing, before someone recognizes me, and we both get kicked out."

"Are you on a Most Wanted list I don't know about?"

Hildy's sigh dislodged one of her curls. "There's a total media blackout, and my last name basically screams 'media.' And since I haven't exactly been flying under the radar, there's no way I'm getting in. But don't worry, I'll be in the wind."

"What?"

"I've always wanted to say that. FYI, there's a burner phone in the garment bag, if they take yours."

"I have zero bars."

"Pictures." Hildy tapped her temple. "Want me to count you down? Three, two—"

"I'm going," Jean snapped, gathering her impractical bag and floppy hat.

"Remember to own it. You're the kind of girl who puts the 'eh' in entitled."

"And the tit." Jean dropped onto the grass. "Tits. Plural. Since I have two." She slammed the door before Hildy could get the last word in.

Two men in western shirts with contrast piping and shiny snaps hurried over, the first going to the trunk while the other greeted Jean.

"Welcome to the Pike Family Ranch. Your name?"

She channeled the attitude of the haughtiest guests she'd dealt with at Dolphin Bay. "I am Eve." A flicker of uncertainty made her add, "Sockless Tommy's niece."

He glanced at the very un-cowboy tablet in his hands, tapping the surface before turning it to face her. "If you could just sign here."

Jean debated raising her sunglasses to read the minuscule lines of text but didn't want him to see the blank look in her eyes.

"Standard NDA," he said, with an *I-know-right* eye roll. Just one of those everyday annoyances, like having to show your passport before jetting to the Alps for a ski vacation. "For everyone's protection."

"Indeed," she droned, in the affectless deadpan that definitely did not qualify as an accent. Between that and the frozen face, Eve's vibe was fully *I am so cool I'm basically a cadaver. Who sleeps in a designer crypt.* Her attitude dared any of these fools to ask her to line dance.

"Thank you. The family would love for you to join them in the main house for refreshments. I'll tell your driver where to park."

Jean inclined her head, as if this were the bare minimum she expected at the many house parties she attended in her life as a wealthy parasite. Er, socialite.

No wonder Charlie thought he could get away with treating the little people like dirt, if he'd been brought up in this environment. About time someone taught him otherwise.

All she had to do was make it to the house in these death-trap platform sandals. They'd looked so alluring on the shelf, before she'd strapped them onto her feet. Definitely no sport mode on these babies.

An attractive middle-aged woman stepped out the front door, already smiling. She was wearing a long denim shirtdress that managed to suggest "western" without making her look like she was waiting tables at a barbeque joint. But it wasn't the low-key elegance that hit Jean hardest. The perfectly layered dark hair was lightly threaded with silver and her eyes looked so much like a certain two-faced snakeologist's, she might as well have been wearing a sign around her neck that said *I'm Charlie's mom!*

"Hello! Welcome . . ." The other woman's smile stayed bright as her voice trailed off in question.

"I am Eve," Jean said again.

The temptation to keep talking was strong, but a central part of the Eve concept was being a conversational black hole. No babbling allowed. Instead of trying to justify her presence by volunteering information, she let other people fill in the blanks.

"Eve! How wonderful to meet you." Before Jean could react, she'd been pulled into a hug. It required all her presence of mind to stay limp and sluglike instead of reciprocating. "I'm Sandy Pike. We're so happy you could join us for the festivities."

"I'm sure."

Mrs. Pike recovered from this ego trip with impressive speed. "What do you do, Eve?"

"I dabble. I'm a dabbler."

"That sounds very . . . creative. Like your clothes!"

Jean side-eyed Mrs. Pike but detected no trace of covert insult. She kept her guard up anyway, in case Charlie's mother was as slick and duplicitous as her son.

"I met Sockless Tommy once. You don't look much like him."

"Lucky me." Jean's jaw felt like concrete. Was she about to be exposed this close to seeing Charlie again?

Mrs. Pike laughed. "All those ex–professional wrestlers have the same sense of style, don't they?" She linked her arm with Jean's so they could walk side by side. "Of course a lovely young thing like you isn't going to have a mullet perm."

"No," Jean agreed, wondering what other fun tidbits Hildy had neglected to mention about Jean's fake uncle.

"Now, do you need a potty break," Charlie's mother asked, with the sweetness of a preschool teacher, "or are you ready to join the others?"

Would Jean have been greeted this warmly if she'd shown up as herself—sometime waitress and reluctant resort employee—instead of the alleged niece of a rich stranger with questionable taste in hairstyles?

The front door loomed ahead. It was the moment of truth—and consequences. For Charlie, obviously. Those butterflies in Jean's stomach were pure performance anxiety, untainted by anything weak and embarrassing like excitement.

Jean flashed back to the last time she'd stood outside a door waiting to see him. She imagined a flamethrower spitting fire across the empty lot of her feelings, burning down any weeds that might have sprouted from the dirt. Then she pictured herself kicking aside the ashy husk that represented the last scrap of her delusions about Charlie "The Snake" Pike.

It didn't matter if he had twenty girlfriends inside. She was here for one thing, and one thing only. "What was the question?"

"I asked if you were ready to go in," Mrs. Pike reminded her, tactfully ignoring Jean's momentary zone-out.

Right. Showtime. Jean squared her shoulders. Prepare for total domination, Charlie. She turned to his mother with a thin smile.

"Bring it on."

Chapter 18

Charlie watched his father roll his shoulders and smooth his hair before reaching for the knob.

A young woman stepped across the threshold, pale-eyed and light-haired. *I prefer dark hair,* Charlie thought, apropos of nothing.

"Welcome!" His dad's voice was many decibels too loud for indoors. "Charlie has been counting down the minutes!"

He frowned at his father before remembering to smile. The new arrival blinked back at him with no discernible emotion.

Charlie's dad cleared his throat. It was almost certainly a cue, but that kind of pressure had never helped Charlie find his words.

"Why don't you step into the living room?" Charlie's father urged their guest. "I need to have a quick word with my son."

She gave the pair of them another cool look before drifting out of sight.

"I don't know what that was, but I need you to make an effort with Emma," his father said when the two of them were alone. "Are you listening, son?"

"Yes," Charlie fibbed. "You said Emma—oh no!" His brain abruptly woke up. "She got out again?" The poor thing must be terrified with all these strangers in the house. He needed to check her usual hiding places. Charlie started to pull away, but his father tugged him back.

"Not *that* Emma." His smile was tight. "Emma Koenig. Daughter of Philip Koenig," he added, when Charlie didn't respond. "CEO of Koenig Industries."

"That's nice," Charlie ventured, not sure what else to say. He should have known his dad wasn't talking about Emma the corn snake. Mr. Pike barely tolerated it when Charlie brought up reptiles of any kind, so he was hardly likely to introduce the subject. "I guess she won't want a frozen mouse."

"Please don't offer Emma Koenig a mouse. Or mention rodents at all." With a visible effort, he left it at that, though Charlie could tell his father was dying to list all the topics that absolutely should not come up in conversation. It boiled down to the same message: *Can you be normal for once, Charlie?*

Jean would have known he was joking. Speaking of irrelevant information. Charlie nodded a silent promise to say as little as possible.

"We need to put our best foot forward with the Koenigs," his father continued, keeping his voice low. "Do you understand what I'm saying?"

Charlie raked his teeth over his bottom lip, stalling. "Maybe?"

"Priority numero uno for you this weekend is getting to know Emma. Shouldn't be too much of a hardship. Can't imagine you had many opportunities to socialize with pretty girls out there in the jungle."

"What do you think scientists look like?" Charlie asked, genuinely curious.

"My point is that it would be a big help if you could at least try to charm Emma," his father said on a sigh. "Like you did with that singer."

Because that turned out so well. Charlie kept the thought to himself, not that his father would have listened. "Maybe I should stay here by the door. Take people's coats."

"It's summertime. And your mother has it handled. You're with me."

He knew his dad had always wanted a son who was a carbon copy of himself, but since Charlie didn't have a showman mode,

he didn't bother to mimic his father's ear-to-ear grin as he followed him to the living room. Once there, they headed straight
for the banquette where Human Emma had settled.

She would make a very convincing ghost, Charlie thought,
now that he'd gotten a better look at her. Even her hair was the
color of the floaty bits you had to peel off an ear of corn. The only
thing missing was a long white dress—and getting her to put
down the apparently riveting book she was reading. Charlie had
to squint to make out the title under the illustration of a shrieking green creature, lips moving as he puzzled it out. *The Ego and
the Mechanisms of Defence* by Anna Freud. Huh. That made him
think of Jean's friend, who studied psychology—

Except that wasn't right. She was a reporter, not a grad student.

"Smile," his father hissed. Charlie gave it his best shot, letting
it drop when she didn't look up.

Mr. Pike cleared his throat. "Emma, you remember Charlie?"

She peered at him over the spine of her book. "From the hallway? Yes." Her voice was so soft, Charlie had to strain to make
out the words.

"The two of you actually met years ago, at a conference in
Salzburg. You ate pretzels together. I'm sure Charlie has fond
memories."

"Uh," Charlie started to say, breaking off when his father
glared a warning. "That sounds . . . well." He swallowed, uncomfortable with an outright lie. "I do like pretzels. The soft kind,
anyway."

Emma's gaze drifted back to her book. Charlie could hardly
blame her for losing interest.

"Is this your boy at last?" asked a new voice, with an accent
Charlie couldn't place. He turned to see a man around his father's age who looked like he should be starring in one of those
historical miniseries Charlie's mom liked to watch, full of mist
and cobblestones and lace.

He placed both hands on Charlie's shoulders, staring deeply into his eyes before kissing him on the cheeks, left and then right. There was an alarming moment when it seemed he might be going for the mouth and Charlie almost jerked back, but he managed to control himself.

"Mr. Koenig?" he guessed. His father looked pleased Charlie had figured it out, but less so when he added, "You seem very healthy."

It wasn't only the strength of his grip. You could practically see the life force radiating from his glowing skin—especially in contrast to his daughter, who looked like she might be getting over a cold. Not that Charlie would have said that part out loud. He felt mean for even thinking it. That was just a lot of sweater for a warm day.

"Call me Philip," Mr. Koenig said.

"Oh, that's—" *unlikely to happen*, Charlie silently finished. "I'm Charlie. Pike." He pointed at himself, aware even before his father sighed that this was not approved alpha-male behavior.

"I bet Emma would like to go outside and get some fresh air," Mr. Pike hinted. "Meet the other young people. Why don't you escort her, Charlie? I heard there might be a volleyball game."

Charlie tried to imagine a less enticing prospect. Paper cuts on all his fingers, maybe. While juicing a bag full of lemons.

"I'm not going out there." Although Emma's voice was barely above a whisper, there was a finality to the words that left no room for argument. "Hay fever," she added, before turning her attention back to her book.

It was an impressive dodge. Short of throwing up in the car, it was almost impossible to derail one of Mr. Pike's "fresh air and exercise" campaigns. Charlie was torn between intimidation and asking her to share her secret.

"Who is that ravishing creature?" Mr. Koenig said. He was facing the other direction, so Charlie couldn't see who he was talking about. Nor did he care, since it was almost certainly another business connection of his father's.

"How do you do?"

Charlie's spine snapped upright, as if a puppeteer had pulled his strings. That voice—

Time slowed to a crawl as he turned.

His brain said *impossible,* but his body was already in motion. Charlie forgot the other people in the room, the bottle of not-beer in his hand, and (most catastrophically) the ottoman that had occupied the same patch of floor for at least a decade. All he could think about was getting to her as quickly as possible.

Which was how he wound up launching himself headfirst over a piece of furniture and landing at her feet. Propping himself on his elbows, he slowly lifted his head.

Jean.

Those were Jean's ankles, and Jean's legs, her knees, her— He jerked his head up to meet her eyes. *Please,* he thought, not sure what he was asking for. She was a life jacket, and Charlie wanted to wrap her around his body before the choppy waters closed over his head. Only not literally, since they were on dry land. (Mostly dry; his hand was touching something wet.)

Before he could unstick his tongue, the sound of laughter penetrated the roaring in his ears.

"For goodness' sake, Charlie." His father's voice was bright, like it was all in good fun, but there was no mistaking the underlying strain. "You're making a mess."

A napkin landed next to Charlie's arm, startling him. Details sharpened: a soggy patch on the carpet where he'd spilled his drink, the bottom half of his body still propped on the ottoman like a human wheelbarrow, Mr. Koenig stepping over him to greet Jean.

Was he going to kiss her? Charlie had a wild impulse to grab the older man's ankle and wrestle him away, but she was already letting Philip Koenig press his lips to her hand. No doubt she'd gotten a good whiff of his incredible smell, like a forest full of saddles next to a seaside cliff. It was enough to make anyone lightheaded. Dammit!

There was an old bottle of cologne on Charlie's dresser. Maybe he should run upstairs and spritz himself. Except that would mean leaving Jean alone with Philip Koenig, which seemed like a very bad idea, what with him being so good-looking . . . and the way he was looking at her. But who could blame him?

She was even prettier than Charlie remembered. How long had it been since he'd breathed the same air as Jean? Way too long. And now she was here, but still so far away. All he could do was stare. Those eyes were like moss agates. Or no, topaz—

"Didn't know your boy was a rodeo clown." The spicy-cocktail guy slapped himself on the thigh, chortling.

"It takes a lot of nerve to step into the arena with an angry bull." It was unclear whether Charlie's father was defending him or implying he wasn't tough enough for rodeo.

While Charlie sopped up the spill, Mr. Koenig led Jean to the sofa, still holding her hand. They sat side by side, too close together for Charlie's comfort. He started to drag himself in that direction, then remembered he wasn't built for serpentine loco- motion and awkwardly swung his legs around. Emma Koenig acknowledged his struggles with a slow blink.

Jean didn't even glance at him. His heart plummeted. It wasn't because she seemed so taken by a smooth older man that she hadn't paid the slightest attention to Charlie. (Well, it wasn't *only* that.) Charlie had just remembered a crucial piece of information. If Jean looked in this direction, she might see *Smithson* through the patio doors.

She would be devastated! And then she would hate it here and want to leave! On top of which Charlie would have to call Smithson out, causing a scene that would give his dad a stroke.

He forced himself to check the patio, gasping in relief when he realized the entire group had migrated out of sight.

"Close your mouth," Mrs. Pike chided, crouching next to Charlie with a handful of paper towels. "You're making Emma feel bad."

How can you tell? Charlie wondered. The younger Koenig was lost in the pages of her book, like nothing else mattered. It was another trick Charlie wished he could learn, though he wasn't looking to hide in plain sight right now. If Jean was in the world, he wanted to be there too.

"I'm going to introduce you now," his mother whispered, "so try to be calm."

Could she hear the frantic pounding of his heart? Calm might as well be the moon for all the hope Charlie had of getting from here to there.

"Charlie, this is Eve."

His smile faltered. "What?"

"Eve. E-V-E. Like in the Bible. She's Sockless Tommy's niece."

Charlie looked from his mother to Jean, waiting for one of them to correct the record. "I don't understand?"

"It's three letters, dear. You'll get there." Mrs. Pike patted him on the cheek. "Eve, this is Emma. She's scientific, like our Charlie."

"Not exactly like," Emma replied, without looking up. "I study more complex creatures."

"My Emma is a doctor," Mr. Koenig informed the room.

"A doctor of psychology," his daughter said. "I can't remove your appendix."

Charlie put a hand to where he thought his appendix was, relieved surgery was off the table.

"She will analyze you," her father warned. "Hard to keep secrets around this one."

"I told you not to try, Papa." Emma turned a page.

"That's a useful skill in business." It sounded like Charlie's dad was congratulating Mr. Koenig on his daughter's degree, as if he'd written the dissertation himself. "Psychology, that is. Unlike snakes!"

"I don't study consumer behavior." Emma sounded mildly offended, as if he'd accused her of working retail.

"I was never one for the books myself," Charlie's father announced, in case any of them had missed his athletic physique. "More of an outdoors type." As if realizing he might be offending Emma, he made a quick pivot. "We here at Pike's are big supporters of science. In fact, we recently funded a research expedition in Australia. They were nice enough to let Charlie tag along. It's good to give the young people a chance to spread their wings before they settle into the business."

Charlie was afraid to look at Jean in case she thought he'd bought his way onto that trip. He was almost positive he'd earned his place.

"Isn't this nice?" Charlie's mother said, ignoring the strained atmosphere. "Charlie and Emma, reunited. Did you know he has a snake named Emma?"

Unlike his dad, Charlie's mom didn't try to sweep their son's interest in snakes under the rug. On the other hand, she still talked about it like a childish hobby, on par with Legos or Pokémon. Not something you'd go to grad school for, much less make a career of.

"Emma means universal," bipedal Emma pointed out. "It's a common name."

"My Emma isn't common. She has magnificent ventral scales."

"I bet he says that to all the girls," Jean murmured, earning a bark of laughter from Mr. Koenig.

"We took him to Reptile Gardens at an impressionable age," Mrs. Pike said, in the tone of someone confessing a childhood head injury. "Somewhere between the alligators and the chickens, he fell in love and never looked back. My Charlie is all about commitment."

Jean made a sound that might have been a snort.

"I have antihistamines," Emma said, sparing her a brief glance.

"How nice for you," Jean replied.

Charlie took a tentative step toward the couch. "What—I mean. When . . . ah. How was your trip?"

"I don't do small talk," Jean said, still not looking at him.

"Sorry." Charlie wiped his hands on his shirt, trying to think of something big to talk about. Death? Religion? Titanoboa, the extinct giant snake?

"You're behaving very strangely," his mother said. "What will Emma and Eve think of us?"

"Eve," he echoed, as if it was a foreign word.

There was a small *hmm* from Emma's direction, like she'd just added a note to his file.

"Shall I show you around, Eve?" Mrs. Pike offered. "There are refreshments on the patio—"

"No!" Charlie yelped.

Even Emma set down her book, as if he'd finally done something interesting.

Charlie swallowed. "I was going to offer her a drink." He took another step toward Jean, stooping to bring himself closer to her level. "Would you like one? A drink?"

"Get her a Pike's Pale," Charlie's dad said, before Jean could express a preference.

"I'm on it," Charlie yelped, hurrying to the bar. He slipped behind the wooden counter, nearly knocking over a stack of pint glasses before managing to pry one loose.

"Everything okay over there?" his mother asked in concern.

"Yes. Very fine." He set the glass under the spigot, taking a quick look at the couch to make sure Jean was still there. Their eyes met, jolting Charlie so hard he yanked on the tap, sending a flood of foamy beer down his other arm. At least some of it made it into the glass.

"Your boy's trigger-happy." It was the spicy-cocktail guy again, mustache quivering as he threw his head back and laughed. Hazard? Hubbard? Horrid? Something like that. Charlie frowned at him before remembering he was pouring a beer.

"Oops," he muttered, trying to wipe off the overflow with his hands.

"Somebody gives a lot of head." Jean's voice arrowed straight to Charlie's ears. He had no idea if she wanted him to hear, or if he was just so attuned to her that everything else was background noise, including the snicker from his mustachioed nemesis.

It was also true that he'd mostly filled her glass with foam.

"Get her a bottle," his dad ordered. "That one's a goner."

Jean stood, sauntering over to the bar with her eyes locked on Charlie.

Although he didn't hold with *The Jungle Book*'s depiction of Kaa (the myth that snakes hypnotized their prey had no scientific basis), Charlie couldn't have moved to save his life. Her silky dark hair swished, teasing his nostrils with a hint of perfume.

Every cell in his body chanted the same refrain: *Jean*.

Not that he could call her that. Somehow, he knew that was part of the game. Charlie couldn't have said what they were playing for or guessed at the rules beyond that one: pretending she was someone else. The message had been right there in her eyes, where he'd hoped to see *I'm so happy to see you* or *I missed you too* or even just *Hello, Charlie*. Instead of which he'd gotten *I dare you*. It wasn't a soft look, but at least it felt like they had a private understanding—their little secret no one else needed to know.

"Eve," he whispered as she slipped behind him. It was only one syllable, but his voice shook.

She didn't touch him. At least not directly, though the swinging fringe of her vest brushed against his legs. Even through a layer of denim it was enough to make his legs tremble.

"What are you—" he started to ask as she pulled out a cutting board, but she held a finger to her lips. Plucking a lemon from the wire basket under the bar, she sliced it into narrow wedges.

Charlie thought of nights in the cottage, watching her shuffle cards or sketch a cartoon in the margins of his field notebook. Plus the other things she'd done with those slender, sensitive, artist's hands.

The dangly bits on Jean's vest swayed as she shifted. Charlie watched his arm move as if it had a mind of its own, the tip of one finger barely skimming the fringe. He wanted to run his hands through it the way she used to let him do to her hair. And then tighten his grip and pull her closer—

The knife hit the cutting board with a sharp *thwack,* making him jump. Jean shot him a look over her shoulder, like she could smell the yearning wafting off him and was warning him to stay back.

"What are you making?" His voice sounded like the croak of a bullfrog.

"Shandies."

That was it, no teasing or long funny explanation. Charlie felt left in the dark, in more ways than one. The next thing he knew, she'd placed six full glasses on a tray, adding a lemon wedge to each.

"I can carry that for you." He started to reach for the tray.

"Are you sure that's a good idea, Charlie?" His mother's worried voice stopped him in his tracks.

It seemed like a terrible idea now that she'd reminded him of his ongoing struggle with gravity. Conscious of Jean watching, Charlie made up his mind, grabbing the tray with both hands.

Was this how tightrope walkers felt? He tried to lock his arms to his sides, but the liquid still sloshed like there was a storm brewing in the glasses. Step by step, barely breathing, he crossed the living room. Just a few more feet to the coffee table, and yet it seemed to take an hour, possibly because he was moving in slow motion.

"Oh thank God," his mother breathed, pressing a hand to her heart when the tray came to rest on a solid surface.

If carrying six glasses from point A to point B was more than his parents thought he could handle, how did they expect him to take over an entire company? He waited until Jean was seated to deliver her drink, hoping to finagle a spot beside her on the couch.

At the last second he lost his nerve, due to the unfortunate placement of a throw pillow and Jean's steadfast refusal to look at him. Charlie wound up hovering at the edge of the group, without so much as a wall to lean against. His parents were probably waiting for him to join in the conversation, but Charlie didn't want to compete with Philip Koenig and his anecdotes about playing polo with minor royalty or sponge diving in Crete. He wanted to talk to Jean, without anyone else listening. That was the only way he could be himself, even if she was being someone else.

His father caught Charlie's eye, trying to telegraph something with jerky head movements and a patently fake *ahem*. Probably he meant *go talk to Emma*, but Charlie was pretty sure that was a doomed strategy. Far more polished people than Charlie would perish on the frozen tundra of Emma Koenig's reserve. Charlie was more likely to annoy her than win her over, which was how he justified his decision to ignore his dad and sidle up to Jean instead.

"Thank you for the drink," he said, showing Jean his empty glass like she was handing out gold stars for finishing first. "It was very refreshing."

Although he probably shouldn't have gulped it down that fast, judging by the beads of sweat breaking out along his hairline. He racked his brain for something to say that would remind Jean of happier times. A coded message only she would understand.

"It's something I'll always *treasure*. Like a winning poker hand. Or . . . a jungle hideaway."

"Charlie," his mother said, in a tone of gentle reproof. "Why don't you take the tray back to the kitchen? *Just* the tray. Leave the glasses."

There was no way to refuse without looking like a jerk. Charlie edged around the coffee table, hunched and shuffling as he tried to avoid sticking his rear end in anyone's face. He was only mildly surprised when he stumbled over an unseen obstacle.

"I'm okay," he said, managing to right himself before he hit the carpet again.

"My shoe isn't." Jean held up her sandal, shaking the broken laces. "You ruined it!"

Chapter 19

You would have thought Jean's strappy platform espadrille was a Fabergé egg from the way they were all carrying on.

"I swear you could fall off a flat patch of grass while standing still," Mr. Pike said to his son. He seemed to have two modes: negging Charlie and talking like a human billboard.

Meanwhile, Euro Daddy was studying the broken strap so intently, Jean wondered if he moonlighted as a cobbler. "Your lovely shoe," Mr. Koenig sighed. "What a pity."

Jean had never had a thing for older men, but there was some serious magnetism coming off this guy. The swoop of hair, the golden skin, those sculpted-by-Michelangelo cheekbones: it all screamed "I spend a lot of time swimming laps in my sleek minimalist pool before sweating out impurities in the sauna." Also, you had to be majorly hot to pull off a western-style shirt with pearl buttons and the faint sheen of silk. He looked like either a European soccer coach or high-end male escort.

His daughter had a totally different vibe, with a face that said shy milkmaid—if you overlooked the sharpness of her gaze. Jean would have to be careful with that one.

Going in, she'd been most worried about fooling Charlie's parents, but they were easy marks compared to Emma Koenig. She seemed most likely to see through the "Sockless Tommy's niece" charade, which was annoying for practical reasons that had nothing to do with the fact that the senior Pikes were obviously pushing a match between Emma and Charlie.

As if Jean cared about that!

She didn't.

As evidenced by the way she had sailed through the first test: seeing Charlie again. She'd played the moment like a champ, supercilious and above it all, as if she ate beautiful beer heirs for breakfast. Jean was in full command of the situation, a haughty hottie.

Extra props to "Eve" on being so convincing no one questioned her identity. If Jean was flustered on the inside, that was forgivable. First-night jitters were part of any performance. At least she'd hit her marks.

All Jean had to do was stick her leg out at the exact right moment and boom! Charlie took care of the rest.

She suspected Emma Koenig knew Jean had tripped him, but thus far she seemed to be keeping the information to herself. Maybe she'd write it up in her next journal article, like the fancy science person she was. That would impress Charlie, in case her booze fortune wasn't enough of an attraction.

Though maybe not as much as Jean's bustier and crotch-skimming shorts. The upside of being dressed like she took a wrong turn on the way to Ibiza while everyone else was doing Grand Ole Opry cosplay was that Charlie had been unable to tear his eyes away. Jean might have been easy to leave, but she was going to make damn sure she was impossible to ignore.

Remember this? That's what I thought.

So far, her plan was working like a charm. And now it was time for phase two.

"I need to change," she announced.

"I can take you." Charlie spoke so fast it was a miracle he hadn't bitten his tongue. "Do you want a piggyback ride?"

"Don't be weird, son." Mr. Pike indicated the door with his chin. "Get the golf cart."

Jean watched from her comfortable position in the passenger seat as Charlie hoisted another piece of luggage into the back of the golf cart. He was red-faced and sweating, darting to the pile of monogrammed suitcases as if they were escaping a burning building with all their worldly possessions.

"I'll have to come back for the rest," he said, wiping his forehead.

"Hmph," Jean sniffed, strongly implying she'd had better service at the last house party she crashed. It was a little concerning that she wouldn't be staying in the main house with the VIPs, but there were bound to be setbacks in any scheme of this magnitude. Like those heist movies where one of the key players gets sick at the last minute and the rest of the team has to improvise with superglue and a department store mannequin.

Charlie dropped into the seat beside her, working his long legs under the steering wheel with difficulty. "Here we go."

As they rolled over the grass, the only sound was the whine of the electric motor. Jean tipped her head back to look up at the blobby red rock formations studding the hilltops. The shapes reminded her of the drip castles her best friend taught her to build with wet sand when Jean first moved to Oahu for college.

Those sunny beaches seemed like a distant memory now. There was a distinct snap in the air as the shadows deepened around them, like cool fingers reaching for Jean's bare skin. The second she was alone, she was ditching this "which way to the rave?" ensemble for something warmer.

Charlie had never told her it was beautiful here. She added that to her running tally of things he'd failed to disclose. It was easier to think about his many failures than his presence beside her.

Now that it was just the two of them, it would be so easy for him to turn to her and say, "Jean," popping the soap bubble of her hoax. Instead he drove as if it required his full concentration, only sneaking occasional glances at the side of her face.

The cart moved slowly around a series of outbuildings. Jean probably could have crawled faster, but then she wasn't hauling a thousand pounds of baggage. Or at least, not the Louis Vuitton variety. They passed a garden, a rushing stream, and a random putting green before reaching an open field dotted with what looked like—

"Are those covered wagons?" Jean forgot to sound blasé. Surely even Eve would be surprised to find this Oregon Trail moment happening. There were a dozen of the wood-and-canvas structures arranged in a loose semicircle, far enough apart that you probably wouldn't hear your neighbor snoring.

What was next, a bout of dysentery? Maybe Charlie could supply a few snakes, to make the experience more authentic.

"It's not a real covered wagon. They're for camping, but fancier," Charlie said. "There's a word for it."

"Vamping?" Jean suggested, determined to be as unhelpful as possible.

His brow furrowed. "I don't know. But I can tell you it has a real bed."

The cart stopped moving as he spoke, so the word "bed" landed like a boulder.

Jean knew it wasn't the rosy glow of the setting sun turning Charlie's cheeks pink as he stammered, "I mean, they all do. The wagons. Wagon tents. You should be very comfortable at night. All of you. In your individual, ah, beds."

"As long as you don't expect me to pee in a bucket." There. Nothing like bathroom talk to squelch any flicker of romantic nostalgia.

"No." He rubbed his jaw, and Jean barely gave a thought to how it would feel without the whiskers. By rights, he should have looked worse now that he'd shaved his scruff, but Charlie could have been a matinee idol in an eight-by-ten glossy.

"The old brewhouse is behind that stand of trees. There are real bathrooms. Showers too." Charlie swallowed, perhaps recalling the last time they'd showered together. It would be a cold day in hell before she scrubbed his back again. Much less his front.

Stumbling from the driver's seat, he hurried up a short flight of wooden stairs to the canvas door, flicking on the battery-powered lantern hooked to the outside.

"Here we are," he said, in case she hadn't figured that out. "Home sweet home."

Jean regarded him with a stony expression, refusing to make this any easier on him.

"I should carry you." The idea seemed to hit him like a thunderclap, sending him bounding back down the stairs to her side. "The grass might be wet. Or if you step on the gravel, that could hurt your foot." He hesitated, arms outstretched. "May I?"

Jean crossed her arms, like it didn't matter to her one way or the other. Shifting her legs ever so slightly, she made room for him to slip his hands under her thighs.

Her practically *naked* thighs, given the shortness of her shorts, now skin-to-skin with Charlie's bare-to-the-bicep arms. As he straightened, cradling her to his chest, it felt an awful lot like Jean's bare ass was pressed against the crook of his elbow. Not a line item on her master plan, but maybe she could work with it, judging by the stutter in his breath as he ducked sideways to get through the doorway.

Inside the wagon, the curved ceiling was too low for him to straighten to his full height, so he hobbled in a slow half circle, looking for a place to set her down. The options were limited to the bed, a luggage rack, and the floor. After another moment's hesitation, Charlie carefully lowered Jean onto the snowy white duvet.

When he tried to extricate his arms, his watch caught in the fringe of her crocheted vest.

"Sorry," he whispered, eyes traveling over her face with a desperate eagerness.

"This is virgin vicuña," she replied in a sultry tone.

"Vir—what?"

"Vicuña," she drawled, puckering her lips. "A very small camel."

"Oh." He was still staring at her mouth.

"It's rare. And expensive."

"That's nice."

"I know. So don't tear it."

"I'll be very careful."

Will you, though? She didn't say that part out loud. It required Jean's full concentration to maintain a poker face while Charlie reached under her thigh to fumble with his watch strap, unfastening it so he could pull his arm free.

"There. All clear." He smiled down at her, seemingly unbothered that he'd lost what was probably an expensive timepiece in her clothing. A lock of dark hair tumbled over his forehead.

Must not touch the hair, Jean's inner drill sergeant barked. She turned her head to avoid temptation. "I need new shoes."

Charlie scrambled backward, straightening to a half crouch. "There's a store about thirty miles up the highway. I could take you—"

"From my suitcase."

"Right!" He dashed out of the wagon, and Jean used the opportunity to suck in a steadying breath. Unfortunately, she could still smell Charlie's clean soap-and-orange-spice scent.

Time to up the ante. Pulling a trial-size perfume from her purse, she spritzed her wrists, rubbing them against her neck and the inside of her knees.

From outside, she heard Charlie mutter to himself, followed by the thump and drag of a heavy suitcase coming up the stairs. Jean leaned back on her elbows, crossing and uncrossing her legs to find the most provocative arrangement.

"I hope this is the right one," he panted, lugging a bulky leather suitcase behind him.

"Open it for me." It was halfway between a command and a complaint, as if she were too weak from shoe loss to do it herself.

Charlie wrestled the bag onto its side, then unsnapped the clasps. Lingerie exploded at him like a jack-in-the-box, silky underthings in every shade springing in all directions.

"Sorry!" He tried to slam it shut, yelping in pain when he caught his fingers in the lid. "I was trying not to look," he explained, yanking his hand free.

Jean glanced at the appendage in question, brows raised. His fingers weren't the only thing he'd pulled out of the suitcase.

"Oh, that's—" He trailed off, blinking at the scrap of silk in his hand. Charlie brought it closer to his face, studying her panties like a scientific specimen. "Is that . . . are they . . . do you—" It seemed to hit him all at once that he was staring at her underwear. Cracking open the lid, he shoved them inside, hurriedly closing the latches like he was afraid something inside might make a break for freedom.

"I'm sorry I touched your, ah."

"G-string?" Jean lifted one shoulder, as if people were constantly pawing at her underthings. "It's not like I was wearing it. That would be a different story." She held eye contact, willing him to imagine the whisper of silk between his fingertips and her skin.

"I'll go get your other bag," he said, face on fire.

"It's the trunk," she called after him. "The heavy one."

It sounded like he was wrestling a bear, or whatever they did for fun around here. Jean watched him shove the trunk to the foot of her bed, a few painful inches at a time.

"I'd help, but I just had my nails done." She held up her hand as evidence.

"That's okay." He wiped his forehead. "Is this the right one?"

At her nod, he carefully opened the lid. "That is a lot of shoes. How long are you planning to stay?"

"I like to have options," she said, ignoring the second half of the question—and the hopeful lift in his voice.

"I suppose it's easier when they're so small," he reasoned, holding up a size six stiletto with a distinctive red sole.

"I don't feel like wearing those."

Charlie picked up an equally ridiculous pink slipper. The feathery fluff at the toe danced as he turned it from side to side, a half smile playing across his face. "Funny to think a grown-up could have such little feet."

"Can you find something that isn't for the boudoir, or are you too busy touching my stuff?"

Charlie dropped the slipper like it was covered in spikes instead of satin, reaching for the next closest shoe. "How about these?"

"Fine," she sniffed, though it was clear he'd grabbed a pair at random. Straightening her leg, Jean pointed her toes.

He stared at her foot. "You—want me to put it on you?"

"Yes. I want you to put it on me." She batted her lashes. "It's only fair. Since you broke the other ones."

"I'm very sorry about that."

"So you've mentioned." She wiggled her toes at him. "Well?"

His dark eyes met hers. "Are you sure?"

"I'll pretend you're my podiatrist."

His warm fingers clasped her ankle before sliding down to cup her heel. A lesser woman might have weakened, but Jean kept her eyes on the prize. Which was—her mind blanked out as his knuckle stroked the arch of her foot.

Revenge! She was doing revenge. And the prize was bringing him to his knees, which she'd technically achieved, considering he was crouched on the ground in front of her. It didn't quite feel like the slam dunk of victory as Charlie slowly slid the satin strap of a midnight-blue heel over her toes. Her heart was beating a little too fast.

"I like a nice tight fit," Jean said, retaking control of the situation. He frowned in concentration. "I'll do my best."

She lowered her leg, watching awareness settle over him. Jean was lying on the bed, his head between her thighs. His gaze tracked from one knee to the other, a slow pan he couldn't seem to control.

She would have given a lot to know what he was thinking. For a few seconds, she indulged herself in an alternate scenario where he turned his face to plant a kiss on the inside of her thigh, then kept going. Charlie had been an eager student in that department, taking to it much more naturally than cards.

"It sure is nice of you to travel all this way." His voice was faint.

Jean was glad she could still affect him this strongly, even if it forced her to feel something too. Lust was a normal human reaction—nothing to be ashamed of. "I like a good time."

"Is that why you came?"

"Why else would I be here?" She let the challenge hang in the air. *Go ahead, Charlie. Explain it to me. To my face.* "Maybe I just really love—" Jean drew out the pause, letting him twist in the wind—"beer."

He had the nerve to look disappointed, as if she was enough of a chump to whisper sweet nothings after he tossed her aside. "And beans, I hope?"

"What?"

"Do you like them?"

"I . . . sometimes."

"Good. Because that's what we're having for supper. Over a campfire."

"I see." She didn't really, but it was important to maintain the illusion that Eve knew everything.

He sat back on his haunches. "It's not very fancy, I know."

She thought of the dinners they'd scrounged together, a buffet of leftovers and vending machine snacks eaten on the floor of his room. Of course, that was before she found out he was heir to a beer fortune. If she'd known he was loaded, Jean would have made Charlie buy his own Snickers.

"I should let you get changed," he said, when she didn't reply. "For tonight."

"Why? You don't like what I'm wearing?"

"Oh no, I like it a lot. It's really—very nice." He swallowed hard. "The long dangly bits are especially interesting. Almost like, you know . . ." He danced his fingers up and down as he searched for the right word. "Tentacles."

"I think it looks like I'm unraveling," she countered. "If you pull one of the strings, the whole top might come apart. And then I'd hardly be wearing a thing."

"That's a different way to look at it." And look he did, from the tips of her toes to the part in her hair. Charlie shook himself. "I should go."

"Aren't you forgetting something?"

"No." He tried to make serious eye contact. "I haven't forgotten *anything*."

"Your watch," she reminded him.

"Oh. It's still tangled up in your—" He nodded at her fringe.

"Then you better get busy." Jean rolled onto her hip, propping her cheek on one hand. That forced Charlie to crawl halfway onto the bed, bracing his knees on either side of her body as he began disentangling his watch. His movements were so cautious, he could have been defusing a bomb.

"That's a nice perfume you're wearing." His voice was unsteady, like there wasn't quite enough oxygen in this tent-wagon, even though the flap was half-open.

She shifted onto her stomach, erasing the polite gap he'd left between his legs and her body. "I know."

"It almost smells familiar."

"Don't tell me your mother wears it."

"No." He inhaled deeply. "It's not that."

"Grandmother?" Jean guessed.

"She smelled like Vicks, mostly. Sinus trouble."

Jean opened her mouth to tell him that *her* grandmother had always smelled like cinnamon gum before remembering she wasn't giving him any more pieces of the real her.

With a last gentle tug, Charlie finished unknotting his watch. "Got it."

She waited for him to move, but he stayed where he was.

"You know, your perfume reminds me of a girl I used to know."

"I doubt that. It's very uncommon."

"So was she."

Alarm bells clanged in Jean's head. She wasn't ready to go there. Charlie needed to leave before he unearthed any of her secrets—like the one stashed underneath all those froufrou undies. So what if she still liked to sleep in his T-shirt? Maybe it was softer than anything else she owned.

"I'm tired. I think I'll take a nap before dinner." Jean pulled her legs out from under him, curling her knees into her chest. "Close the door on your way out."

She kept her eyes squeezed shut until she felt the stairs shake under his weight.

I'll Have What She's Having

Goss & Go, Hollywood News and Views

Sitcom star Bryn Boone, whose performance in the Cannes-bound indie *Say My Name Twice* is generating awards-season buzz, says she's only dating noncelebrities from now on.

"Look at Adriana Asebedo. I saw her out with her new man, and you could tell he was there for her, not the cameras. It's so smart getting a guy who isn't using you to launch his career. And obviously he's also super unselfish in the bedroom, which yes please! More of that."

Chapter 20

It was official: Charlie was a fool.

Not only because of his outfit, though that was enough to make anyone question his sanity. Fringe looked great on Jean, but it made Charlie feel ridiculous. Especially the thick white variety currently bristling from every seam of his clothing. And he didn't care what his mother said about "red" suiting his complexion. This shirt was dark pink. A color better suited to a prom dress or raw meat. Charlie would bet his hat (white, too tight, suspiciously shiny) that a real cowboy wouldn't be caught dead in this thing.

It was too late to go back in time and tell his parents to choose a different theme. Not that they would have listened to him when apparently Smithson was the hero of the hour. Besides, there was a bigger worry circling his head like a swarm of gnats.

What if he'd already blown it? Instead of using their alone time to hopefully, maybe, walk things back to how they'd been before, Charlie had the distinct feeling he'd made Jean mad. Even more than she was to begin with.

Had he overplayed his hand? Tried to rush things? Jean once told Charlie he had a bad habit of telegraphing his move before he laid down a card. Should he have tried harder to bluff?

I have to change too, he could have said. *Into a humiliating outfit I wish you weren't going to see. Except I'd rather see you in the outfit than not see you at all. Unless we were both not wearing outfits, if you know what I mean.*

Even imaginary Charlie was terrible at acting suave.

Someone tapped him on the shoulder and Charlie took a

hopping leap sideways before turning. "Mugsy! Where have you been? You're not going to believe what happened!"

"Someone got maimed in a freak square-dancing incident?"

"No! She's here, Mugsy!"

"You know?"

It was a gratifyingly dramatic response, especially by Mugsy standards. Charlie had been afraid he'd need to convince her it was a big deal. "Yes! I saw her at the house."

"She—oh. You mean Emma Koenig. She seems cool."

Like a glacier, in Charlie's humble opinion. Before he could explain that he wasn't talking about Emma, they heard a loud, "Hey, hey!"

Smithson was strutting in their direction.

Mugsy sighed like she'd taken a sip of spoiled milk. "If he asks me to take a memo or fetch him a snack, there will be blood," she warned.

"He's bad news," Charlie agreed. "Do you think we could get him to leave?"

Mugsy shook her head. "He's so far up your dad's butt he could count his fillings."

Charlie shifted uneasily, and not just because of the disgusting image Mugsy had conjured. "Why is he looking at me like that?"

"Sizing you up," Mugsy replied. "I've got you. Don't worry."

"Is this our guy?" The booming bray was worse at close range, especially when Smithson wrapped Charlie in a bone-crushing hug. "About time you got here, brother. You almost missed all the fun."

He pulled back far enough to grasp Charlie's hand.

"Smithson Oliver Barrett," Charlie ground out.

"Been reading up on me, Chuck?" The pressure around Charlie's knuckles increased. "I've been reading about you too." His smugness was almost as potent as his cologne. "You and Adriana, huh?" He laughed like it was a punchline.

Mugsy made a noise, but Charlie didn't need her to fight this battle for him. Grimly, he returned Smithson's viselike handshake. Charlie knew a thing or two about constrictors and their prey.

"There's Emma," Mugsy said. "Let's go say hi."

Smithson released Charlie's hand so fast it was all he could do not to stumble after him as he spun around. "Where?"

"I wasn't talking to you."

"Too late." Smithson took off without another word, pulling his shoulders back to make his chest stick out.

"I should rescue her," Mugsy said, as they watched Smithson saunter up to Emma Koenig's side. "Unless you want to?"

"I'm good," Charlie said.

She frowned at him. "You sure? It's not too much?"

"Nope," he said, a little too quickly. "I'll be fine over here," he added, toning it down so Mugsy wouldn't get suspicious. "The smoke bothers my contacts."

That had been one of his father's first requests. *Lose the specs, son.* At least it gave him an excuse to sit over here, where he had a decent sight line to Jean's wagon. Charlie wanted to be sure he spotted her first. That way he could warn her about Smithson, apologize for costing her a job, keep Mr. Koenig from monopolizing her attention, and make sure she didn't feel lonely. All very important and worthy tasks.

You just want to see her again, he admitted to himself. It was hard to think about anything beyond that. Distantly, Charlie understood that he should be wary of her motives, but all those things Mugsy said about Jean were like dusty mismatched socks tossed into the deepest darkness under the bed. Charlie knew he should get down on the floor and try to fish them out, but it just didn't feel like a priority. There were other socks. Better socks. His favorite pair.

Because Jean *must* like him at least a little if she'd come all this way. That was Charlie's working hypothesis: she was giving him a second chance. Everything else was a ball of dust in comparison.

"Where is the lovely Eve?" Mr. Koenig propped his boot on the hay bale Charlie was using as a lookout.

How was it fair that Mr. Koenig's all-black western gear looked sleek and lived-in, like he was about to hold up a train, when according to Charlie's father, the Koenigs were from Copenhagen?

"I'm sure she'll be here."

"Who could resist?" On that ambiguous note, the older man departed. He was immediately swallowed by the crowd of multinational grown-ups dressed in some approximation of frontier wear, including the first suede pantsuit Charlie had ever seen. Spicy-cocktail man was wearing two-tone denim, studded with metal rivets. It looked like one of the machines had gone haywire in the jeans factory.

There was only one Jean who mattered to Charlie, and there she was, stepping out of her wagon. He watched her glide across the grass, still wearing the sparkly shoes he'd picked out for her. As she moved into the light from the campfire, his throat went dry.

That was some dress.

Two perfect semicircles had been cut from the fabric between her hip and rib cage, like the designer knew exactly where a person would put his hands if he wanted to pick her up and set her on a piece of furniture. Or when he needed her to hold still for a few seconds because the sensations were too much, and he had to slow down to feel them all.

Her skin was bright as snow against the dark fabric, glowing in the flickering firelight. Charlie pressed the back of his fingers to his forehead. His face felt flushed despite the cool evening.

The musicians his parents had hired struck up an unfamiliar tune full of twanging banjos. They could have been playing "Happy Birthday" and he wouldn't have recognized the melody.

"Jea—" he started to say, swallowing the rest of her name when she glared a warning. "I mean, *gee*, it's nice to see you again, *Eve*."

"I know." She started to move past him.

"Could I talk to you about something?"

There was a pause before she answered. "I don't know. Can you?"

Definitely a trick question. His eyes caught on Jean's painted toenails, peeking out from under the thin strap of her fancy shoes. "It's about the guest list." *Not this other thing you're doing,* he tried to telepathically convey. *Or what happened before . . . between us.*

He took a few steps away from the campfire and the dangling string lights, glancing back to see if she would follow. With a sigh, she joined him in the shadows, one dainty foot tapping with impatience.

"My parents hired a consultant. To help with the centennial and, um, branding."

She waited for him to go on, the furrow of her brow saying, *And?*

"His name is Smithson. Smithson Oliver Barrett. His family is . . . also in the beer business."

Jean spun around before he could gauge her reaction. She stomped a few paces, keeping her back to the rest of the gathering. It was hard to give her space when she looked so alone and small standing there. What Charlie really wanted was to tiptoe over and give her a hug, but he knew how it felt to need time to put yourself back together. Also a hug wasn't something you should spring on a person stealthily, in the dark—unless you were playing naked hide-and-seek, which as far as Charlie knew was something Jean had invented. And that was more of an indoor game.

"A branding consultant," she repeated, whipping around. "This was his idea? The cowboy schtick?" Jean looked Charlie up and down, as if noticing his outfit for the first time. Her mouth opened and then closed again, but at least she didn't laugh.

"People from other countries tend to like that stuff." Charlie wasn't sure why he felt the need to be fair to someone like Smithson, who he would just as soon blame for all the world's problems. "The hats and boots and all of that—"

"Rhinestone cowboy nonsense?"

Charlie nodded. That was about the size of it.

Jean started walking toward the cluster of people gathered around Smithson.

"What are you going to do?" he asked.

"I don't know." She didn't slow down.

"Okay." He took bigger steps to keep pace with her, almost bumping into her when she suddenly rounded on him.

"You're not going to tell me to stop and think?"

"I wasn't planning on it." Whatever happened next, he was sure Smithson deserved it. Jean squinted at him a moment longer before resuming her march. Charlie stayed half a step behind, ready to serve as her second-in-command.

"That's why I'll always be a deep-sea guy," Smithson was saying as they approached. "When you bring in a giant swordfish, it's a fight to the death." He did some flexing and bending to illustrate. "But no shade to fly-fishing. I'm sure standing in a creek is nice too. Especially with a cold beer." He raised his bottle to a brewer from Montana.

"Patronizing, party of one," Jean muttered as she stepped into his line of sight.

Smithson flashed her what he probably thought was an irresistible grin. "Hello, hello. Smithson Oliver Barrett." He held out a hand, which Jean pointedly ignored. "Who's your daddy?"

Two hay bales to Charlie's right, Emma Koenig jotted a few lines in a pocket-size notebook.

"Seriously?" Jean said to Smithson.

"Go on. What's your poison? Tequila? Rum? Something a little spicier?"

The hot-cocktail guy yodeled an ear-piercing, "Yeehaw!"

"In case we end up doing business together." Smithson did some twitchy things with his face, like the "business" in question might not actually be business related. There was no indication that he recognized Jean from their high school days, which was even more incomprehensible to Charlie than the catchphrase *Get Piked*. Should anyone be that excited about getting stabbed?

"That's not going to happen."

Smithson kept talking as if Jean hadn't spoken. "You're with the Finns, aren't you?" He flicked a finger under his nose, implying that their Finnish guests were either snobs or recreational drug users. "Tell your dad I have some ideas he'll want to hear."

"Oh, right. Because I couldn't possibly be running my own business. I must be here with a man."

"My bad." Smithson pretended to slap himself on the cheek, unfortunately stopping short of actual contact. "Feminism, wut wut. For real, though. Who are you with?"

Jean's smile was dangerous. Charlie had never seen this side of her, but like most parts of Jean, he found it more than a little exciting. "You don't recognize me?"

"Mmm, nope. You have an OnlyFans?" Smithson sucked on his beer in a way that made Charlie want to yank it out of his hand and dump it over his head.

His father joined them too late to hear that charming remark. Smithson's posture changed as he greeted Mr. Pike.

"If it isn't the man of the hour. You having a good time, sir?"

"Couldn't be better. It's the perfect mix of paying tribute to the past and celebrating the future." Charlie's dad spread his hands to indicate the young people gathered around Smithson.

"Everything old is new again." Smithson delivered this bit of wisdom as if he'd come up with it himself. "I'm helping them recontextualize to reach a younger demographic," he told Jean.

"We're telling a story about legacy," Mr. Pike chimed in. "Family. Honoring our roots. It's not every business that can say it's been around for a hundred years."

"And we want to keep it around for a hundred more." Smithson leaned forward to fist-bump Charlie's father. "Leave it to me, C-Money. Where I lead, people follow."

Charlie had never found occasion to fist-bump his dad. The few times it felt like they were seeing eye to eye, it turned out to be more like when a bird thinks, *hey, a friend* right before crashing into a reflective pane of glass.

"Cards, anyone?" No one was more surprised than Charlie to hear the words fly out of his mouth. He just wanted Jean to be happy, and ideally also to change the subject so Smithson would stop monologuing about his personal awesomeness.

"What are we playing?" Emma asked, setting down the notebook in which Charlie imagined she'd been writing *SMITHSON SUCKS* over and over.

"Um, poker?"

"That's for tomorrow, sweetheart." Mrs. Pike handed him a basket of cheese straws, tipping her head to indicate he should pass them around. "We're taking everyone up to Deadwood to see a real saloon. But good for you, being sociable," she added, patting him on the arm.

"How about horseshoes? Would you like to play with me, Eve?" He felt the color creeping into his cheeks when he heard how it sounded, but hopefully no one else could tell by firelight. At least it wasn't cornhole, a name Charlie could never say without cringing.

"I had you down as more of a library warrior, Two Buck." Smithson laughed, but Charlie had seen the mean look in his eye, and knew it wasn't a friendly nickname. "Two Buck Chuck. Get it?"

Before Charlie could answer, Smithson turned to Mr. Pike. "About time for the announcement, don't you think, big guy?"

Charlie's dad had always been sensitive about his height. Mugsy's theory was that many of the problems in their relationship stemmed from the fact that Charlie was several inches taller than Mr. Pike. Whether or not that was true, Smithson had cracked the code for sweet-talking Charlie's father, who rubbed his hands together in delight.

Uh-oh. Charlie had a bad feeling. Mugsy joined them, frowning at the geometry of the scene: Smithson and Mr. Pike over there, Charlie standing apart.

"They're about fifteen minutes out," she informed Charlie's dad.

Jean glanced sharply at Mugsy, then at Charlie, before lowering her head so her hair fanned in front of her face.

Smithson handed his beer to a guy in a flannel shirt with the sleeves cut off. "Listen up, y'all. Everybody getting their cowboy on tonight? I feel like Kevin Costner!"

"Hear, hear!" said Mr. Pike.

"Give it up for the Pike family, for putting on this spread. Charles and Sandy, and of course my boy Chuck." He hit Charlie with double finger guns. "Let's show them some love." There was a smattering of applause.

Jean shot Charlie a furious look.

"I'm not his boy," he whispered. "He's just saying that."

"Now, we promised you entertainment," Smithson went on, like this was his show. "Some of you had your suspicions about our special guest."

"Reba," Haggard of the red-hot cocktails bellowed.

Smithson frowned. "It's not Reba."

"Crystal Gayle?" one of the Canadians asked.

"Never heard of her." Smithson circled a finger in the air. "Come on, people. It's obvious. Huge star. Totally on brand with the fam."

"You have Dolly?"

Charlie thought that might have been the whiskey guy, but it was hard to tell once everyone started buzzing about Dolly Parton. A tuneless rendition of "Jolene" was floating through the crowd when Smithson clanged a cowbell he must have pried out of the hands of one of the musicians.

"It's not Dolly. Or The Chicks. Or Beyoncé," he added when the pear brandy guy from Oregon raised a hand. "Hit it," he yelled at the band.

Mugsy rubbed her mouth. Charlie wasn't aware she felt that way about bluegrass, but maybe mandolin music was like cilantro: either you liked it, or it made you physically ill. Between the warbling and the jangling and the whine of the harmonica, it took a few minutes for his brain to travel from "that sounds familiar" to "oh no."

He watched awareness spread through the group, more and more of them turning to stare at him. Charlie's dad was clapping along, encouraging everyone to join in, like this wasn't a song about his son's alleged sex life. Overshadowing the embarrassment was a sharp prick of fear: Did Jean know? He tried to catch her eye, but she was staring at the ground, spine rigid.

So that was a yes.

"That's right," Smithson yelled, "Adriana Asebedo is playing a private concert, right here, Sunday night!"

While everyone celebrated around them, Charlie turned to Mugsy. "Did you know about this?"

Her wince said it all.

"Why didn't you tell me?"

"You had a lot on your plate. I didn't want you to panic."

Jean dumped the contents of her tin cup on the grass.

"You're leaving?" Charlie asked when she stood.

"Why, is there another big announcement? New single dropping? An engagement?" Her eyes flashed as she glared up at him.

"No!" It was hard to concentrate when she was standing this close. "It's nothing like that."

"Do I know you?" Mugsy interrupted.

"I'm Eve. Sockless Tommy's niece." Jean twisted a strand of hair around her finger, pulling it in front of her face.

Mugsy looked like she had more questions until her phone buzzed, distracting her.

"Is she here?" Smithson demanded, shoving a path through the crowd. "I should go welcome her. Help her get settled in."

"It's a tour bus," Mugsy said.

"That's basically a house on wheels," Jean added. "All you have to do is park."

She and Mugsy exchanged a look of reluctant allyship, as though surprised to find themselves on the same side of the argument.

"I need you here." Mr. Pike clapped Smithson on the back. "The party's still going strong. Why don't we let Charlie handle this? I'm sure he and Adriana have catching up to do." The part he didn't say, but Charlie heard loud and clear, was that no one really needed *him* to stick around.

Smithson's smile was forced, but he followed Mr. Pike back to the buffet, where the other guests were filling plates with grilled wild game sausages and beans.

"You should eat something," Charlie said, in a desperate bid to keep Jean from disappearing. "Or we could take a walk? To look at the stars."

"Those stars?" She jabbed a finger skyward, where pinpricks

of light were scattered like glitter. "Sounds like you have your hands full anyway."

Emma Koenig came to stand beside Mugsy. "I've never been a fan of sausage."

"Are you a vegetarian?" Charlie asked.

"That too," Emma said, with another glance at Mugsy.

Charlie had the distinct impression there was a second conversation happening under the surface, but he didn't have time to figure it out because Jean was walking away.

"Wait," he called after her.

"No," she answered.

Mugsy grabbed his arm when he made to follow. "You heard her, Charlie."

"I know, but I really need to talk to her. She thinks . . . something that isn't true." He tried to say the rest with his eyes. It was tricky in the dark, especially with Emma standing right there, ready to write a diagnosis in her notebook.

Lovesick fool. Symptoms: repetitive thought patterns. Difficulty regulating body temperature. Mood swings.

"Whatever it is, you can sort it out tomorrow," Mugsy said. "First things first."

The dismissiveness hurt, until Charlie remembered that Mugsy didn't know the girl in the blue dress was Jean—*his* Jean—not the random relative of a booze tycoon. Maybe not the best moment to open that can of worms.

His father flicked two fingers in a *run along* gesture. He was probably banking on a romantic reunion between his son and a chart-topping pop star, perfectly timed to coincide with the company's centennial. The weight of his father's expectations pressed down on Charlie, driving out a sigh.

"Fine," Mugsy said, misreading his reluctance. "I'll go with you."

She said good night to Emma before leading Charlie away from the campfire.

"The wagons are over there," Charlie pointed out. "Also, I should probably go alone. Since the two of you just met—"

"We're going back to the house."

"What? Why?"

"Because then your dad will think you did what he wanted."

"Mugsy, I don't have anything to say to Adriana."

"I know, Charlie. That's why I'm going to talk to her for you."

"And I can sneak back to the wagons?" He glanced behind them, calculating the stealthiest route.

"Absolutely not. You're going to hide in your room, so no one sees you *not* hanging out with Adri." Mugsy shoved him in the arm. "And you can get your alone time. You're welcome."

She picked up the pace, putting a conversation-ending gap between them.

Lost Weekend EP: Anatomy of a Heartbreak?

Liner Notes: Behind the Charts

While there's been no official word from Adriana Asebedo's camp, fans agree that the surprise midnight release of a four-song EP was inspired by the dissolution of her relationship with reclusive beer heir Charlie Pike.

Will this be Adriana's *thank u, next* or a blip on her chart-topping career?

Time will tell.

Chapter 21

Jean pressed her fingers over her eye sockets. What a strange night, and not just because Charlie had been dressed in watermelon-pink satin, like a cross between a children's TV host and a very niche stripper.

Fucking Smithson, that little shit. And he hadn't even recognized her!

On some totally irrational but hard-to-shake level, it felt like Jean was being punished—as if telling Charlie the story had somehow manifested Smithson's reappearance. She should have kept a lid on all of it. Her past, her feelings, her very short list of People to Trust. Her life had been perfectly fine before Charlie bumbled onto the scene.

Fine-ish.

Her stomach cramped. Jean couldn't blame the beans because she'd left without eating any. Maybe there was something fundamentally wrong with her, hence the pathological attraction to dishonest sons of beverage magnates. Not that her teenage crush on Smithson bore any resemblance to what she'd had—correction, *thought* she had—with Charlie. With Smithson, at least fifty percent of the pull had been his status. Her fling with Charlie was purely about wanting *him*. Or rather, the person he'd pretended to be.

Speaking of lying, Adriana Freaking Asebedo was about to roll up in her blingin' bus with her perfect skin and those mile-long eyelashes and her dance moves and her millions. The tiny part of Jean still holding out hope that the Charlie/Adriana story was a tabloid rumor had officially shriveled up and died. There was no way a star of her magnitude would play a beer festival in the back of beyond if she didn't have a personal connection to the Pike family, not even speaking of the guilty-as-sin look on Charlie's face.

Jean kicked her legs up and let them land like bricks. That felt pretty good, so she pummeled the bed with her bare heels a few more times. Then she added a groan, with a little growl in it, flopping back and forth on the squeaky mattress.

This was way more fun than analyzing feelings.

Scratch, scratch, scratch.

The noise was coming from just outside her wagon.

Did they have bears here? Wolves? Mountain lions? Was she about to be eaten, on top of everything else? What a perfect chaser to a fabulous evening!

Although it was really more of a tapping sound, now that she thought about it, so unless it was a weirdly polite bobcat, odds were her visitor was human.

A little voice inside her whispered *Charlie*, and Jean didn't care to scrutinize whether it was coming from her head or her heart. Was he back to perv on her shoes while conveniently forgetting to mention that his other girlfriend and his *other* other girlfriend were coming to this party? Because Jean had no doubt Charlie was still attracted to her, on a purely physical level. It was a low bar, but it pleased her to know she still held some sway over him. Power was power. You could use it.

"Come in," she called, in her sultriest voice. He could try giving her the puppy-dog eyes, but Jean would stay strong. While also taunting him with a glimpse of what he couldn't have.

Hildy stuck her head in, glancing around before stepping inside. "I was afraid I might be interrupting something. You know what they say—if the wagon's rocking, don't come a-knocking."

"All clear," Jean said stiffly, unwilling to admit that the only action happening was a temper tantrum. "Where have you been?"

"Chilling with the caterers. I make a mean garnish. Those little tomatoes carved like a rose?" she added, at Jean's look of confusion.

"Why do you know how to do that?" It was hard to imagine Hildy Johnson working in food service.

"Boarding school," Hildy tossed off, the way someone from Jean's world might have said, Trader Joe's. "There's a whole underclass of PAs and valets and whatnot at these things. Nobody gave me a second look. But enough about my adventures."

Hildy sat on the edge of the mattress, making a *scooch over* gesture. As soon as Jean moved, Hildy stretched out next to her, claiming one of the pillows. "Give me all the juicy details. Is he eating out of your hand yet?"

"I'm working on it. It's a delicate operation . . . not a smash-and-grab."

"Speaking of smashing, you could also torture the guy by hooking up with someone else right in front of him."

"Like who?" Jean had barely noticed the other guests, beyond Smithson (who she'd rather stab) and the older Koenig, who was certainly more willing than his daughter but not in a way that raised Jean's temperature. It was hard to get in the mood for a sexy fling when you were still sorting through the rubble of the last one.

"Whoever you want. My point is that we can get a story even if you don't want to fully commit. To the role."

Obviously Jean knew what she meant; there was no other type of commitment on the table. The offer still rankled.

"You don't think I can do it. Because of Adriana."

"I never said that. Who am I to tell another woman what she's capable of? Especially a force of nature like you."

Jean grunted, only partially appeased.

"But if you do have a change of heart," Hildy continued, "we can still give the people what they want."

"Meaning?"

"Seeing Adriana back with her Silent Storm." She was careful not to look at Jean.

"Why does anyone care? They don't even know him." The person who had a right to an opinion was Jean. Not that she really knew him either, except in the Biblical sense.

"Or we push the love triangle with this other chick," Hildy said, correctly reading the wagon. "How long has it been going on? Does Adriana know? Was she the girl-next-door who got cast aside for the glitter of fame?"

"I can tell you one thing about her. She was at the resort with him."

"Ouch," Hildy said.

"It's whatever. Doesn't make a difference where she's from."

"You don't think having a history matters?"

"How can she compete with Adriana Asebedo? Even that ice maiden is going to have her work cut out for her, and she's some kind of Booze Princess."

"Especially if someone new catches his eye," Hildy hinted.

"Who?" If there was another frosty beer heiress swanning around this place, Jean was going to riot.

"You."

"Oh. Right." Jean rubbed her temples. "If anyone's taking him for a ride at this little rodeo, it's Eve."

"Literally," Hildy agreed.

"If it comes to that." Jean tried to sound noble, like she was a spy behind enemy lines prepared to make the ultimate sacrifice.

"No, I mean an actual ride. On horses."

"What?"

"Trail ride, baby. Didn't you look at the schedule?"

"I was a little busy establishing my cover."

"Good thing you have me. It's almost like I really am your PA." Hildy sounded strangely excited by the thought. "So yeah.

Tomorrow morning. I wonder if he'll help her get on the horse. And then her mount gets spooked, and he has to go charging after her to save her? Some of that early-morning mist, everyone's breathing hard—" Hildy broke off with a hiss when Jean pinched her.

"It sounded like you were having an episode."

"You know what we need?" Hildy gripped Jean's wrist. "A *picture*."

"Right now?" It wouldn't be the most inopportune moment Hildy had chosen for a selfie, but Jean wasn't sure she could dredge up a smile.

"Tomorrow. Of Charlie and Adriana, preferably on horseback."

"You want me to do it?"

"You're going to be closer than I am."

"Yeah, but I don't know." It was one thing to talk a big game about spilling Charlie's secrets. Sneaking a photo of him in a private moment felt a lot more deliberate. Jean's vision for revenge was more about the personal touch. Messing around with him one-on-one.

"I guess it is a bit early to risk getting busted. Let's let things play out a little longer. Watch and wait. Can I ask you something?"

"Knock yourself out."

"What do you really want from him? When all is said and done."

Damn. Somebody wasn't pulling her punches. "I want—" Jean broke off, waiting for an answer to surface that she could bear to admit. "I want him to take it back."

"Something he said?"

"All of it." Who he'd pretended to be and what he'd made her feel—the good parts and the bad. Jean needed more than an apology from Charlie. It had to be a complete rewrite of the past if she was ever going to get rid of this creeping sadness.

"Sounds like we have our work cut out for us," Hildy said

on a yawn. She rolled over, tucking her hands underneath the pillow.

Long after her companion's breathing slowed, Jean lay awake in the dark trying not to imagine what Charlie was doing at that moment. Sipping champagne with Adriana? Having a cozy family meal with his other lady friend, who his parents clearly knew and liked? Talking mergers and acquisitions with the ice maiden?

It was only Jean who had to show up under false pretenses, skulking around with a borrowed name because the real her wasn't good enough to bring home to mama. Maybe if Jean had been rich or connected or famous, she wouldn't have been swept under the rug with the rest of the trash.

The rush of anger had a calming effect. She was doing what needed to be done.

If that meant kicking off her villainess era, so be it.

Trail Rides with Ranger Mitch

Welcome.

My ethos is simple. Time spent in nature is a privilege.
Horses are better than any of us deserve.

Don't fuck it up.

Happy Trails,

Mitch

Chapter 22

Charlie had a hunch the guide who greeted them at the trailhead the next morning had spent more hours on a military base than a ranch, and not just because he kept referring to the time of day as "oh-seven-hundred hours." There was also the buzz cut, and the warning not to let their horses go "AWOL," and the way he kept pointing two fingers at his eyeballs and then at Smithson.

"I want this to go smooth and by the numbers," the man who'd introduced himself as Ranger Mitch informed them. "No tricks and no screwing around. Let's move out."

The horses, who clearly had a better idea of what was going on than their riders, ambled into a neat single-file line.

"So no reverse cowgirl?" Smithson joked, presumably for Emma's benefit, since none of his cronies had gotten out of bed for this outing. Charlie suspected they were still sleeping off the effects of last night. It was mostly the older crowd today, plus himself and Smithson, looking a little worse for wear, as well as Mugsy, Emma, and Jean.

No one laughed at Smithson's off-color remark, though Ranger Mitch, who apparently had supersonic hearing, winged a pine cone at him.

"I have eyes on you," their guide said, somewhat redundantly given the jabby fingers.

Charlie would have enjoyed the moment more if he wasn't deep in a memory of Jean explaining that particular position. She was a good teacher, offering a quick conceptual overview followed by plenty of hands-on learning. He still preferred the regular cowgirl, because he liked seeing Jean's face, and Charlie had always had simple tastes, but the variation was also fun.

It was never *not* fun, being with Jean.

And there was so much more he could have learned. She'd promised to show him something called the flying Pamchenko once he was ready for more advanced curriculum. Only they'd never gotten a chance, because apparently it required a running start and two days later, he was on a plane, separated from Jean by an ocean.

Now that she was here, a different kind of barrier stretched between them. Plus you probably couldn't do something like the flying Pamchenko in a covered wagon, even if he did manage to win back Jean's favor.

The odds of that seemed slim right now. It felt like he'd lost ground since yesterday, and it wasn't hard to guess that it had something to do with last night's big announcement. Unless it was because Jean hated it here, or he'd missed a cue and wasn't playing the game right, and now she was bored and wanted to leave.

The problem was that he couldn't ask about the game without forfeiting, because the whole point seemed to be *not* acknowledging they were playing. And since Charlie wasn't sure how long Jean would stick around if she wasn't entertained, he needed to find a clever way to let her know the truth without letting her know that he was letting her know.

The first step would be getting her to acknowledge his existence. So far, he might as well be a tree as far as Jean was concerned. No, that wasn't fair. She was looking at the trees, and the rocks, and the sky overhead. The scenery interested her; it was Charlie she was blanking out. Every time he so much as thought about moving closer, Jean drifted away.

"What are you doing?" Mugsy asked, pulling up alongside him.

"Nothing! How did it go last night?"

"Fine." She stared straight ahead.

Apparently neither of them was in a sharing mood. That saved Charlie from admitting he'd been speculating about the logistics of the flying Pamchenko, which would have been awkward for them both. He was pretty sure Mugsy still thought of him as a teenager half the time.

"I wanted to talk to you about that girl."

Charlie glanced at her sharply. If Mugsy meant Adriana, she would have said her name. Same for Emma Koenig. "What about her?" He tried not to sound too eager, even though he'd been dying to talk to someone about Jean.

"I think I recognize her. From the resort."

If he hadn't been clutching the reins, Charlie would have fallen out of the saddle. "You saw her?"

"I'm not one hundred percent. I kept thinking there was something about her—"

"Her clothes, maybe. They're very interesting, aren't they? Or her face? Since she's so, you know." He dropped his voice to a whisper. "*Pretty.*"

Mugsy frowned at him. "I mean she looked familiar. But it was dark the first time I saw her, and I was a little distracted, so I don't want to go off on one of your guests if I'm wrong."

"When exactly was it? That you saw her." It killed Charlie to think he'd missed a last glimpse of Jean on his way to the car.

"She came to the door. For turndown service."

"Turndown—" He caught himself before it turned into a question. "Right. That." Charlie swallowed. All this time he'd thought Jean stood him up that night, when in fact she *did* come to the cottage. Which made Mugsy's claim that Jean sold him out and did a runner once she had what she wanted a lot less convincing.

"Only I don't see why the niece of the Schnapps King would be working at a hotel," Mugsy continued, oblivious to the rearrangement of Charlie's brain, "so either it's not the same girl or there's something shady going on."

"Like what?"

"She's a spy."

"Here to steal . . . beer secrets?"

That earned him an eye roll. "Your privacy, Charlie. And Adriana's. That's what I'm afraid she's after. Somebody could have planted her here to spy on *you*."

"Wouldn't she be trying to talk to me?" he pointed out. "Instead of ignoring me?"

Mugsy huffed at that, probably because she couldn't argue. "I couldn't find much about her online. Either she scrubbed all her content, or she's got dummy accounts."

"That doesn't have to mean anything sinister, Mugsy. Maybe she was applying for jobs."

"I bet."

"Or—graduate school." Charlie stared at the pommel of his saddle, in case Mugsy was giving him a pitying look. "She could have hidden ambitions."

"Maybe." It wasn't quite a sigh, but Charlie could tell she was humoring him. "I've got my eye on her. You watch your step too."

He nodded, fully intending to pay extremely close attention to Jean, even if it wasn't the way Mugsy had in mind.

The trail passed out of sight as they rounded a bend, so it felt like an ambush when Charlie saw his dad waiting ahead. His hand tightened on the reins, an unconscious movement that had his mount nickering softly as if to say, *get ahold of yourself.*

"Ride with me, son." As far as Charlie knew, this was his father's first time on horseback, but you'd never guess from his confident handling of his mount. Anything athletic came easily to him. Too bad those genes had skipped Charlie. "You don't mind, do you, Mugsy?"

"Maybe Mugsy should be in on this," Charlie said. "If it's business talk."

"This is more of a father-son discussion." Charlie's dad nodded at Mugsy, who slowed her horse to let Charlie and his father pull ahead. Several long minutes passed before his father spoke again.

"Your mother said I should talk to you." That answered Charlie's first question: why are you hanging out with me instead of someone more important? "Thank you for not hiding in your room last night."

"Sure." Guilt mixed with the weak coffee in Charlie's stomach. It wasn't loyalty to the business that had drawn him to the campfire. "Is that what you wanted to talk to me about?"

They didn't chat often enough for this to feel like a casual conversation, even without the lurking-in-wait aspect.

"You know, Charles, there's nothing more important to your mother and I than passing on the legacy of Pike's Brewing to the next generation."

Charlie waited for his father to go on, but he seemed to expect a response. As if there could be any doubt what point he was making. "Meaning me."

"That's right. Knowing that you're provided for, and the Pike's tradition will carry on, is all we ask from this life."

That wasn't strictly true. His dad had a dozen hobbies, and his mom had always wanted to travel. Charlie nodded anyway. It was the accepted storyline of their family.

"It's really something to think back on your great-great-grandfather brewing the first batch of Pike's. The hills were crawling with prospectors, everyone itching to make their fortune in gold, but did Great-Gramps spend his days with a pickax and a pan?"

"No." Charlie did his best to sound interested in a story he'd heard a million times. Although he suspected it had been embellished over the years. The first Pike had probably been a moonshiner, but this version sounded better. Or, at least, more legal.

"That's right. Our forefathers spotted an opportunity, and they went for it. What does a prospector want at the end of a hard day's work? Pike's Pale, the real gold in them thar hills."

Charlie made an appreciative noise, like he hadn't seen that coming. On some level he understood that his father preferred to tell stories with a high probability of success, even if that meant repeating the same ones over and over. But this particular tale carried extra weight.

"You know who likes working at the brewery?" Charlie ventured. "Mugsy."

"Yes, she'll be a great help to you when you take over. Few things are as important as selecting the right team. Mugsy can be your fixer. She's good at that."

"Actually, I think Mugsy might want to do something more creative. Take things in a new direction—"

"Plenty of time to talk about that later," his father interrupted. "If we're still in business."

Charlie started to nod before the substance of the words hit. "What do you mean?" His father wasn't above occasional dramatics, but this time he sounded serious.

Mr. Pike glanced over his shoulder, where Philip and Emma Koenig were arguing about a bird, taking it in turns to mimic its call.

"Why do you think they're here, Charlie?"

"For the centennial?" Even as he said it, Charlie knew that wasn't the answer.

His father huffed a laugh. "We survived Zima, wine coolers, hard lemonade. Made a tentative peace with Red Bull. But I tell you this: I have nightmares about those alcoholic seltzers."

"I didn't know that." He thought of sharing a nightmare of his own, like the one where he had gills but was stuck on dry land, except his father wasn't finished.

"Tough times, Charlie. That's what the last five years have been. We put a good face on it, but I don't know how much longer we can go it alone. Do you hear what I'm saying?"

"Not . . . exactly," he admitted.

"The Koenigs run a multinational operation. With their backing, we could expand our brand instead of watching it shrink down to nothing."

"What about all the other people?" He tried to surreptitiously indicate the Canadians in their sun hats, flanked by the cider makers from France.

"Consolation prizes. We need deep pockets and global reach. Anything else is a Band-Aid. Might stave off the inevitable for a few years, but eventually it's goodbye to generations of blood, sweat, and beers. And then what happens to you?"

Charlie couldn't suppress a flicker of curiosity. What *would* happen to him if the shadow of Pike's Pale Ale wasn't looming on the horizon, as it had been his entire life? He shoved that thought aside, not wanting to buy his freedom at the cost of his dad's beloved business.

"Why didn't you tell me?"

"You weren't there, Charlie."

"Sorry."

"It's okay, because you're here now. And together, we can turn this ship around."

He made it sound like they'd done this kind of thing before—as if Charlie and his dad were an established team with an impressive record of wins, as opposed to two people who awkwardly coexisted when they couldn't use Charlie's mom as a go-between. Sometimes Charlie worried his father confused the uplifting movies he watched on cable with real life.

"I'll try my best," Charlie said, because that much was true. "How can I help?"

"I need you to be here, playing the part of my son and heir."

"I am your son."

"Then it should be easy. Philip Koenig is a family-first kind of guy. He'll respect that we're keeping the Pike legacy alive. With Smithson's help."

"About that, Dad—"

"Look alive," his father said, cutting him off. "You want to help? Go talk to your girl." Like most of Mr. Pike's suggestions, it was an order in disguise. Rather than waiting for Charlie to comply, he smacked Charlie's horse on the rump, sending mount and rider trotting ahead—on a collision course with Adriana Asebedo.

Chapter 23

Jean had seen some horrifying things in her day, but the sight of Charlie galloping toward his beloved on horseback rocketed straight into her top three. What did they think this was—a rehearsal for Adriana Asebedo's next music video? Maybe they could CGI a carpet of wildflowers into the background. Add a slo-mo effect to her hair.

Not that Adriana needed the help. She looked natural in the saddle, like she spent her weekends cantering through meadows instead of wearing sequins on red carpets. Jean vaguely recalled that the pop sensation came from humble roots, maybe even someplace rustic enough to include horses. That had been part of her aesthetic in the early days, though obviously now she was much more sophisticated. Hard not to be when you were a kajillionaire.

As much as she wanted to look away, Jean found it impossible not to stare. It was borderline uncanny to encounter someone in the flesh whose face was so familiar from seeing it on a screen. Jean's brain immediately cued up a slideshow of every random tidbit it had collected about Adriana Asebedo: the red dress she wore to her first VMAs; her transformation from cute teen singer to sultry adult; how she sold out every stop on her latest tour; the TV actress she was rumored to be dating in her early twenties; that time one of her songs casually confirmed Adriana was bi and everyone lost their minds, in the positive and negative sense; and of course the video for "Silent Storm," which Jean definitely had not pored over like a crime scene investigator after CharlieGate, looking for clues. Too bad she hadn't studied

Adriana's love life a little more carefully *before* Charlie flashed his tattoo.

It would have been a lot to take in, even without the flames of jealousy slow-roasting her from the inside. If Jean squinted at her sideways, it was almost possible to pretend Adriana was an ordinary person. Pretty, but not inhumanly so—a girl next door with expensive clothes and professional styling who did not subsist on junk food and restaurant leftovers. The two beefy dudes trailing her, who looked like they'd be more comfortable riding tanks, changed the vibe, but maybe everyone was supposed to pretend they were invisible.

Jean wondered if the security detail could hear what Adriana was saying to Charlie. The pop star was smiling, but it looked like a serious conversation. *I missed you. I missed you too. I love you. I love you more. Let's go be rich and beautiful together. I thought you'd never ask.*

That was just a guess. Despite her best attempt at reading lips, she had no idea what they were discussing—especially after Charlie's other lady friend rode up beside her, blocking Jean's view.

"Eve, huh." She didn't phrase it as a question, but Jean heard the undercurrent of suspicion. "Sockless Tommy's niece."

Jean tensed. "That's right."

"Why do they call him that?" the other woman asked, clearly testing her.

"Probably because he doesn't like socks." As if Jean was going to be tripped up that easily.

Adriana Asebedo's laughter floated through the air, making it impossible not to look back at her and Charlie. It didn't sound like a fake giggle. This was husky and delighted, a full-throated burble of amusement. The knife twisted in Jean's gut. Sleeping together was one thing, but making each other laugh? That was hard to forgive.

"You seem very interested in what's happening back there."

"Aren't you?" Jean shot back, because she wasn't the only one trying to sneak a peek.

Sure enough, the other woman gave a guilty flinch, followed by a wary look at Jean. "I don't know what you're talking about."

It was a transparent lie, but Jean opted not to call her on it. A truth standoff was apparently in both their interests. Maybe this chick didn't want Adriana to find out Charlie had been running around on her, like the player he was.

"Don't mess with him," the other woman warned.

"Are you his bodyguard?" Jean asked, as if she didn't know better.

"No, I'm his everything guard. And I don't like it when people take advantage of him."

Jean was surprised she didn't crack her knuckles for extra menace. Maybe she didn't need to, with a glare like that. "He's a big boy. He can fight his own battles."

"You don't know him."

There was no way to argue without exposing herself as a fraud. And besides, she had a point. Jean didn't really know Charlie at all, did she?

On that depressing note, Emma Koenig joined them, reining in her horse to ride next to Charlie's lady friend.

"I was hoping we could continue our conversation about the local flora, Margaret."

So that was her name. Naturally, Charlie had never mentioned her.

There wasn't room to ride three abreast, and since Jean had no desire to spend more time with Charlie's mistress *or* the girl his parents were pushing on him, she found herself riding next to Sergeant Cowboy.

"Love is hard," he said, out of the blue.

"How did you know?" It was deflating to learn she hadn't been playing it as cool as she thought.

"I've been around the sun a few times." He fell silent, contemplating the trail ahead. "They do have powerful chemistry."

Following the direction of his gaze, Jean realized he was referring to Emma and Margaret.

"I guess," she said, almost disappointed he wasn't talking about her romantic tribulations.

"Hard to fight that kind of thing."

"Yeah." Chemistry was a bitch, all right. It messed with your head and made you do ridiculous things. Believing in someone too good to be true. Chasing him halfway around the world. Rubbing your own heart over the cheese grater of his double life.

"Keep your chin up," Sergeant Cowboy said.

"Because it gets easier?" Jean guessed.

"No. But it's almost snack time."

"I catch one of you deviants littering, you'll be picking garbage out of the pine needles with your teeth," Sergeant Cowboy said when they reached the clearing where a breakfast buffet was waiting.

Jean slid off her horse, landing hard. It was more of a controlled fall than the neat leg swing Emma had just executed, or Adriana Asebedo's exuberant hop, but Jean's priority was speed, not grace. She needed more coffee stat.

"I was going to help you," Charlie said, sneaking up behind her.

"Eve has ridden plenty of horses." Eve was also the type to refer to herself in the third person. She must be a blast at parties.

"Good, good." Charlie frowned at the ground. "Would you like to get a cup of coffee?"

"Yes." She charged ahead, ignoring the implied *with me.*

"Beautiful morning," Charlie tried again, joining her at the table.

Jean glared at him over the rim of her tin mug. "Is it?"

He could make those doe eyes at someone else. Adriana Asebedo, for example. Once she finished the tense discussion she was having with Margaret. Maybe they were negotiating a new custody agreement, alternating weeks with Charlie.

"Are you having a good time?"

"Peachy."

Charlie ignored the sarcasm. "It can be relaxing to get out in nature. Alone—or with other people. Whose company you enjoy." He tried to give her a significant look, but Jean wasn't having it.

"It's hard to relax when you don't really know the people around you. Or if you can trust them."

"Oh, you can," he said at once.

"Even if they've lied to you?" she asked sweetly.

"Maybe it only *seems* like a lie."

"If it quacks like a duck, it's a duck," said Sergeant Cowboy, who happened to be passing by with a manly fistful of trail mix.

"Quack, quack." For reasons she couldn't explain, Jean made flapping motions with her elbows.

"Did you know that bread isn't good for ducks?" Charlie asked, with an air of desperation. "Too many empty calories. They fill up on bread and stop foraging for more nutritious food."

"I guess they don't know any better. Ducks are easy to fool. But once they wise up, look out." She narrowed her eyes at him in case he thought the duck part was literal.

"The truth can also be hard to swallow," Charlie countered. "If you don't know how the . . . duck will react. Or you're afraid it will change things. Between you and the duck. If you've had a bad experience in the past. With ducks."

"Well maybe it's unfair to judge a duck because you happen to be paranoid."

"Unless the reason you feel paranoid is that you like that duck so much, you can't imagine anything worse than losing them."

That brought Jean up short, but only temporarily. How dare Charlie say things like that with a straight face? "If you like a duck that much, why run away from it?"

"I—I'd guess the person was scared."

"Of ducks?"

"Not all ducks. Just the one very special duck. With the most beautiful feathers." His eyes didn't move from her face, even when Sergeant Cowboy's bellow rang through the clearing.

"We ride in five, greenhorns. Let's get this place shipshape."

Jean looked away first, draining the rest of her lukewarm coffee.

"Do you think we could talk more later?" Charlie asked, as she turned to drop her mug in the plastic bin provided for that purpose.

"Won't you have your hands full?" she hinted. "With all your other *guests.*"

He blinked at her, like he didn't know what she was getting at. Please. Did she look like that big of a sucker?

"I'll probably have a headache." She meant it as a transparently BS excuse, but Charlie's face flooded with concern.

"Is it bad? Did you get too much sun? I shouldn't have been talking your ear off. Do you want me to see if Ranger Mitch has any aspirin?"

"I think Sergeant Cowboy would tell me to cut my head off with a rusty machete before he gave me painkillers."

Charlie still looked worried. "Do you need more coffee?"

She shook her head. "I'll take a nap when we get back."

"Want some company?" Smithson asked, sliding between Jean and Charlie.

"You've stepped in it now," Charlie observed.

Jean assumed he was referring to the verbal evisceration she was about to deliver until she noticed he was looking at the ground. More specifically, Charlie had his gaze trained on the fresh horse droppings Smithson had walked right into.

Cursing, Smithson wiped his shoe on the grass, loudly informing everyone in hearing range how much he'd paid for his stupid loafers.

"That was your first mistake," Sergeant Cowboy said. "The rest of you, mount up."

"What about me?" Smithson whined.

"You can follow when you get yourself cleaned up. The horse knows where it's going."

"Are you kidding me? I'm supposed to trust a horse to get me home?"

"Ever seen a horse step in a pile of crap?"

"No," Smithson snapped, like that was the stupidest question he'd ever been asked.

"That's right. Horses are too smart for that shit."

Chapter 24

Short of adding spinning saw blades or a cloud of poison gas, it was hard for Charlie to imagine a less appealing environment than the party bus Smithson had commissioned to bring the younger members of the group to Deadwood that evening. Between the flashing lights and mirrored chrome, a stereo system that vibrated from the carpeted floor up to the base of Charlie's skull, and the general stickiness of every soft surface, he couldn't find a safe place for his eyes to land, much less the rest of his body.

Worst of all, Jean wasn't there, having declined on the grounds that she wasn't feeling well. Charlie hated the idea of her alone in her wagon with a headache—or worse! He'd wanted to call a doctor, but his mom suggested a care package instead, filled with painkillers, dark chocolate, a romance novel, fluffy socks, and several of Mugsy's teas. He'd have to hope it was enough.

This bus was the last place anyone would want to convalesce, fluffy socks or not, so in that sense Charlie was glad Jean had been spared. And yet he felt every added mile between them as if it were yanking on something tender inside him that would snap if it stretched too far.

"You are sighing," Emma Koenig observed, peering at him from across the aisle. She'd had the foresight to bring sunglasses on this after-dark excursion, so maybe this wasn't her first time riding a party bus. Beside her, Mugsy was taking the old-school approach, closing her eyes while her lips moved in what was either a prayer for serenity or a curse on Smithson.

Someone turned the music up even louder, eliciting cheers

from the front of the bus. Drinks had been flowing freely all day. Not unexpected with this many liquor distributors gathered in one place, but another source of anxiety for Charlie. Human behavior was hard enough to predict without throwing the mood-altering volatility of alcohol into the mix.

At least the thundering bass meant no one expected him to make conversation. Even Mugsy and Emma, seated side by side, were reduced to touching each other's arms and hands when they wanted to point something out.

Only Smithson seemed undeterred by the background noise, yelling at his pack of followers like he was delivering a TED Talk on a dance floor. Charlie caught snatches of his monologue and was surprised to find that he was discussing business. Stock options, import taxes, market penetration: all the buzzwords Charlie knew he should care about, that inevitably turned to white noise whenever his father mentioned them.

"Hey, Two Buck," Smithson shouted, cupping his hands around his mouth like a megaphone. Charlie braced for a pop quiz he was bound to fail, about MOQ or ISO or any of the other acronyms he could never keep straight. "How come your girl isn't riding with us?"

"She has a headache," Charlie answered without thinking. "Which is none of your business." He could have kicked himself for revealing anything about Jean to her old enemy.

"I got the deluxe bus for her." Smithson spread his arms wide, like they should all be grateful to him for sourcing this traveling hellscape. "Hey, maybe she's coming on horseback. That girl can *ride* . . . but I guess you already knew that, eh Chuck?"

There was a round of chortling and hand slapping, in case Charlie had missed the double meaning. Then Smithson grabbed the driver's microphone and started singing over the PA system.

"Silent storm, you rocked me—"

Mugsy stomped up the aisle and grabbed the handset. "Grow up," she said to Smithson, her voice echoing through the speakers. "This isn't your frat house." After offering what looked like an apology to the driver, she returned to her seat, still muttering.

"If this is the future of the industry, maybe I don't want to be part of it."

Charlie reached across the aisle to touch her shoulder. "Don't let them spoil it for you, Mugsy. You're worth twenty of them—especially Smithson."

She blew out a long breath, like there was a cake full of candles in front of her. "You're right. Screw them. And the horse they rode in on."

Emma dipped her sunglasses to peer at Mugsy.

"What?" Mugsy fidgeted under her gaze, smoothing her hair.

"I admire your passion."

"Oh. Thanks."

Emma nodded, sliding her dark glasses back into place.

"Sorry if I offended you ladies," Smithson bellowed. "That includes you, Chuck."

Mugsy started to stand, but Charlie shook his head. "He's not worth it."

She frowned at him but must have seen that Charlie wasn't too upset, because she lowered herself back into her seat. Jokes about that song were nothing new. And at least Jean wasn't here to get the wrong idea.

At last, the bus rumbled into Deadwood, circling around Main Street to park behind the casino Smithson had rented out for the evening. Charlie hadn't been here for years, though he had fond memories of the history museum and the hilltop cemetery where Calamity Jane was buried. He wondered if Jean would want to see that, before remembering it was nighttime, and she wasn't here.

They entered the building through a back door. Even with the lights and sounds from the slot machines, it was a welcome respite from the bus.

"That was like the before part of a migraine commercial," Mugsy grumbled as she stepped past Charlie. He held the door for Emma, who surveyed the scene with typical detachment. Machines of varying size surrounded them, with a quieter cluster of felt-topped tables at the other end of the room.

"I learned how to play poker," Charlie said. "When I was in Hawaii. Jean taught me." If he thought Mugsy would be impressed, her scowl quickly set him straight.

"How much did she take you for?"

"We, uh, didn't play for money." Was it warm in here? Charlie's face felt flushed. Fortunately, Mugsy didn't ask for details. "I've been thinking. Maybe I could reach out to her. Jean." It was a sideways version of the truth, but Mugsy had never responded well to a frontal assault. "She shouldn't be that hard to find—"

"Charlie."

There was a world of *no* in her voice, mixed with equal parts *you can't be serious* and *do I really have to tell you why that's a bad idea?*

Emma Koenig had turned her body slightly, as if fascinated by the design of the nearest slot machine, but Charlie could tell she was listening. It didn't stop him from trying again.

"I'm not sure she did what you think she did. And even if she did, what did she really tell them?"

"Your location," Mugsy reminded him. "And I'm sure they paid her plenty for it."

"Allegedly. But she could have given them a lot more than that. If you know what I mean."

Mugsy made a strange noise.

"Are you grinding your teeth?" Charlie asked. "Remember

what Dr. Hall said. There's no point wearing your mouthguard at night if you're going to abuse your molars during the day."

Her nostrils flared, in what he hoped was a calming breath. Maybe she needed time to adjust to the idea. Before he explained that Jean was already here.

"I would like to try this sarsaparilla," Emma said. Even though it was quieter in the casino, she still touched Mugsy's arm to get her attention. "Is it like one of your teas?"

Charlie was surprised Emma had tasted Mugsy's teas. She didn't share them with just anyone.

"Not quite in that league, but it's drinkable," Mugsy replied. She glanced at Charlie. "You'll be okay?"

"Yes, Mugsy." He kept the sigh inside. "I'll manage." Especially since they'd booked the entire building. Charlie wondered how much that was costing his parents, on top of all the other expenses of the weekend.

After they disappeared up the stairs to the saloon area, Charlie looked for a quiet corner. Not to hide; just to be alone with his thoughts.

"Hey, Two Buck." Smithson's wide-legged strut was even more pronounced than usual. Maybe he was feeling the effects of their morning on horseback. "Hope you brought your wallet."

"Do you need change for the slots?" He reached into his pocket, emerging with a handful of loose coins. It was a sincere question, but Smithson looked annoyed, especially after one of his sidekicks laughed.

"I'm not playing the nickel machines, Chuck. It's blackjack time. A man's game."

In Charlie's experience, it was much more of a woman's game, but he didn't see any point in arguing with Smithson. The two of them were never going to see eye to eye, even if they were seated across a small table from each other. Which did not sound like Charlie's idea of a good time.

"Actually," he started to say, looking around for a bathroom or other likely excuse.

Smithson leaned closer, lowering his voice. "Your dad made me promise not to let you be a wallflower."

And here Charlie had assumed Smithson was torturing him for his own amusement.

"Let's go, bro." He draped an arm around Charlie's shoulders, ignoring his flinch. "It'll be fun. Smart guy like you, I bet you'll clean up." It was clear from his tone that he did not, in fact, believe that Charlie had a prayer of holding his own.

It seemed there was one thing he and Smithson agreed on after all.

Chapter 25

Jean stepped onto the grassy shoulder to allow the slowly approaching vehicle to pass. She'd gone for a walk assuming everyone else had already left the premises, only to find herself caught in a rural traffic jam (one human, one automobile) within minutes of abandoning her wagon.

"Nothing to see here," she said through her fake smile. "Keep on moving."

Like everyone else in her life, the driver ignored Jean's wishes, pulling up alongside her and rolling down a tinted window. Her first thought was that Hildy must have commandeered a luxury sedan. She seemed like a person who would change cars for the evening the way other women swapped handbags.

"Need a ride?"

Jean blinked at Adriana Asebedo, alone in the back seat. The sensible answer would have been *no, I want to commune with the dusty gravel and my sad feelings*, but once again Jean's curiosity got the better of her.

"Where to?"

"Deadwood."

"Why not?" Resisting temptation had never been Jean's strong suit, which was why she seldom tried. Might as well do a little recon behind enemy lines. And if that failed, it would be worth it for storytelling purposes. When the hell else was Jean going to be in a car with a megacelebrity?

The front passenger door opened and one of Adriana's burly security guys stepped out. "Phone?"

She shook her head. It looked like he wanted to pat her down, so she turned out the pockets of her sleeveless tunic, lifting the hem to show there were no hiding places in her faux leather leggings, unless he wanted to do a cavity search.

He opened the rear door, waiting until Jean fastened her seat belt to close it behind her. For a guy with a neck the size of a tree trunk, he gave off strong nanny energy.

"So what's your story?" Adriana asked, before Jean could sort through her mental list of Top Five Conversation Starters for Pop Stars. "Are you one of them?"

"The booze crew? No. I'm an artist." It felt good to tell the truth, like wiggling your bare toes after peeling off sweaty socks at the end of a long shift.

Jean half expected Adriana to zone out after that perfunctory show of interest or turn the conversation to herself. Instead the other woman studied her in silence.

"Did you design that?" She pointed to the tattoo peeking from under the strap of Jean's tunic.

"Yeah." Jean stuck her arm out to give her a closer look. "It's my drawing. I didn't ink it on myself."

Adriana lightly touched the outline of the plumeria with the tip of her finger. "Cool."

"I know."

The singer smiled, more in understanding than amusement. And why not? They were both creative people, and art existed on a higher plane than a romantic rivalry—if that was even the right word, since Jean wasn't sure they were competing for the same prize. Maybe she should quit pussyfooting around and straight up ask. *Seen any other good tattoos lately? Like maybe a snake?*

"So why are you here?" Adriana asked, before Jean could throw a metaphorical glass of water in her face.

"Unfinished business, I guess you could say." If you didn't want to sound like an unhinged person frothing at the mouth about REVENGE!

Adriana's lips curved just enough to display her famous dimples. "I guess that makes two of us."

Oh, so she wanted to play the charmingly self-deprecating card? Good luck with that. Jean wasn't going to give her the satisfaction of asking. Obviously they were both talking about Charlie, not that Adriana seemed to be aware of that. Unless she *did* know, and Jean was about to be dropped in a ditch along a deserted stretch of highway.

"Not just here for a beer party in the boonies, then?" Jean kept her voice light, like a person with no personal stake in the answer. Just makin' conversation. Tra-la-la!

"It's not my usual scene," Adriana agreed. "I'm trying to fix my karma. Or maybe it's selfish. I don't know."

"Am I an angel or a devil?" Jean asked rhetorically. "Story of my life."

Adriana gave her another considering look, twisting one of her rings around her index finger. "You were riding with Margaret this morning. Are you two friends?"

Oh boy. Even though she kept her voice steady, Jean heard the twinge of emotion. It wasn't a casual question, which meant Adriana most likely knew about Charlie and Margaret.

"She's very beautiful, don't you think?" Adriana added, looking at her lap.

Make that *definitely* knew, hence the probing for intel about the competition. Jean felt a surprising reluctance to be the bearer of bad news. Something about those big round eyes that looked a little tired, like someone as famous as Adriana should be immune to human frailty.

"Sure, I'd paint her. Whoever she is. Another beverage person, presumably." Jean added a vague hand wave, hoping that would be enough to introduce reasonable doubt.

"She makes teas," Adriana corrected. "Really good ones. Not alcoholic."

"Oh yeah." Jean nodded as the realization struck; that must have been what was in the get-well basket Charlie had left at her door, before tiptoeing away with the exaggerated motions of a mime. His criminal instincts were clearly limited to the romantic arena. "Very soothing. As much as I can be soothed." She glanced at the security guards. "Not that I'm a dangerous person."

"You tried her tea?"

"It was in a hospitality basket." No need to mention she'd gotten it from Charlie.

"Ah." She seemed weirdly relieved. "Not a custom blend?"

"Nope." Maybe focus less on the tea and more on who your man is seeing behind your back, Jean thought at her. A little friendly suggestion.

"And the blonde girl?"

"Emma the frost maiden?" Jean shook her head. "I don't see that happening."

Adriana jumped on that, like she wanted to believe but needed hard evidence. "Why not?"

"One, old people suck at matchmaking. They're way too obvious, like a cat in tap shoes. And two, I don't get the impression Emma has much use for other humans." What Jean didn't say, because it would have been weird, was that no one could compete with Adriana Asebedo. Charlie was probably dumping Margaret right now, if he hadn't already. Jean needed to hustle if she wanted to bring her evil plans to fruition before Charlie and Adriana rode off into the sunset together.

Fortunately, she thrived under pressure.

"You don't think there's anything there?" Adriana pressed.

"Nah. Here today, gone tomorrow."

The singer fell silent, fiddling with her rings again. "It's not always like that, though. Sometimes you meet a person and it's lightning. It marks you. The burn is so bright, you can't get it out of your head afterward."

"Like your retinas are fried?" Jean knew she was deflecting, and maybe Adriana did too, because she gave her an arch look.

"That's never happened to you?"

"If it did, I'd find a way to get it out of my system." *And I'd sure as hell never admit we were both talking about the same guy.*

"And how would you do that?" Adriana sounded equal parts dubious and intrigued.

"Obviously it would depend on the situation. Like in your case, you'd probably write a song. Let it all out in the lyrics."

"And hear it played everywhere I go for the next ten years? No thank you."

"Huh. That would suck." *Like seeing Pike's Pale Ale everywhere, for the rest of Jean's life.* "Option two would be to hate them instead."

Adriana pulled her glossy ponytail over her shoulder, running her fingers through it like she was checking for snarls even though every strand was perfectly smooth, not a split end in sight. "Really hate them or just pretending to yourself?"

Damn. Adriana Asebedo, straight for the jugular. "You should be on *60 Minutes.*"

"I have been on *60 Minutes*. Twice."

"As the host, not the guest. Bringing the hard-hitting questions."

"Turn the tables," Adriana mused. "Force someone to talk to me about their innermost feelings."

"Exactly!" Jean didn't think they were at the high-five stage yet, so she smacked her own palm with the back of her other hand. "Give people a taste of their own medicine."

Adriana considered this, lips pursed. "I guess that's something to think about. If Plan A goes tits up."

"It's good to have options," Jean agreed.

A few minutes later, they parked in a dark lot that was empty apart from a party bus with blacked-out windows, equally suited to prison runs or pub crawls. Adriana's security detail led them into the building, alert for threats. Maybe they were worried about a raccoon ambush.

"We're going to have dinner upstairs," Adriana said. "Do you want to join us?"

It was flattering to be asked, even though Jean had no desire to watch the Charlie-and-Adriana show at close range. "I think I'll hit the tables."

"Then I hope it's your lucky night."

Jean couldn't bring herself to say, *you too!* "Thanks for the lift."

As soon as Adriana and her entourage were out of sight, Jean wandered deeper into the casino, past the slot machines and video consoles. All of these booze nepo babies had money to burn, so Jean might as well win some of it from them at poker.

Speaking of ripe for the plucking, she heard Smithson badgering another player and was surprised to see that it was Charlie. So he wasn't having dinner with his long-lashed love after all.

As she approached the table, Jean sized up the situation. Charlie looked pale and uncertain, while Smithson was gloating as he raked an armful of chips over to join his pile of winnings.

Oh hell no.

"Deal me in," she said, pulling out a chair.

Chapter 26

Charlie had given up hope of his luck turning, at poker or anything else. The only bright spot on the horizon was that eventually this outing would be over, and Smithson could beat his chest and feel superior because he'd triumphed over a table full of drunks.

Though in Charlie's case, it wasn't cocktails clouding his judgment. A solid half of his attention had jumped back to the last time he'd played cards. When he caught a whiff of Jean's perfume, he assumed it was an olfactory hallucination, brought on by how intensely he was concentrating on the past. But then there she was, climbing into the seat beside him. He leaped up to help her push the tall chair back under the table, since he doubted her feet would reach the floor.

"You here to watch the master at work?" Smithson spun one of his chips.

"I'm here to wipe the floor with a bunch of amateurs," Jean corrected.

"Yeah, okay." Smithson's laugh died out when she stared back at him without smiling. "You don't have any chips."

"She can have mine." Charlie made a snowplow with his hands, pushing his meager stash over to Jean.

"Tapping out, Two Buck? Can't stand the heat?"

Charlie scratched the back of his head, considering how to respond to Smithson's taunting. "Yes and no," he finally settled on.

"What does that even mean, dude?"

"It means he's done, and the reason is none of your business, because I'm here to take his place." Jean propped her chin on her knuckles. "Unless you're afraid to lose to a girl?"

"Like that's going to happen," Smithson muttered, nodding at the dealer. "Let's do this."

Charlie edged around the table, looking for a vantage point with a clear view of Jean's face.

"Hold up." Smithson set down his cards, twisting to glare at Charlie. "Are you trying to see my hand?"

"He doesn't cheat," Jean said without looking up from her cards. "Not at poker, anyway."

That was . . . a perplexing remark, but Charlie decided to be grateful she'd stuck up for him and wonder about the rest later. He drifted a short distance from the table, creeping back once the game started. If he couldn't look at Jean's face, he could at least stand behind her. The contrast between the slender whiteness of her neck and the dark line of her hair reminded him of a delicious black and white cookie. He wanted to bite her there. Very gently, so it was more of a nibble, because the human spine was much less resilient than a snake's. It was one of her ticklish spots, a fact Jean always adamantly denied even while twitching and squirming if he so much as blew on her neck . . .

"You want to sit on her lap, Chuck?"

"I'm fine here."

Smithson snorted into his drink. "Guess you're good at being arm candy."

The line of Jean's shoulders tightened, though Charlie doubted anyone else had noticed the microscopic movement.

"Am I bothering you?" he asked in a low voice, bending closer to her.

"Hmm?" She rearranged three of her cards, for no reason Charlie could ascertain. "Oh. I barely noticed you there."

Jean rubbed the end of her nose. She did that sometimes

if she was holding in a joke or a surprise or any other type of secret. It was one of her tells—not that Charlie would ever tell her that.

So he stayed where he was, and the game continued. After a few minutes, it occurred to Charlie that he wasn't nervous, despite the dirty looks from Smithson. His faith in Jean was that strong. She would either win or do something so fabulous, the outcome of the game was irrelevant. He tried to follow the ins and outs of who played which card and when but found his attention wandering.

Had there ever been anything as enticing as the hint of Jean's tattoo peeking over her shoulder in back, offering that teasing glimpse of flowers and feathers?

Should he get another tattoo? Something bolder and less hidden?

Would Jean be willing to draw it for him—or *on* him?

"I win," Jean announced, scooping more chips into her growing pile. "Again."

Smithson looked significantly less cocky. "I had a bad hand."

"Whatever you have to tell yourself." She thanked the waiter who had just dropped off a fresh drink. "Ready to cut your losses?"

"You'd like that, wouldn't you?"

Jean tipped her head to one side, considering. "I think I'd rather keep dominating you, actually."

Charlie imagined a whistling sound effect from an old Western, or a movie samurai wielding her sword. Jean had the instincts of an apex predator, scenting weaknesses and setting traps with deadly speed and accuracy. Some of the other guys started to rib Smithson, which only riled him up more.

"What did you say your name was?" he asked Jean. Charlie wondered if he'd finally put it together.

She kept her eyes on her cards. "I didn't."

"I'll tell you what it's not." Smithson paused for effect. "Adriana Asebedo."

"How clever of you to notice," Jean replied, sipping her drink. "If only you paid that much attention to the game."

"You think if you fight his battles for him, he'll choose you?" Smithson jerked a thumb at Charlie.

"This isn't a battle." Jean made a tutting sound with her tongue. "It's a beating."

"We'll see about that," Smithson said, over the hastily smothered laughter of his crew. "You're on a hot streak now, but my luck always turns."

Either Smithson was wrong about his luck or it was no match for Jean's skill, because he kept losing. Finally the other beverage bros got bored and headed upstairs to smoke cigars, giving Smithson the excuse he needed to fold.

"FYI, Two Buck, a real man doesn't get his sidepiece to do his dirty work," Smithson said, tossing down his cards.

"I love statements that start with 'a real man' or 'a real woman.' They're always so progressive," Jean mused.

"And she's not my sidepiece," Charlie added.

"Call it what you want, bro. You might be hitting that, but I don't see you telling your daddy she's your woman." He jerked a thumb at Jean, and Charlie had the urge to bend that digit backward until Smithson apologized.

The anger was so strong, he was shaking with it. "I would never call her *my* woman—"

"Oops," Smithson sneered, as Jean pushed away from the table, hiding her face from Charlie.

Before he could explain that he only meant no one could own another person—least of all a free spirit like Jean—she was gone.

Chapter 27

Jean returned from a solo nature walk—which wasn't nearly as relaxing as that kind of thing was supposed to be—the next afternoon to find a note from Hildy on her pillow.

Hope you're ready for cowboy poetry night.

Ominous.

Or maybe that was the lingering bad mood from last night talking. So what if Charlie had repudiated her in public? Today was another day, full of fresh opportunities to make him regret his choices.

Time to weaponize some rhymes.

Jean's wardrobe was better suited for an evening of Slutty Conceptual Art, so she chose the outfit most likely to torture Charlie: a neon mesh sheath over a sculptural fuchsia bra and high-waisted panties. Was it subtle? No. But if ever there was a look that said, *eat your heart out, triple-timer*, this was it.

She checked her reflection one last time before leaving the wagon, snapping a selfie for posterity. Posting it was out of the question, but Jean imagined the caption she would use if she could.

Twang this, bitches.

When she reached the main house, Jean discovered that the far end of the Pikes' spacious patio had been converted into a stage. The emcee—face barely visible behind a mustache that probably had its own zip code—stepped to the mike as she approached.

"Git yerselves right on up here now y'all, we're about to have us a rootin' tootin' good time."

A guitarist and a fiddler played a jaunty tune as the crowd drifted toward the stage. Jean glimpsed a head of dark hair zigzagging through the sea of bodies, which gave her a few seconds to compose herself before Charlie appeared.

"Eve." He paused to catch his breath. "You look incredible."

"I know."

"Oh, um, good." He blinked a few times, like he was trying to unscramble his thoughts. "I wanted to thank you. For last night."

A tequila purveyor (Jean recognized him by the bolo tie) glanced curiously at them.

"I have no idea what you're talking about." She started to edge past Charlie.

"Do you have an identical twin?" he asked, sticking to her side.

"No." Although that would have been a good angle. Next time, maybe. If she ever found herself in a situation remotely resembling this one.

"There might be dancing later," he tried again.

It was her turn to frown at him. "You dance?"

"I guess there's a caller who tells you the moves."

"I'm just here for the rhymes," she said, like she was some kind of cowboy poetry purist.

"But—"

Jean shushed him as the first performer took the stage.

Forty-five minutes later, they'd heard poems about cows and dogs and horses, pickup trucks and tractors, snowstorms, spring mud, sleeping under the stars, and sharing a bed with a "yeller-haired temptress."

To Jean's delight, Sergeant Cowboy opened the second act.

"I call this 'The Secret to a Good Life,'" he announced, before settling onto a stool behind the microphone.

> *"A man isn't a man if he can't man his own ship.*
> *From mess halls to rest stops, I eat my vittles and grits.*
> *Sometimes life gives you a lickin'—"* he pointed to his scars.
> *"And you come back so mad you're spittin'*
> *But get yourself a dog and a nice warm fire*
> *When winter storms blow, put on your good tires*
> *Pour yourself a whiskey, or maybe some gin—*
> *Tomorrow's sun still comes a-risin'*
> *Sure as shootin'."*

He busted out a harmonica, wailing a plaintive melody in time with the stomping of his boot.

"Talk about a man with layers," Jean said when the applause died down. "I would kill to know the story behind those neck scars."

"Hot coffee," replied Charlie, who hadn't left her side. She pretended not to be aware of his presence, as if she were serving up witty asides for her own amusement.

"I assumed it was a bar fight. Or a helicopter."

"Like—the blades?"

"I don't know. Maybe something with explosions." Jean mimed a fireball expanding between her hands.

"The lid came off his takeout cup, and the coffee scalded him."

Jean sucked a breath through her teeth. "That must have hurt. Not as much as a propeller, but still."

"The silver lining is that he got a big settlement from the fast-food chain, and that's how he started his trail riding business."

"Huh."

"What are you thinking about?"

"Which body part I would sacrifice for fuck-you money."

"Please don't." He grabbed for her, not seeming to realize he'd done it until she glanced at the place where his fingers wrapped around her arm. "I like your body the way it is," Charlie whispered, letting go.

She smoothed a hand over her midsection, noticing how his eyes tracked the movement. "As an independently wealthy heiress, I don't have to worry about selling my organs on the black market. But I appreciate your concern."

"An heiress named Eve," Charlie added, like he was cramming for a test.

"Exactly. And Eve has it all. She doesn't need anyone or anything. Because nothing touches her."

Charlie hesitated. "I don't know how we got to talking about scars and organs and helicopters. And not needing people."

Something you'd rather discuss? Your other girlfriends, perhaps? It wasn't like Jean to censor herself, but she was in unfamiliar territory, in more than the literal sense.

On stage, the emcee tapped the microphone. "And now, cowpokes, things are going to get wilder than a tumbleweed in a windstorm. It's open mic time. Come on up and show us what you got! It's a hell of a lot easier than ridin' a bronco."

"Easy for him to say," Charlie muttered.

"You're not going to do it?"

"Me? Go up there?" He pointed from himself to the stage, in case she needed the visual aid.

"It's your hoedown."

"Not really *mine*," he started to protest, but she got there first.

"It will be. All of this is going to be yours." Because Charlie had a number after his name like the rich boy he was, and would eventually inherit a whole freaking business and a fancy house, none of which he'd seen fit to mention even though they were sleeping together.

"I don't think of it that way. It's not who I am."

Jean gave him her steeliest look.

"It's one part," he conceded. "But there are other parts of me that are more important. Those are the things I'd want someone to know. The real me is not . . . this." Charlie gestured at the crowd.

With a sniff, Jean turned away, crossing her arms to show she wasn't buying what he was selling. "I know some people have a fear of public speaking," she relented, after a stony silence. "It's one of the most common phobias. Right up there with claustrophobia."

"I don't have that." Charlie sounded relieved to cross at least one off his list.

"Arachnophobia. Fear-of-heights-phobia."

"Acrophobia," he supplied. "Unless there are people who are afraid of being afraid of heights."

Jean didn't laugh. Her attention was fixed on Smithson, sauntering up to the microphone with his hands in his pockets. Charlie's father cheered from the front row.

"My name is Smithson Barrett. My poem is called 'Eye of the Tiger.'" Smithson cleared his throat directly into the microphone, triggering a shriek of feedback.

"*I have the eye of the tiger—*" He paused, mouth slightly ajar. "*Two eyes. That's what I got. Both of them are fierce fighters.*"

"Is he still talking about his eyes?" Jean asked Charlie, not bothering to lower her voice. "What are they, like those betta fish that attack each other if you put them in the same bowl?"

When Smithson covered his mouth with both hands, Jean assumed he was copying Sergeant Cowboy's harmonica solo.

"*Tikatikatika poom poom poom,*" he grunted into the mike.

"Is that beatboxing?" She could hardly believe her ears.

"*Tsss-t-t-t-tssss,*" Smithson vocalized, thrusting his hips. "*Chukka chukka wowwow.*"

"He put a dance break in his cowboy poem," Jean marveled. "Am I dead? Because this might be heaven."

There was another interlude of *chukkas* and *tssss*, plus a few *dvvvvts*, before the next verse.

"*Hey now, I'm an all-star.*
I make it rain.
Hire me and your company will go far.
My mad skillz save you money pain."

He made a few more buzzing sounds, then collapsed into a bow.

"Wow," Jean said over the polite applause. "I would have paid to see that, but no! He did it for free." Jean shook her head. "Money pain."

Charlie was staring at her face, like all he'd ever wanted out of life was to see her smile. She almost felt the teensiest bit warm inside, like one of her organs was turning to taffy. But just a small one, like the gallbladder. Maybe a kidney.

Was she really that easy? All he had to do was stand next to her on a summer evening, when he could have been talking to a dozen more important people, a good percentage of whom he was probably sleeping with, and suddenly she was all heart-eyes. Somebody needed to throw a drink in Jean's face, stat.

"Charlie."

He jumped when Margaret tapped him on the shoulder, turning to face her with a guilty flush. "Oh, hello. Um. We were just watching the poetry—"

Margaret held up a hand before he could dig a deeper hole. "Your dad needs you." *And I'm not interested in your weak excuses*, her expression added.

"Can I talk to him later?" Charlie asked.

"He wants you to do a poem." She tipped her head at the stage. "About Pike's."

Charlie was shaking his head before she finished. "I couldn't."

"That's what I told him, but he said it was already written and all you had to do was read it." She spared Jean a millisecond of side-eye. "Excuse us."

"I think he'll be great," Jean called after them. Charlie glanced back at her, probably trying to guess from her face whether she was being sincere or snide.

Ha! As if she knew.

Chapter 28

"That was very rude, Mugsy. I wish you'd try to get to know Eve a little—"

She treated him to her fiercest scowl. Even tossed over her shoulder while in motion, it was enough to singe his eyebrows. "That's what you're worried about right now?"

"It's one of the things." He could have listed the rest of his top five, but they were loud enough inside his head without giving them extra air. Was he going to make a fool of himself in front of Jean? Would it be worse to say no and look like a coward? Did his father not know him at all, or did he just not care about Charlie's feelings? Was everyone going to stare at Charlie and think *Smithson did it better*?

"There you are!" Throwing an arm around Charlie's shoulders, his father herded him closer to the stage. Maybe he thought Charlie would make a break for it if he didn't keep a tight hold. At least they didn't stop for the usual round of, "this is my son, Charlie. I prefer to speak for him, so he doesn't embarrass me," introductions, since his dad was in a hurry.

"Uh, Dad? Can I talk to you?" Charlie asked, nodding at the wine importer his father had just pointed out.

"No time. We need to get you in place."

"About that. Are you sure it's a good idea? Me going up there."

His father waved this off. "Smithson already pointed that out. Change of plans."

"Oh." Charlie would not have described the feeling in his chest as relief, exactly. It was too mixed up with the uncomfortable awareness that his dad didn't think he could stand on a stage and read someone else's words.

"Stay right here," Mr. Pike said, angling Charlie's shoulders so the light from the stage caught his profile. "Adriana's up next."

"Adriana Asebedo?"

"Yes, Charlie." His father managed to sigh without dropping his smile as he nudged him forward. "People will want to see your reaction."

"I thought you wanted me to get with Emma."

"Smithson said we'd get more social media capital out of pushing the Silent Storm angle."

That sounded like Smithson. Crass. Calculating. Wrong. "I don't know, Dad—"

Mugsy tapped him on the shoulder, shaking her head. Charlie took that to mean *don't bother,* because Mr. Pike was too deep in the zone to hear what he had to say.

"Let's hope this doesn't turn into a mosh pit," Mr. Pike joked.

Philip Koenig smiled politely. Either they didn't have mosh pits in Denmark or he didn't find it funny.

Charlie scanned the crowd, trying to see if Jean was still standing where he'd left her. An elbow poked him in the side.

"Quit frowning, son. We're having fun." Mr. Pike led the applause as Adriana took the stage.

Charlie was close enough to see her eyes ping-pong back and forth, almost as if she were nervous. That didn't seem possible for someone who had played sold-out arenas all over the world, but Charlie knew some fears didn't respond to logic. He smiled at her, just in case. None of this was her fault.

"I hope it's okay I brought my guitar." Adriana flashed her dimples, and the crowd laughed. She was charming in a way that reminded Charlie why he'd liked her in the first place. Adriana was good at making you feel like you were seeing something special and private, like the inside of a geode, even though she was also sparkly on the outside—and like tonight, there was almost always a much larger audience than one.

"You all have inspired me with your lyrical stylings, so I thought I'd try out something new." She looked down as she strummed a single chord. "It's hard to find the words to speak what's in your heart, but I'm going to give it a shot." When she raised her head, her eyes were bright. "Sending this out to a special someone who's here with us tonight."

The whispers started even before Adriana fixed her gaze in Charlie's direction. There were a few gasps and one *aww* that seemed to come from the spicy-cocktail guy.

"*Honey baby,*" she began, not quite singing.

"*You said you had to go*
I begged you to stay.
You said we had our fun
I asked for another day.
If I travel the world and don't find another you
Will you still tell me what I feel isn't true?"

She paused to strum another melancholy chord.

"*Time didn't fade this hunger.*
And we're not getting any younger.
Give me a chance to be part of your life.
You don't have to make me your wife.
I just want to be near you, as much as I can."

Her voice was stronger now, the tempo increasing as she sang the final line.

"*I came all this way to tell you, honey baby, I'm your number one fan.*"

She flashed another wistful smile, plucking a delicate melody on the guitar. Sergeant Cowboy chimed in on the harmonica, the fiddler adding a piercing vibrato.

After a final flourish, Adriana placed her palm over the

strings, silencing the guitar before hurrying off the stage to a burst of thunderous applause.

Charlie's dad clapped him on the back. "What a moment. They'll be talking about that for years. Good work, son."

"I just stood here."

"And that was perfect," his father agreed. "We made the magic happen."

All around them, misty-eyed beverage moguls chattered like squirrels, watching Charlie with varying degrees of subtlety. When he turned, ready to escape attention he neither wanted nor deserved, Charlie came face-to-face with Mugsy. If the rest of the audience looked like their hearts had melted, his oldest friend was a block of ice.

"Are you okay, Mugsy?"

She blinked twice. "I have to go."

Charlie would have followed, but Mugsy was a former all-state track star who still ran twenty miles a week. He didn't have a prayer of catching her.

"It's going to be hard to top that. My word."

Charlie wanted to tell his father he was laying it on too thick until his dad said, "Maybe we should call it a night?" and Charlie nodded in full agreement.

"Not so fast." Mr. Koenig gestured at the stage. "It appears the lovely Eve has something to say."

From behind the microphone, her eyes met Charlie's. It was only a moment, but he felt scorched by the contact. Not in a sexy way.

It's not what you think, Charlie tried to convey with heated eye contact of his own. But Jean refused to look at him. Lowering her mouth to the microphone, she spoke in a husky monotone.

"I call this 'You Mess With the Bull, You Get the Horns.'"

After smoothing a hand across her forehead, she began.

"Across a sea . . . a sea of grass.
I rode a lonesome cowboy, who showed his ass.
Kissing at midnight, chasing that happy trail.
He pretended I was the only one he wanted to nail."
She paused to let the hooting die down before continuing.
"Turns out he was a filthy liar,
And now I want to set him on fire.
All that's left are bitter regrets.
Why into my pants . . . did he I let?"

Charlie was spellbound. Even when she sounded like Yoda, Jean was the fiercest person he'd ever met. Watching her gave him a sharp thrill, like hiking to the top of a mountain and struggling to catch your breath while the view blew your mind: pleasure and pain, all wrapped up together.

She glanced at him before launching into the next verse.
"I wish I could tell you how he played me for a fool.
But it's too big a mystery why I trusted that tool."

Charlie started to raise an arm to get her attention, wanting to interject, but Jean had her eyes closed, cradling the microphone with both hands.
"Yeehaw. Flippity-flap. Git along little doggy.
You're just a child and your diapers are soggy."

Raising one arm, she snapped twice before leaving the stage.

It hit Charlie in waves. She was going. She thought the worst of him. She would be gone.

Distantly, he heard his father's voice calling after him.

"Where are you going, son? There's someone I'd like you to meet—"

He didn't turn back. Onward and upward. All the way to the stage.

The only good thing about standing on a raised platform in front of a rambunctious crowd was that the light was in his eyes, so he couldn't see all the faces staring back at him. Also, it meant he'd made it this far without falling on his face. That was one fear overcome.

"Hello," Charlie said, wincing when the sound echoed across the crowd. "The title of this poem is . . . 'Untitled.'" Because he hadn't paused long enough to come up with a name—much less any words to go with it.

"Okay, well. Thank you for listening."

"Is that part of the poem?" someone yelled from the darkness. Charlie suspected it was Smithson.

"No. That was just me. Thanking you." Except not Smithson. "This is the poem. Right after this." He took a deep breath.

"*I like snakes.*

And some people.

Especially the one who . . . my heart did take.

My feelings for her are more than double.

They're treeple."

Charlie gave serious thought to diving off the back of the stage and rolling across the grass until he landed in the creek. Why had he convinced himself he was capable of this? Jean might not even be listening. She could be back in her wagon by now, well out of hearing range. There was nothing for it but to go on. And pray for a power outage.

"*When we're together, I'm like the open prairie.*

Wide and rolling and endless. With lots of . . . plants.

If you think I like being alone, on the contrary!

Until she came along, I didn't understand the meaning of romance."

"Nice one," Sergeant Cowboy called. "Steady on." Charlie nodded his thanks for the support.

"*If there's a tree in the garden with only one piece of fruit,*

I'd give it to her—and that's the truth."

Bending, Charlie slapped his thighs a few times, because he thought he'd seen that in a movie once. Then he pretended to crack a whip before saying, "*Rawhide!*"

Hopefully that was cowboy enough.

As he walked off stage on wobbly legs, people clapped. It was better than booing, though most likely their guests felt obligated to applaud because of who he was. They would have done the same if Charlie had been the type of seven-year-old who wanted to put on a show for his parents' guests after dinner, as opposed to fleeing to his room.

His mother was the first to reach him. She folded him into a hug, then leaned back to search his face, still holding on to his shoulders. "Oh honey, I had no idea. Is it Mugsy? I thought you knew she preferred women."

"Of course I know that. It's Mugsy."

Mrs. Pike looked confused.

"I mean Mugsy is Mugsy. My best friend. It would be strange if I didn't know something that important about her."

"Yes, Charlie, but you're not always tuned in to that kind of thing."

He added that to the stockpile of unflattering beliefs his parents held about him. "Well, I wasn't talking about Mugsy, so you don't have to worry. If you'll excuse me, there's someone I need to find."

Charlie detoured around another group of aging businessmen in pristine cowboy boots. Where was she?

"Somebody's whipped," Smithson called after him. Charlie ignored him, doubling back to see if he'd missed Jean in the crowd.

A couple decked out from head to toe in rhinestone-encrusted leather veered toward the refreshment table, and Charlie found himself face-to-face with Philip Koenig.

"Charles," he said, in his stateliest, you'll-never-guess-what-I'm-thinking manner.

"Mr. Koenig," Charlie replied, unable to bring himself to use the other man's first name.

"It is an act of bravery to put your heart on the line." Mr. Koenig raised his beer. "I commend you."

Charlie saw his father approaching, expression shifting when he overheard Mr. Koenig.

"Didn't know you had it in you." Mr. Pike playfully punched Charlie's arm. "That was fire, as the kids say."

"I wasn't talking about Mugsy," Charlie hastened to inform him, in case both of his parents were confused on that score.

"I should hope not," Mr. Koenig said. "Emma would be so disappointed."

"Who knows which way the wind is blowing with these crazy kids?" Mr. Pike shook his head. "I'm sure we both played the field in our day. Make hay while the sun shines, am I right, Phil?"

The answering smile was enigmatic.

"Young love." Mr. Pike raised his glass. "Shall we toast to that, Phil?"

"I'll drink to love at any age," the other man replied.

"I have to go," Charlie said, because he couldn't drink to love without Jean.

And Jean, he was forced to conclude after finishing another circuit of the crowd—including the apple pie station, bathroom line, coat check, sound board, backstage area, and an awkward hug from Sergeant Cowboy—was gone.

The last dregs of adrenaline ebbed away. He'd gone all in, making a desperate bid to impress someone who'd already left. Once again, his best wasn't good enough.

Too little and too late, Charlie thought. The story of his life.

Chapter 29

"Quaint alert! Who gave this place the right?"

"*So* cozy. Did I tell you I stayed in one of these at Joshua Tree?"

The voices trickled through the fog of sleep until they pricked the edge of Jean's consciousness. Her eyes flew open.

People were in her wagon.

"That one had a hot tub though," the second voice continued.

"Nice."

"I know."

"Too much to expect around here. It's like we're playing Prairie Dog Village."

Snorting and cackling ensued. The intruders didn't sound dangerous. Rude, maybe, but if Jean held very still, they might leave, and she could go back to sleep.

"You're so funny. Are you using something different on your skin?"

Jean frowned, failing to see the connection.

"Yes! Thank you for noticing. It's a clean beauty company my cousin started. Very niche. I could probably get you on the list—"

"Excuse me," Jean interrupted, sitting up. She was tired of playing dead while a multilevel skincare marketing scheme unfolded next to her bed.

Two lithe young noncowboys stared back at her. One had a cascading black ponytail and the other's hair was short and acid yellow. Judging by the not-from-around-here outfits, they had also been expecting a different kind of festival, with fewer chuckwagon suppers.

Ponytail clutched her chest. "Jump scare."

Jean had the distinct impression she was waiting for an apology. "This is my wagon."

"We thought it was empty," the one with short hair said. "Everyone's at breakfast."

"Can you imagine?" Ponytail turned to her friend, Jean's existence forgotten.

"I bet it's that gray gloop they put on biscuits." Short Hair gave an exaggerated shiver.

"What even is that?" Ponytail asked, sounding genuinely curious.

"I don't know." Short Hair leaned in. "Should we try it?"

"You are so bad," Ponytail replied, with a little kitten swipe at her friend's arm. "They are so bad," she added for Jean's benefit. "I really shouldn't, but I probably will."

"I might eat bacon," the one with Mountain Dew hair confessed, eliciting a gasp from Ponytail at their daring. The pair exited without a word of farewell.

"Bye," Jean said to the empty wagon. "Don't let the door hit you on the way out. I'll be here in my bed, trying to get some sleep. Even though two randos just walked in and had a whole-ass conversation about breakfast foods."

Not that Jean was hungry, or ever would be again. She settled onto her back, pulling the covers up to her chin. Being awake didn't appeal, because then she'd have to think, and thinking would mean remembering, so she closed her eyes and tried to recall every relaxation technique she'd ever heard about. Breathing exercises. Finding her third eye. Singing that ninety-nine bottles of beer song—nope. No beer.

Out of desperation, she started counting sheep. She'd made it to thirty-seven when a loud *beep-beep* disturbed the early-morning quiet. It sounded like a garbage truck backing up. With her luck, it was headed straight for the wagon.

Jean considered lying there and letting it haul her to the

dump, but she still had her pride. Some of it, anyway. Sighing, she dragged herself out of bed to peek through the door.

It was not a garbage truck after all. Someone was delivering a portable toilet.

"A little on the nose," she told the forklift operator, who wouldn't be able hear her over the noise. Jean knew her life was in the crapper. There was no need to rub it in.

The extra facilities were probably for Adriana Asebedo's full crew, who were due to arrive today. Her prebreakfast visitors must've been the first wave.

Adriana "Charlie Is My Honey Baby!" Asebedo.

Retch.

Jean shoved down the memory of almost kind of liking her on the ride to Deadwood. All that was in the past. Now she hated everyone, including herself.

It had felt good in the moment to call Charlie out, spewing the magma of her anger in a lightly cowboy-coded rant. Where did he get off leading her on all over again? What was he doing following her around and bringing care packages and being handsome in her general direction? That wasn't just dishonest. It was mean.

Only then, as Jean was leaving, she'd heard Charlie's voice— speaking into the microphone, of all things. For such a mild-mannered guy, he managed to shock her with disturbing frequency. Jean should have made him play truth instead of dare, back in that bungalow of lies. It would have saved her a lot of heartache.

I could leave right now. There was a sliver of comfort in the thought, until she remembered that her best friend was out of town, her apartment sucked, and she'd need to find at least three new jobs the second she got off the plane.

And the odds of ever seeing Charlie again once she flew home were pretty much nil. Unlike Eve, Jean didn't run in the same circles as a future beer baron, much less the pop star girlfriend he pretended not to have. This was basically her last chance to get any kind of satisfaction from him.

"When the going gets tough, the tough . . . don't go," Jean announced to the empty wagon. Not the most stirring battle cry of her life, but she wasn't in peak form at the moment. Surely she'd feel better when she finally accomplished what she'd come here to do.

There was only one way to find out.

It took four outfit changes to settle on the right look for the occasion: another tissue-thin bodycon dress with a wrist full of jangling bracelets.

On her way to the house, Jean passed scurrying roadies unloading thick cables that absolutely did not make her think of snakes. Golf carts buzzed back and forth, a counterpoint to the distant sound of hammering.

She nodded at the security guards stationed at Charlie's front door. It was the same pair she'd met on the casino outing, which must mean their boss was inside.

Too late to turn back now. Jean pictured herself storming in like Maleficent, patron saint of uninvited guests.

Following the sound of voices, she found most of the younger members of the house party in the living room. Adriana gave her a nod of greeting, which Jean forced herself to return with a tight smile.

Not her fault, she reminded herself. *This is one hundred percent on Charlie.*

Dragging her attention from the pop princess, Jean noted that even the normally standoffish Emma and Margaret the grump had been pulled into Adriana's orbit. Though at least in Margaret's case, she appeared to be uncomfortable in such close proximity to a megacelebrity. Guilty conscience? Either that or she was wincing at Smithson's attempt to "charm" their special guest with a monologue about sailing. Good to know he hadn't upgraded his material in the last decade.

Conspicuously absent from the group was Charlie. Probably still in bed, after a strenuous night with one (or more!) of his girlfriends. Jean swallowed the acid at the back of her throat.

As if summoned by her thoughts, Charlie clattered down the stairs. Jean waited for him to lock eyes with lover girl and share an erotically charged smolder, but he didn't so much as glance in Adriana's direction—or Margaret's. Charlie seemed more concerned with the floor.

"Has anyone seen Emma?" he asked.

"She's right there." Smithson jerked his thumb at Emma Koenig. "Talking to me. Take a number, Chuck."

"Untrue," Emma said, without looking at Smithson.

"Not that Emma." Charlie bent to look under a side table. "My snake. She's not in her habitat. I think she might have gotten loose again."

Amid the general commotion—shrieking, jumping onto furniture—Jean noticed several interesting facts. The first was that Smithson screamed like a teen girl in a slasher movie. The second was that Adriana Asebedo turned to Margaret first, even though she had two gigantic bodyguards in shouting distance. Then again, her protection detail looked freaked, while Margaret remained stoic as always. No doubt she was used to snake-related emergencies from spending so much time with Charlie, whereas that kind of thing didn't come up as often on stadium tours.

"Can we go to your workshop?" Adriana asked. Margaret shrugged, not meeting her eyes.

Emma (the human one) stood. "I will join you, if I may."

Smithson opened his mouth, and they all knew what was coming next.

"In your dreams," Margaret snapped, before he could ask. "Don't you have work to do?"

"Excuse me," said Charlie, pushing past him. "I think I saw something move. Under the couch."

That cleared the room in record time, with Smithson leading the charge, in the sense that he shoved in front of the women.

"What a hero," Jean muttered.

Charlie looked at her questioningly.

"Not you. Him."

"Oh." He shifted his feet, staring at the rug. Jean didn't know if he was looking for snakes or avoiding her gaze. "Did you sleep well?"

"Not really."

"Good, good." He shook himself. "I mean, not good. I'm sorry to hear that."

"Are you?"

He hesitated, as if sensing a trap. "Yes?"

Jean sniffed. "How about you? Did you have a restful evening?"

"No." Charlie rubbed his jaw.

"Something troubling you?"

"Yes." He seemed relieved she'd guessed.

"Pangs of regret, perhaps?"

"More like things left unsaid. Or possibly said but not heard?"

"You mean your poem." Jean let him sweat. "If I had heard it, who's to say any of that was the truth?"

"It was all true." He frowned. "Except the 'Rawhide' part. I don't know where that came from."

How could he stand there blushing and stammering like her sweet snake guy when all evidence pointed to him being Charlie the Casanova instead? Enough of this confusion.

"I'll help you look for your snake."

His face lit up. "Really?"

She shrugged, like the Good Samaritan she was pretending

to be. "We should probably start in your room. The scene of the crime."

"Oh. Good idea." He stood there, smiling shyly at her.

"I don't know where it is," Jean reminded him.

"Right! Sorry." Charlie spun around so fast it was practically a hop. "This way."

She followed him up the winding staircase, ignoring his frequent backward glances. What did he have to worry about? *Jean* wasn't the one who made a habit of disappearing.

When they reached his door, Charlie stood aside to let her enter first.

Jean was glad he couldn't see her face as she got her first look at his childhood bedroom. Not because it was horrifying—the aesthetic was lonely science nerd, as expected—but to keep him from realizing how curious she was about his past.

"I thought you'd have one of those beds shaped like a rocket ship." She leaned on the corner of his queen-size mattress with the heel of her hand, bouncing a little like she was testing the springs.

Charlie blushed. "I never wanted to be an astronaut."

"Snakes, snakes, and more snakes, huh?"

"I guess I'm predictable that way."

She sniffed, moving to the other side of the room to inspect his bookshelf. Lots of nonfiction, the bright yellow spines of National Geographic almanacs and junior encyclopedias interspersed with more serious reference books. Unless he had a stash of comics and dirty magazines under his bed, predictable was not the first word that came to mind. Where other guys might have hung a band poster or something from the *Sports Illustrated* swimsuit issue, Charlie had an old sign for Reptile Gardens Wild Animal Park.

He straightened from checking behind the curtains, watching

her pick up a plastic trophy with a plaque at the bottom engraved with the words, *The Hurricanes, Peewee Soccer.*

"You played?"

"I was on the team. Technically. Everyone who registered got a trophy."

Jean was going to ask why he was still hanging on to something that didn't seem to hold much meaning for him when Charlie spoke again. "My dad was the coach. He thought it would be a fun thing for us to do together."

"Ah." Setting down the golden cup, she inspected a Rubik's cube, a Lego minifig dressed all in green, and a plastic dog that looked like a kid's meal prize. A rolled sheet of paper caught her eye, tucked behind a set of plastic binoculars. Jean started to reach for it, pulling her hand back when she recognized the Dolphin Bay letterhead.

It was her treasure map. Another souvenir of an encounter that meant about as much to him as a four-pack of chicken nuggets.

"It's kind of a museum," Charlie said from the other end of the room. He brushed a layer of dust off a high shelf, then wiped his hand on the back of his pants. "I don't usually live here."

"Oh?" She pitched her voice like it was a polite response, not something she was dying to hear more about.

"It's a pretty out-of-the-way place, as you probably noticed. Good for hiding out—until things die down."

In what universe would people ever stop caring about Adriana Asebedo's love life? Unless he planned to lie low at his parents' house forever, Charlie must have weighed the loss of privacy and decided his sexy songbird was worth the sacrifice.

Jean liked to think she could take Adriana Asebedo in a fair fight. (For Charlie's affections, that is—everyone knew the singer studied Muay Thai.) But surely there was more to life than being glamorous and jaw-droppingly successful. Jean had plenty of things to bring to the table. She was unpredictable, for starters. Full of sudden impulses.

"I already checked under the bed," Charlie said when she headed in that direction.

"What about *in* the bed?" Jean kicked off her shoes before throwing back the neatly arranged covers. Dropping onto the mattress, she pulled the sheet over her head. It took some writhing, but eventually she managed to pull her dress off and shove it to one side.

"Are you okay?" Charlie asked, as she divested herself of lingerie.

"I need your help." She raised the edge of the sheet. "In here."

Jean couldn't see his expression, but his lower body quickly moved into view. "Take your shoes off first," she ordered. "And your outside clothes."

"Oh." He hesitated only briefly before stepping out of his pants.

"Glasses," she reminded him.

"Right," he said, in a *silly me* tone. Charlie climbed under the covers, scooting down until they were both hidden beneath the top sheet.

"We're not wearing clothes," he said when the rustling subsided, like he needed confirmation.

"Fewer places for a snake to hide."

"Ah. Do you think she's in here?" he whispered.

"I sure hope not."

"Should I get a flashlight?"

"We don't need it."

"Pit vipers are really good in the dark."

The blood in Jean's veins turned to ice chips. "Are you telling me Emma is a viper?"

Her question seemed to amuse him, which made one of them. "Oh no. She's a corn snake. Very sweet. Loves to burrow."

Slowly, Jean drew her knees into her chest, removing her vulnerable toes from the darkness at the bottom of the bed.

"It's just an interesting fact about certain types of snakes," Charlie continued, like they were standing in front of a display at a nature museum. "Boas and pythons do it too—hunting in the dark by sensing the body heat of their prey."

"Awesome."

"It really is. The theory is that they use the pit organ—" He broke off when Jean's questing fingers found his mouth. "Too much snake talk?" he mumbled into her hand.

"It's the context." She removed her hand. "I don't like thinking about deadly creatures that hunt in the dark when I'm in the dark."

"Don't worry. You're much more likely to run into a rattlesnake around here."

He couldn't possibly mean that the way it sounded. "You have a rattlesnake in your room?"

"No, I meant it's the only venomous snake in South Dakota. The prairie rattlesnake, to be more specific. *Crotalus viridis viridis.*"

Although hearing Charlie speak Latin usually did it for her, this was not how Jean had envisioned the scene playing out. She slid her hand across the sheet until it hit flesh. A little more poking identified it as an arm.

When she ran the pads of her fingers up to his shoulder, he stopped breathing.

"Charlie."

"Yes?"

She wormed closer, hips then shoulders, straightening her legs to press her whole body against him. "You're into me." There was no mistaking the evidence.

"Yes." He inhaled, deep and unsteady.

They stayed like that, breathing in and out, his chest expanding against hers. It felt like wave after wave washing over her, the sensation of being skin to skin with Charlie. What was the plan again? The strategic part of her brain had turned to white noise.

The bed shook as he scooted down. Jean sensed his mouth seeking hers (and thought briefly of pit vipers) as his breath fanned her lips.

"Wait." She flattened her palm against his chest, pushing him back a few inches. "Are you seriously about to sleep with her?"

"Who?"

"Eve."

He hesitated. "Not if she doesn't want to?"

"But you would if she's willing." She bucked her hips against his. "That's pretty obvious."

"Yes," he admitted. "Or we could just be here together and talk."

"Since she's not good enough to be your sidepiece?"

"I didn't say that."

"Pretty sure you did."

"But I didn't mean it like that."

"So what, Eve is like number four on your list?"

"What list?"

"Of people you're sleeping with."

"How can it be a list when there's only one person on it?"

"Then what do you call this?" She grabbed his hand, dragging it down her chest from collarbone to belly button.

"Uh, you mean the sternum? Or I guess you could say sagittal plane." He hesitated. "Unless you were talking about the breast . . . er, the right breast. No, left! Sorry, I got my directions reversed. It's hard to think when I'm touching you."

"I'm talking big picture, Charlie!"

"The torso?" he ventured, sounding profoundly uncertain.

"You can drop the act. We both know what this is about."

His hand was still pressed against her stomach, long fingers nearly spanning the distance between her hips. "I might need one more clue."

"There's a naked woman in your bed."

"Yes." It was barely a whisper, like he was afraid to wake himself from a dream.

"But she's not the only one burning up your sheets."

"You mean because there are two of you?"

The confirmation stung, but Jean pushed past it. "Uh, *duh*. At least. Starting with Adriana Asebedo."

"I'm not sleeping with Adriana Asebedo."

"Not yet maybe, but I'm sure it's only a matter of time before you get back together, *honey baby*." She removed his hand from her body, letting it flop back onto the mattress. "And then there's the other one," Jean continued, before he could deny it. "How long have you and Margaret been a thing?"

"Margaret?" He sounded genuinely confused. "You mean *Mugsy*?"

It was a good thing Jean was lying down because her head was spinning. "Wait. You're telling me *Margaret* is Mugsy?"

"Mm-hmm. Mugsy is a nickname."

"Huh. It suits her." Better than Margaret, anyway. Mugsy the babysitter. No wonder she acted like she was in charge of Charlie. Jean closed her eyes, hoping that would slow the flood of irrelevant thoughts. "And Emma? The human one?"

"Oh, no. I would never. And neither would she," he added.

Somehow, his excuses made Jean angrier. She didn't want to be rational or understanding. Charlie owed her *something*, and even if she wasn't sure what that was or how to ask for it, Jean was spoiling for a fight.

She grabbed his hip, squeezing hard. "What about me?"

"Which you?"

"The one in front of you right now."

"My one and only." His hand cupped her cheek.

She shook him off. "Meaning Eve."

"If you prefer."

"So you'd cheat on me with her?"

"That's hard to say." He was clearly trying to avoid incriminating himself, whether he meant it or not.

"And yet here you are," she pointed out, "in bed with her."

"But Jean, sweetheart, I know she's you. Or you're her. Both, I guess." He traced the shape of her ear, following the line of her jaw to her chin.

She grabbed his wrist. "You didn't know if I knew that you knew it was me. How do you explain that?"

"I thought—um. Well. I guess I didn't know that you knowing I knew was part of it. Or me knowing that you knew that. About what I knew . . . or didn't. And also you." He made a sound of frustration before trying again. "I thought I was doing what you wanted?"

"So it's my fault?"

"No! I assumed it was part of the game."

"Is this a game to you?" she demanded.

"Never! Unless you want it to be. I just want you to stay."

"Then why did you leave? You didn't even say goodbye." It felt like yanking out a chunk of her own hair, asking such a vulnerable question.

"I was afraid."

"That your girlfriend would find out you were two-timing her?"

"I would never two-time you."

"I'm not talking about me!"

"You mean . . . Eve?"

"No! I hadn't even invented Eve yet." Honestly. Did she need to bring in a whiteboard?

"Jean."

"Is that my name?" she asked, waspishly.

"I think so, yes." He cleared his throat. "Why are we arguing?"

"Because you tricked me. Several times over. And then kicked me to the curb like I was worthless." It sounded like the beginning of a cowboy poem. "Why? Is there something you'd rather be doing right now? Am I messing up your plans?"

"I want to kiss you." His thumb pressed against her bottom lip. "I've been dying to, ever since you got here. It's all I can think about."

Her heart banged against the inside of her rib cage like it was trying to stage a jail break. "Fine. If you insist." Closing her eyes, she puckered her lips like a cartoon character.

Charlie trembled as their mouths met. Jean forced herself to lie there like a mannequin, stiff and unresponsive.

Undaunted, he pressed glancing kisses to one corner of her lips and then the other, while his knuckles brushed the underside of her chin.

"Jean," he sighed against her mouth, all heat and relief and desperate longing.

"Maybe."

The brattiness backfired when Charlie took advantage of her parted lips to deepen the kiss, his tongue sliding against hers. A sound that was part groan and part laughter rumbled in his throat.

"I missed you so much," he whispered, barely lifting his mouth from hers.

She kissed him again to keep from saying it back.

The next time her brain came online, Charlie was flinging back the sheet. Daylight poured across the bed, illuminating a compromising position: Jean's shoulder blades flat against the mattress while Charlie braced on his elbows to keep his full weight from crushing her.

There was a sudden stillness as they hovered on the brink of this do-it-or-die moment. Jean read the question in Charlie's eyes, right above his goopy smile.

"So how do you see this playing out?" She tried to sound serious and unaffected, even though her breathing was shallow.

He blinked several times, adjusting to the shift in tone. "I was hoping you would let me make love to you. If that was something you wanted."

Jean narrowed her eyes. "And then?"

"We could cuddle?"

"What about after that?"

Charlie looked increasingly uncertain. "Snacks? Or we could play cards—"

"Wrong answer," she grunted, shoving him aside.

"Wait. Don't leave!" He reached for her, but she was already up and moving.

"Not so fun when the shoe's on the other foot, is it? I'm not even going to explain what you did wrong. I'll just take off. That's your game, isn't it? Love 'em and leave 'em. Wham, bam, thank you, ma'am." Because Charlie had made it abundantly clear he didn't see a future with her. A quickie in his childhood bedroom was all she was good for.

"But Jean," Charlie said, all earnest confusion, "why did you tell them where I was if you didn't want me to leave? I couldn't stay after that."

"I didn't tell anyone, Charlie."

"It's okay," he assured her. "You could do a lot worse than that to me and I'd still forgive you."

"First of all, no one is *settling* for me like I'm damaged goods. 'Oh well, she's kind of an asshole, but I'll make do.' And second!" She fished her bra from beneath a pillow, shaking it at him for emphasis. "How could I tell someone *where* you were when I didn't even know *who* you were?"

He looked crestfallen. "I'm sorry. I should have been honest."

Jean waited for him to justify his behavior, but Charlie had come to a full stop. It was a real apology.

"You could have stuck around and asked me to my face," she said. "At least given me that chance."

"You're right. And I'm so sorry about your job, Jean. I didn't mean to mess up your life."

She considered telling him the job was the least painful thing she'd lost that night but didn't want to fold while she had the upper hand. "I'm a strong independent woman. I'll figure it out."

"But you could be a strong independent woman with friends."

"I have friends."

"Special friends?"

"Wouldn't you like to know."

He folded back the covers on her side, smoothing the flap like he was the one who worked at a hotel. "Maybe you could come back to bed? Just to talk."

Jean snorted. "Like that's going to happen."

"The talking or—?"

"I'm not going to sleep with someone who thinks I'm a terrible person. Just because I haven't got barrels of beer money doesn't mean I have no standards."

"I never thought you were terrible."

"Save it." Jean fastened her bra, then reached down for her dress, yanking it over her head. She paused with one arm through a sleeve. "You know what?"

He shook his head.

"I *should* have sex with you right now." She yanked the dress off again, dropping it on the floor before reaching for the clasp of her bra.

"Oh." His eyes were very wide. "That is—"

"And then I'll walk out that door," she said, over the sound of his sputtering, "never to be seen again. It would serve you right!"

He didn't say anything for several long moments. "Would it serve you?"

Jean wondered if he could hear the pounding of her heart. "How should I know? That's why I'm freaking out."

"It's your choice."

Even his niceness rubbed her the wrong way. "Why? Because you don't care?"

"I didn't say that."

Storming back to the bed, Jean took a running leap onto the mattress. She was practically breathing fire. Charlie didn't resist as she shoved him onto his back, or when she climbed over him, balancing on her hands and knees as she stared down into his eyes.

He should be petrified. Jean was in a dangerous mood. Nipple twisting was the least of what she could do to him. But Charlie just looked up at her, patient and hopeful, his gaze skating from her eyes to her lips. To her annoyance, he started to smile.

"Jean?"

"What?" she snapped.

"Is this the flying Pamchenko?"

"Don't try to be cute." Who was she kidding? It was too late for that. He was revoltingly adorable. Horribly and unfairly irresistible. What was wrong with her?

Striking like a cobra, she bit his bottom lip, immediately following it up with a hard kiss. Instead of whimpering in terror, Charlie opened his mouth and let her ravage him.

She changed the angle of her lips, worked her hands into his hair, sucked hard on his tongue. Again and again she kissed him, waiting for Charlie to beg for mercy. She was going to dominate him, and he would have no choice but to give in.

"Jean," he sighed.

There! He was already murmuring her name like she owned him, body and soul. It was all going—there was a plan—and Jean felt—so *good*. She was letting go, giving in, her mind emptying as her body took the wheel. When he gripped her waist with both hands, she started to lower herself onto him until a last tattered thread of awareness slapped her between the eyes.

"Oh no you don't." She scrambled away from him, landing on her ass.

His hand came up to touch the side of her face, thumb brushing her cheekbone. "Don't cry, Jean."

Of all the ridiculous accusations! She rolled to the edge of the bed and jumped to her feet, grabbing her dress with one hand and reaching for her shoes with the other.

"For your information, this is victory sweat, not tears. Because I win. And winners don't cry."

She swiped at her face, ignoring the slick of moisture. It was hard to execute a quality stomp barefoot, but Jean gave it her best shot, pausing only to point at Charlie in case he planned to follow. "Don't even think about it."

Chapter 30

This time, Charlie didn't do as he was told.

He had to stop for pants, but the second he was decent he took off at a run.

"Jean!"

She spun to face him, barely slowing as she speed walked backward. Curving her fingers into fangs, she hissed at him before shaking her wrist to rattle her bracelets. Whipping around again, Jean broke into a run.

Charlie started to give chase, faltering when one of Adriana's roadies wolf-whistled at him. He couldn't go charging after her barefoot and shirtless, not with every booze bigwig from here to Tokyo on the premises. If he could wave a wand and send them all home, he would do it without a second thought. He needed time alone with Jean to explain, and none of these people were helping.

On second thought, if he had access to magic, Charlie would zap the two of them back to their cottage, before everything got twisted and confusing.

"Uh, Charlie?" Mugsy had emerged from her workshop, followed by Emma Koenig. "What's going on? Did you find the snake?"

"Not exactly."

She frowned at his bare chest. "Did you try to catch it with your shirt?"

"That's sort of a long story. But I do have some other exciting news."

"About snakes?" she asked, with a certain fatalism.

"No, this is about people. One person in particular. Although technically she's been two people, but not anymore."

Mugsy blinked at him. "You lost me, buddy."

"It's Jean. She's here!"

"Where?" Mugsy was already digging out her phone. "I'll get security."

He touched her shoulder. "She's been here all along. You've seen her! It's *Eve*."

"The girl you met in Hawaii is Sockless Tommy's niece?"

"No, Jean is Jean. Eve was more of a character she was playing."

"You mean she was in disguise?" Emma asked.

"Sort of." Maybe he should have rehearsed this part. Or at least put on a shirt, so he'd know what to do with his arms.

"She *is* the girl I saw that night." Mugsy's frown intensified. "And you knew who she was all along. Why didn't you say something, Charlie?"

"Because I was happy to see her." And I didn't want you to scare her off, he silently added.

"She must have followed you here," Mugsy said, piecing it together. "Hoping for another score."

Emma Koenig gave her a significant look. "The past has a way of returning."

"You mean people make choices. All by themselves, without asking permission." For some reason, Mugsy sounded defensive. "It doesn't mean we have to repeat the same mistakes."

"It wasn't a mistake," Charlie assured her. "She's the best thing that ever happened to me."

Too late, he noticed the new addition to their party. Adriana Asebedo had come up behind Mugsy in time to hear Charlie's last remark.

"Am I interrupting something?" Adriana asked.

"Minor security issue," Mugsy replied.

Adriana looked at Charlie. "The snake?"

"You could say that," Mugsy muttered. "In the low-down, good-for-nothing sense."

"That's unfair," Charlie protested. "To both of them."

"You mean her multiple identities?"

"No! Jean and Emma. The snake."

Mugsy turned to Adriana. "It's under control."

"Okay. I trust you." She hit Mugsy with both dimples.

"Actually, I'll take care of it." Charlie realized he had his hand raised like they were in a classroom and quickly lowered it.

Mugsy shook her head. "I don't think so."

His father waved at him from the patio. "Come over here, son."

Charlie sighed. "Promise me you won't do anything without me, Mugsy."

"This feels messy. I don't like it."

"Sometimes life is messy. You taught me that." She'd been talking about a spilled glass of orange juice, but the principle was sound.

Mugsy still looked like she had a mouthful of vinegar. "There's something else I need to tell you."

"If it's about Jean, don't bother. I know what you're going to say, and I've made up my mind. Some risks are worth taking."

"And some things are too important to gamble on a passing fancy."

"I don't think we're talking about the same thing." Charlie tried to read Mugsy's expression, which was locked down even tighter than usual. When he glanced at Emma and Adriana to see if they understood, he got the distinct impression there was another storyline playing in the background, and he'd missed the first four episodes.

"*I'm* talking about using your head," Mugsy said. "Considering the long-term consequences and making sensible choices."

He was pretty sure that was in reference to the family business, and Charlie's duty to keep it going. But even if his future was here, he wasn't going to give all of himself to Pike's Pale Ale. Not tonight, anyway.

"I need to lead with my heart," he told Mugsy. From the corner of his eye, he saw his father beckoning. "Just as soon as I figure out what Dad wants."

Heaven and Ale: Pike's Brewing at 100

Brewer Magazine

One of the country's first microbrews, Pike's Pale Ale has long been synonymous with the laid-back lifestyle of the American West. While other brands experiment with maximum IBUs and cask-conditioned porters, Pike's has continued to peddle the classic taste of their eponymous ale, alongside a few welcome seasonal variations.

Will nostalgia and solid middle-of-the-road flavors be enough to carry them through another century? Current CEO Charles Pike III is confident in the leadership of the next generation.

"My son Charlie was born and bred to this business. Beer is in his blood. We're all excited to see where he takes Pike's next."

Chapter 31

"To recap, there was no revenge banging?" Hildy asked, peeling another strand off her string cheese. Apparently she'd found a stash in the kitchen while everyone else was out having their initials branded into fancy leather belts.

"I choked," Jean confirmed. "Which pisses me off even more."

"Because you're sexually frustrated?"

"No!" Although that was also true. It was hard to fast after an all-you-can-eat buffet. "I'm mad because I was all over the place emotionally. Like a little bitch."

Jean's self-image did not allow for woe-is-me waffling. Her whole identity was about being bold and tough, with a take-no-prisoners attitude. It was Charlie's fault she'd turned gelatinous on the inside.

"And he denied the Adriana thing? We're supposed to believe she's not here for him? Even after she did that poem?"

Jean waited in case Hildy wanted to stab her again. "He claimed he wasn't sleeping with any of them."

Hildy crumpled her cheese wrapper. "There's something else going on here. With Adriana. Something we're not seeing. I can smell it."

"Yeah, it smells like horseshit to me." This was a lie; Adriana smelled like ginger and cloves, and Jean had no reason to believe the pop star was pretending. Her performance at cowboy poetry night had seemed pretty direct.

"Even if they're not together now, there's no way he chooses me instead. 'Sorry, smokin' hot superstar, I prefer this random hotel employee I met on vacation.'"

"You don't give yourself enough credit."

"I give myself plenty of credit." Jean pounded her breastbone with the flat of her hand, as if she could drive the words home. "I like who I am. Confident, freaky, talented. I don't need to jeopardize all that by going after someone like Charlie. Why would I set myself up to fail?"

"So you're afraid," Hildy translated.

"Immune to reverse psychology is what I am." Jean touched her bottom lip. Her mouth was still tender from kissing Charlie, but how long would the feeling last—a couple of hours at most? Their time together was a Polaroid in reverse, already fading back to black.

"It's not even the losing that gets me," she admitted. "I don't like it, but I'll survive. The problem with the Adriana Asebedo situation is that it changes who I thought he was. Knowing he was with her rewrites everything I thought I knew about Charlie. Like now he's partly hers."

Instead of all mine.

Jean had never considered herself a touch-him-and-die type. But Charlie had made her believe she meant more to him than anyone else *ever*, past or future. Finding out about Adriana Asebedo threw that certainty into doubt. Even Jean's self-esteem was hard-pressed to imagine Adriana hadn't left a permanent mark, her initials carved somewhere on his heart.

After all, there was a freaking song about it.

"It doesn't matter what's going on with those two," Jean reminded herself. "I'm supposed to be making a dramatic exit."

"About that." Hildy tugged one of her curls.

"What?"

"I might have rear-ended someone." She made a pinching motion with her thumb and forefinger. "A teensy bit."

"How? When?"

"I had to move the Jeep so they could unload the trucks. It

was chaotic. Also, what kind of car doesn't have those little sensors that tell you when you're about to crash into something? There should have been beeps or flashing lights."

"But you're okay?"

"Fine." Hildy fluffed her hair, confirming that her most important body part had come through unscathed.

"I take it the car is not?"

"My family is extremely lawsuit cautious. My uncle sent someone to tow it back to town, just in case. We'll let insurance handle it." Hildy waved a hand like that solved the problem.

"We're stuck here—no way out?"

"It's not like we're locked inside a haunted house with a serial killer on the loose," Hildy said in her most soothing tone.

"What about calling a Lyft?"

"Fun fact: there are zero drivers available at this location. Isn't that interesting? I didn't know there were still places on this continent you couldn't get service. Hey! Maybe I should do an article on the last rideshare deserts. You could be one of my sources."

"I'm not thinking quotable thoughts right now, Hildy."

"Sure, I get it. But that would add a killer opening. 'POV: You just got dumped and desperately need to get away from your ex. But instead you're trapped in the quicksand of modern dating nightmares: no cars available.'"

"Catchy," Jean said.

"Sorry. I'll switch to my solutions mindset." She made a swiping motion in front of her face. "Maybe you could borrow a horse?"

Someone had been soaking up too much frontier ambience. "I'm going to go for a walk. See if something comes to me."

Jean left the wagon without a clear plan. It felt like being seven again, running away from home with her pillow and half a pack of cookies because her parents wouldn't let her stay up to watch

Grey's Anatomy. At least her grievances had gotten more legit with age.

As she walked, Jean considered her options. Daddy Koenig might be willing to help, but she didn't want to give him the wrong idea. Sergeant Cowboy would tell her to tough it out. Weirdly, the person who seemed most likely to offer assistance was Adriana Asebedo—but you couldn't ask someone to rescue you when they were part of your problem.

Two names that did not cross her mind were Mountain Dew and Ponytail, her early-morning visitors. And yet that was exactly who appeared in her hour of need.

"Hey," Ponytail said, grabbing Jean's arm. "What are you doing?"

"I have absolutely no idea," Jean replied, honestly.

They laughed like she'd said something funny.

Mountain Dew stared into Jean's eyes for a borderline uncomfortable stretch before giving a decisive nod. "You're coming with us."

Which was how she ended up partying with Adriana Asebedo's dancers and backup singers all afternoon. If by "party" you meant yoga and meditation, a chair massage, and a gloppy-yet-surprisingly-tasty green drink that was allegedly better for her than "a vitamin IV," though they made her promise to also try one of those ASAP.

"It's like being reborn," Ponytail (whose real name was Jessica) promised, and Jean had to admit she liked the sound of that. Bonus points if they could also do a memory wipe of the last month of her life.

Conspicuous among the sci-fi stylings of the beauty tools and health supplements were the humble mason jars of Mugsy's teas. From what Jean could tell, all the creativity went into the beverages themselves, because the handwritten labels gave off strong "I don't have time for this nonsense" vibes. Much like their maker.

"I'm surprised they didn't hook you up with beer," Jean said.

"Too bloating before a show," Mountain Dew (aka Pax) told her. "And these teas are Adriana's favorite, if you know what I mean." Pierced eyebrows arched, assuming Jean understood the subtext.

She connected the dots easily enough. Being nice to his beloved former babysitter would get you plenty of bonus points with Charlie. Not that Adriana Asebedo needed to exert herself to impress anyone. All she had to say was, *Want to hold my Grammy? Or Let's fly to Belize for the weekend!* Shelling out for homebrewed teas was the equivalent of buying a candy bar for Jean.

"Adriana doesn't eat with you?" she asked Pax, over the light-yet-satisfying lunch the tour's private chef had prepared for the crew. It was hard to resent someone who regularly treated her employees to restaurant-quality food, but Jean was trying.

"She needed some alone time." This was relayed in such a gossipy hush Jean knew it was code for "she's busy ripping off Charlie's clothes."

You'll have to put them back on him first, she thought, with a bitterness that rivaled the Meyer lemon vinaigrette on a dish that had suddenly become unappetizing.

"I don't suppose any of you have a car?" she asked, trying to look trustworthy. "Or a truck? Windowless van? Anything faster than a lawnmower."

"You need a ride, babe?" Jessica patted her on the head, because apparently she saw Jean as a feral kitten they'd found in a barn. "We have room on the bus. How far are you going?"

"To the airport."

"No problem. You mean Denver?"

Jean shook her head. "The little one in Rapid City."

"Ohhh." Jessica wrinkled her nose. "That's trickier. You should just stay with us until our next stop!"

That was a profoundly bad idea for many reasons, but Jean

wasn't in a position to be picky. She could always ask them to let her out at a gas station along the highway. "When are you rolling out?"

Please say tonight, she silently prayed, crossing her fingers behind her back.

"It's up to Adriana," Pax said with a shrug. "She has things to figure out first."

Significant looks ricocheted among the members of the crew.

"What?" Jean asked, giving up on deciphering their facial expressions. This was a group that had dramatic reactions to most topics of conversation, from "best fabric softener scent" to "near-death experiences on our last tour."

"We want Adriana to be happy," Jessica said. A chorus of nods affirmed this truth. "But at what cost? It's the eternal question. Career or love?"

"And it's not like happiness is guaranteed," Pax chimed in. "How is it going to be any different this time? They have the same obstacles as before."

Everyone had an opinion, voices climbing over each other as they discussed Adriana Asebedo's love life. It was like the comments section on a fan website, only not mean. Jean couldn't quite tell if they shipped Adriana and Charlie or not, because she was doing her best to tune out the details.

"What do you think? Knowing the other side of the story." Jessica touched Jean's knee.

That was an easy one: *I think Adriana should leave, and Charlie should choose me.* Jean couldn't say that to Team Asebedo, so she pretended to be a neutral bystander. "As long as everyone involved is a consenting adult, where's the harm?"

Here, she thought, answering her own question. *I'm the injured party.*

Sighing, she dragged herself off the plush banquette. "I'm going to go see if I can flag down a truck or something."

"No." Pax pointed at the seat Jean had just vacated. "Why get murdered and stashed in someone's freezer when you could stay and watch a private concert by Adriana Asebedo and her amazing dancers?"

On cue, everyone in hearing range struck a pose.

"This is a super rare opportunity," Jessica added, dropping the hands splayed on either side of her face. "I grant you the setting is a little weird, but cows are better than war criminals."

"Gigs like this are usually for a baby oligarch's Sweet Sixteen," Pax translated, adding a fist-clenching fake cheer. "Woo-hoo! Let's all celebrate the dictator's great-niece."

"Adriana would never." Jessica pressed a hand to her heart.

"She has standards," Pax affirmed. "Trust, many are the billionaires who've begged Adriana to play their sad little soiree."

"We're only doing this because of the personal connection." Jessica leaned into Jean's space. "Also, it's going to be a historic occasion. You didn't hear it from me, but Adriana *might* launch a new single tonight."

"Is it about beer?" Jean asked, only half joking.

Her new friends laughed. "It's an Adriana song," Pax told her. "You know it's going to be about *love*."

It felt like Jean had downed two meatball subs with extra cheese instead of a protein bowl. Some of her internal discomfort must have shown on her face because Jessica sent Pax an *aha!* look.

"Bad breakup?" Jessica guessed.

Jean nodded.

"Are they going to be here tonight?"

"The odds are pretty high."

She placed her hand over Jean's. "Then it's obvious what you need to do. And running away is not it."

"For sure," Pax agreed.

"So then—what?" Jean asked, glancing between them.

"Makeover montage," they sang, before clapping at their own brilliance.

Jean let them mess with her hair and do her nails, but when they brought out the big guns—an eyeshadow palette the size of a picnic table, the airbrushing sprayer, body paints—Jean couldn't be their Barbie any longer.

First she convinced Jessica to let her paint iridescent scales along her forehead and one cheek, after which Pax requested "something you'd find on an old Led Zeppelin album." The next thing Jean knew, she was covering half of Adriana Asebedo's crew in body art.

The process was so absorbing Jean barely thought of the scene she'd painted on Charlie's back. Twice, tops.

"You should do this professionally," Pax said, twisting to inspect the winged creature on one shoulder.

"Is there a lot of demand for face painters? Outside the school carnival circuit."

"I'm serious. You're really good."

"Thanks." Jean took the praise with a grain of salt. This was an uplifting crew, possibly because of the time spent in a hyperbaric oxygen chamber. Over the last few hours, Jean had also been told that she should be a stand-up comic, a magician (she knew one trick), and the flyer in a cheerleading squad.

It was nice of them to try to boost her spirits. Jean recognized the kindness, even though she was a long way from having anything to cheer about.

Eventually her new friends had to get ready for the sound check, so Jean hid out in the bus until it was time for the concert.

Pax and Jessica had made her promise to stay at least for the first set, on the grounds that it would be something to tell her grandchildren. Or the neighborhood kids daring each other to ring the doorbell of her creepy spinster hovel on Halloween, to choose a more likely scenario.

Jean waited until the thumping bass suggested the preshow was underway before leaving her sanctuary. Maybe the free booze and loud music would dull the edge of her aching loneliness.

After sneaking through the web of cables, she snagged a pint glass from one of the banquet tables before creeping around the other concertgoers to find a secluded spot beyond the reach of the lights.

Okay, she could do this. Listen to Adriana Asebedo sing about her love affair with Charlie, endure some beer propaganda, then get the hell out of there. At least she didn't have to pretend to be having a great time. This persona was kind of a vibe. A phantom with a tortured past, gliding through the shadows unrecognized—

"Jean!"

Shit.

Chapter 32

Charlie almost fell over from the relief of spotting her, and also because one of his shoes had come untied.

"I looked everywhere for you. I thought you were gone! There was a girl with curly hair in your wagon, but she claimed not to know you even though she was wearing your clothes."

Jean sipped her beer. Charlie almost asked if she liked it, possibly even enough to stick around for a while, but those were questions for later.

"I guess we all have secrets," she said, mysteriously.

He turned that over in his head a few times. "Are you talking about something specific or is that just a thing people say?"

"I'm talking about relationships."

"Right." Charlie hesitated. "Which ones?" He'd been hoping to go straight to discussing the two of them, but judging by Jean's sigh, the timing might not be ideal.

"Cards on the table?"

"Yes, please."

Jerking her head at him to follow, Jean led the way farther from the nearest concertgoers, where they could hear each other without whisper-shouting.

"Are you getting back together with her or what?" She gestured at the stage, where a giant black banner featured the overlapping double A that was Adriana Asebedo's logo.

That was an easy one. "No."

Jean narrowed her eyes at him, like she was shooting a truth ray directly into his soul. "What were you talking about on the trail ride? The two of you looked pretty cozy."

Charlie hesitated, trying to decide if he was violating Adriana's privacy. "She wanted to apologize."

"For what? I thought *you* broke up with *her*."

He shook his head. "That song is just a song. It's not about me."

"Really? You're telling me you're not the one who got away."

Jean made it sound like he'd tried to sell her an acre of swamp. "Listen." He stepped closer and was immediately distracted. "Is that a new perfume?"

"More of an essential oil. Keep talking."

"Okay." Charlie sighed, wishing he could say something that would paint him in a better light. "We barely dated. A couple of dinners, a baseball game, and then that one beach where everyone lifts weights and rollerblades. I got a sunburn." It felt like his skin had shrunk a size, even before it started peeling. His most vivid memory of that time was an itchy discomfort verging on physical pain.

"There are like a million pictures of the two of you together. And she's wearing different outfits."

"She changes clothes a lot. If they spot her in a dress, she can put on jeans to sneak out the back."

"Sounds exhausting."

That was an understatement. "We never even slept together. In case you were wondering."

"Do I strike you as a prude?"

He shook his head. "Because we didn't know each other that well. That's what I'm trying to tell you. Plus I panicked."

"About having sex with a pop star?"

"All of it. Camera flashes and people yelling, like they're mad at you. It was a nightmare, only you were never going to wake up." Maybe that made him weak, but he didn't want to lie to Jean about who he was. "That's what she was apologizing for. She was sorry about how it changed my life. The attention that came with being in her orbit."

"So you told her you couldn't take it and that was the end?"

"Not in so many words."

Jean looked horrified. "You ghosted her too?"

"No! I did run away. Not my finest hour. But not quite so suddenly."

"Lucky her."

Charlie winced. "I deserved that."

"Maybe, maybe not. Jury's still out. Tell me the rest."

"There's nothing more to tell."

She rubbed her forehead. "I don't get it. If you weren't in love and you didn't have epic sex, why did she write that song?"

"Must have been about someone else. Or she made it up. The songs can't all be about real people." It didn't matter to Charlie, apart from wishing whoever it was would come forward and take the spotlight off him. "I like Adriana. She's a nice person. And very talented."

"Yeah, okay. Don't get carried away."

"I think she might be lonely. That's what made me feel like there was a connection, at first. Even though she's a star and I'm just me."

Jean frowned at him. "So she didn't come here to win you back?"

"She never won me in the first place, Jean. Not like you."

Her huff was skeptical. "You prefer *me* to Adriana Asebedo?"

"Yes! I'm not pining for *her*."

"A dozen tabloids beg to differ."

"Well, they don't know me. I'm telling *you* that it was never that big of a deal—for either of us. She probably thought I was a nice, boring person who didn't have an embarrassing past, so why not? But we both figured out pretty quickly I wasn't qualified for the job of being Adriana Asebedo's boyfriend."

"It's not like it was on your CV: 'Celebrity wannabe.'"

"She understood that. Adriana wasn't upset when we ended things. Mugsy said she took it very well."

"Mugsy? Why was she there?"

"I was a mess. Didn't leave my room for days. So Mugsy flew to California and talked to Adriana."

"You mean, Mugsy broke up with Adriana for you?" Jean's silence was deafening. "Did you ask her to do that?"

"Well, no. I was too caught up in it to see a way out."

"And you didn't feel like that was overstepping? By a lot?"

"She meant well. And it was such a relief, like she pulled me out of a hole in the ground."

Jean grumbled under her breath.

"It was for the best," Charlie assured her. "The publicity was great for business, and my parents finally let me go to Australia, as long as I agreed to come back here after. But at the last minute I couldn't do it, so I got off the plane, and then I met you." He longed to reach for her hands but wasn't sure Jean was ready for that. "I was so happy when you didn't know anything about me except . . . me."

"Perks of answering the door naked."

Charlie didn't remember answering the door. He'd looked up, and there she was—and all he really wanted out of life was to keep being surprised by Jean.

"When this is over, would you consider giving me another chance?"

"Who's asking?"

"Me. Charlie."

She poked him in the chest. "Charlie who?"

He grabbed her hand, holding it in place. "Charlie who loves you."

Chapter 33

It was like their first meeting all over again, only with more clothes. Jean could only stare at Charlie, who had taken her attempt at a knock-knock joke and turned it into so much more. This was a different kind of nakedness, but she was transfixed all the same.

A drumbeat started on stage, slower than the pounding of Jean's heart. "Your dad's looking for you," she told Charlie, since he wasn't paying attention to anything but her.

It felt like she was walking on lily pads, barely maintaining her footing on the shifting surface of this conversation. She needed time to wrap her head around everything he'd told her about his past before she could dig into her present feelings—much less discuss the future.

"You should probably go over there," she said, hoping he wouldn't spot it for the evasion it was.

"Only if you come with me."

So much for her plan to sneak off and scream at the moon until the churning in her head subsided. She nodded at him to lead the way.

From behind, Jean watched Charlie's shoulders tense the closer they got to the stage. The music grew louder with every step, the lights more blinding. She slipped her hand into his, giving a quick squeeze to say *I'm right here.*

Mr. Pike was vibrating with excitement when they finally reached his side.

"This is it, Charlie boy. Everything we've worked for. What a moment! Are you loving this or what, Phil?" he asked, turning to his other side.

Daddy K gave Jean one of his bedroom looks, gaze flitting to the hand Charlie was still holding before he smiled at her again.

A guitarist joined the drummer on stage, adding a new layer to the staccato beat of the drum. Anticipation was building into something thick enough to bite, colored lights flashing their own rhythm. Even this audience of middle-aged beverage moguls was caught in the swelling tide, joining in on a slow clap that was almost in sync.

Girlfriend knows how to make an entrance, Jean thought as the dancers and backing vocalists took their places one by one. She cheered for her new friends, and Pax waved back as the clapping turned frantic. A flurry of movement at the far end of the stage could only mean one thing.

A spotlight flared to life, illuminating . . .

"Smithson?" Charlie said, as Jean's least favorite person walked over to the microphone stand.

"Talk about anticlimactic." She couldn't believe he was doing the intro instead of Charlie or his dad. Then again, making himself the center of attention was vintage Smithson.

"Dad—" Charlie started to say. Mr. Pike shushed him, staring at Smithson like he was about to explain the secret of life.

"Can I get the lights up?" Smithson held a hand over his eyes, squinting into the darkness. The audience muttered as floodlights turned the atmosphere from rock concert to high school football stadium.

Pent-up excitement leaked away like a public fart. Jean caught the dancers and musicians shooting each other WTF looks.

Not good said her instincts. Beside her, Charlie shifted restlessly, apparently sharing Jean's sense of impending doom.

Smithson held up his hand for silence. "Folks, I'm afraid I have some bad news. The concert is canceled."

Mr. Pike laughed, like it was a joke.

"I know it's disappointing." Smithson made a fist, pressing it to the center of his chest. "We've got a major security breach on our hands. Someone violated the NDA, and Adriana isn't comfortable performing under those conditions."

Jean's bullshit detector was blaring. It wasn't just the phony heartfelt delivery. She didn't believe Adriana would have gone to Smithson for help. He was much too smarmy to fool someone who'd cut her teeth in the entertainment industry.

"Gentlemen, you know what to do." Smithson pointed into the audience.

Like everyone else, Jean looked around to see who he was talking about. It wasn't until she'd been flanked by the twin monoliths of Adriana's security detail that it hit her. *She* was Smithson's target.

"That isn't Sockless Tommy's niece," Smithson announced, with unmistakable relish. "Not only did this stranger infiltrate our gathering, she also smuggled in a member of the press."

Oh please. Jean rolled her eyes at the gasps of dismay. It wasn't like she'd exposed their secret sex cult. She would have bet her last five dollars this was payback for beating his ass at poker.

"Sorry, kid," the shorter guard said. "It's time to go. Your friend's waiting at the house."

Her friend? Oh shit. Hildy. Jean hoped her wince wouldn't be taken as an admission of guilt.

Charlie looked from his shell-shocked father to Jean, expression troubled. She waited for him to throw her under the bus. From what she'd seen of their father-son dynamic, there was no way he was going to defy his dad. It might even be a bonding moment for them: disposing of the riffraff.

He drew himself up to his full height. "She's not going anywhere."

It took Jean a few seconds to process the words. "I'm not?"

"Unless you want to," Charlie amended. "It's your call."

Smithson hopped down from the stage, pushing people aside until he reached Mr. Pike. "What's the holdup?"

"She's my guest," Charlie said. "And I don't believe she did anything wrong."

"Or at least not *that*," Jean put in. "The NDA thing."

Charlie nodded as if she'd made his point for him. "Jean can stay as long as she wants."

"Sounds like this is a family matter," Mr. Pike said, loud enough for all the people staring at them to hear. "We'll take a brief intermission and be right back. Why don't you all have a drink? Try the first ever batch of Silent Storm Centennial IPA!"

Jean didn't know whether to be impressed or skeeved out that Charlie's dad had managed to turn the moment of crisis into a PR opportunity. Naming a beer after his son's reputed sex ballad was certainly a choice.

"Dad—"

"Not here," Mr. Pike said through a toothy grin. "We'll talk about this inside."

Chapter 34

Charlie had spent countless childhood afternoons in his father's office. He was good at being quiet, even as a little boy. His dad probably thought Charlie was soaking up important business facts, but mostly he'd been lying under a table, reading about reptiles.

As the years went by, it felt less like a treehouse than a submarine, outside pressure squeezing from all sides. His dad wanted him to take the helm; Charlie couldn't wait to pop the escape hatch.

Tonight was different because Jean was there, which meant Charlie wasn't alone. He wondered what she thought of all the Pike memorabilia, the old beer signs mixed in with black-and-white family photos, as if the people and the promotional campaigns were telling the same story.

The bouncy-haired young woman from Jean's wagon was sitting on the loveseat under the bay window. She waved sheepishly at Jean, mouthing a "Sorry."

Jean shook her head. "Not your fault."

The French doors burst inward, Mugsy hurrying over to Charlie. "You should have let me handle this," she said, scowling at Jean. "Before it blew up."

"Jean is not the problem," Charlie said, before Mugsy could steamroll him. It was easy to be firm when you felt strongly about something. Mugsy looked taken aback, and then thoughtful, giving Jean a second, less hostile look.

"I trust one of you is about to tell me what the problem is,"

Charlie's dad said, sinking into his leather chair as the rest of a ragtag group that included both Koenigs, Smithson, and Sergeant Cowboy filtered into the room. "How in heaven's name did an event one hundred years in the making go kaput?"

That struck Charlie as a slight exaggeration, but his dad had always been prone to hyperbole when stressed.

The girl with the curls glided across the room, beaming at Charlie's father.

"Hildy Johnson of Johnson Media." She reached over the desk to shake his hand. "It is such an honor to meet you. My uncle is a big fan."

His father's face seemed to be at war with itself, the mouth trying to smile while the eyes stayed tight. "Your uncle?"

"Richard Johnson. Also of Johnson Media. He enjoys a pale ale after a hard day of golf."

Mr. Pike laughed, obviously flattered—and charmed. Charlie decided to seize the moment.

"Dad, I'd also like you to meet Jean."

"Oh Charlie," his mother sighed. "I've told you and told you. Her name is Eve."

"Never mind her name, who is she?" his father demanded, tensing up again.

"My girlfriend. I hope." It was ridiculous how much Charlie enjoyed calling her that. "We haven't really discussed the terminology."

"What about Adriana?" His father rubbed his forehead with both hands. "She came here for you, Charlie."

Smithson pushed off from the wall, hooking his thumbs in his belt loops as he flicked his unmoving hair. "Technically, that was my get."

"Of course," Mr. Pike agreed. "Credit where it's due."

Mugsy looked like she was going to explode.

"What is it?" Charlie asked.

"Remember how I needed to tell you something?" Mugsy said under her breath.

He nodded.

"This is about that."

"Right now?" Charlie whispered. They were beginning to attract attention, specifically from Emma Koenig.

"I should have told you before." Mugsy sounded miserable.

He knew that feeling, when not speaking felt worse than the fear of what would happen when you did. "Then go ahead, Mugsy. Let it out."

"You remember when I went to California, to talk to Adriana?" She rubbed her throat, like there was something caught in it.

Charlie nodded.

"We spent some time together. Adriana and me."

"Okay." Maybe Adriana had been angrier than Mugsy let on or said something mean that she didn't want him to know about, because Mugsy was always trying to shield him from the harsh realities of life.

"There was a connection, I guess you could say." The words emerged like Mugsy was winching them up from the bottom of the ocean. "It was unexpected."

Charlie could tell she felt bad, which made no sense. "There was no reason for you not to like her. I liked her too."

Mugsy winced. "I know. That's sort of the issue."

"Whatever it is, I'm sure it's fine," Charlie told her.

"I didn't plan it." She looked straight into his eyes, so he could see she wasn't hiding anything. "I had no intention of anything like that happening, ever. I just . . . fell into it."

"Fell into what?"

"Uh, Adriana it sounds like." Smithson snorted at his own joke. "You hooked up with her? Day-um." He shook out his hand like he'd touched something hot.

Charlie tuned him out, focusing on Mugsy. "When you said you had to stay because there was all that flooding and flights were canceled, that wasn't the real reason?"

"The weather was really bad." She sent him a pleading look. "It rained for days."

"Rain on rain," Charlie said, as the pieces fell into place. "A silent storm."

Mugsy gave a reluctant nod.

Charlie glanced at Jean, whose wide eyes told him he was on the right track.

"That's why Adriana agreed to come! It had nothing to do with me, or him." Charlie flicked his fingers in Smithson's direction. "Because you're the one she wrote the song about."

Mugsy's blush confirmed his hypothesis.

"Which means she's also Honey Baby," Jean filled in, like they were a team of detectives.

"Because her skin is golden or the sweetness of the taste?" Emma Koenig's tone was as clinical as ever, so there was a lag before the full meaning registered.

"I knew there was more to the story!" Jean's friend Hildy lowered the fist she'd just pumped. "Sorry. Pretend I'm not here."

Smithson snorted. "I should have guessed you weren't rocking Adriana's world, Chuck."

"Zip it," Mugsy told him, as the patio doors opened again. Adriana entered the room, a few paces ahead of her security team.

"Is everything okay?" She looked to Mugsy first.

"I don't know." Mugsy seemed to be having a hard time meeting her eyes. "Are you mad at me, Charlie?"

"Not mad," he said slowly. "Maybe a little disappointed. I wish you would have talked to me."

"You had barely broken up. I didn't know what you were feeling, and the last thing I wanted was to hurt you." Mugsy blew out a breath. "I thought if I never saw her again, that would be my punishment."

Charlie gave up trying to puzzle that one out. "How would that work exactly?"

"Then we would both be unhappy. And it wouldn't be like I took something from you."

"Why would I want you to suffer, Mugsy?"

She smiled sadly at him. "You wouldn't. I wasn't being logical."

"As I tried to tell her, before she blocked my number," Adriana said.

Funny how he and Mugsy had both run away and been chased here by the women they—well, he couldn't speak for Mugsy, but Charlie knew how he felt about Jean. He hoped Mugsy would give happiness a chance, but it wasn't for him to tell her what that meant. For now, she still looked like her conscience was scratching her like a sandpaper shirt.

"Some things are too personal to share," he told his oldest friend. "I know how that feels. And I'll always love you, so stop worrying."

Mugsy cleared her throat. Emma handed her a lace-edged handkerchief.

Smithson tapped his gigantic watch. "You know I get paid by the hour? The sexy part is over, so let's wrap this up." Crossing his arms, he turned to stare at Jean.

"I'm not scared of you, Smitty the Shitter." She stuck her tongue out at him.

"What did you call me?" He took a step toward her.

"You heard me. Did you really think people were going to believe someone left a whole Toblerone on the seat of your bumper car? Please."

"How do you know—uh, what are you talking about?"

"You really don't remember me? Maybe if you search that tiny little organ you call a brain, it'll come to you. Travel back to your high school days." She made wibbly-wobbly fingers in his face. "A little burger joint you trashed."

He squinted at her. Jean stared back.

"Holy shit. Cheese Fries? I can't believe it's you. Didn't recognize you without the uniform." Smithson looked her up and down. "Are you stalking me? You always were kind of obsessed."

"No, you absolute dipshit. I'm here for Charlie. He's the one I'm in love with!"

Mrs. Pike gave a gasp that turned into a sigh of delight.

Sergeant Cowboy clapped. "Speak your truth, short stack."

Several phones dinged at once. Mr. Koenig frowned as he checked his notifications.

"What is it?" Mr. Pike asked, fumbling for his own phone. "Pike's Past Its Peak." His voice faded as he read. "That's . . . quite a headline." He blinked rapidly, as if trying not to cry.

Charlie didn't have an alert set up for brewery news, so he borrowed Mugsy's phone to see what had pushed his father to this unprecedented state. It was short but to the point:

The beer company better known for the private life of scion Charlie Pike IV is on the auction block, according to inside sources.

You didn't have to be a business genius to know that wasn't the image his father had been desperate to project this weekend.

"What did I tell you?" Smithson slapped Mr. Pike's desk with the flat of his hand. "Somebody's been talking to the press, and I think we both know who it was."

Jean's friend Hildy glanced over Mr. Koenig's shoulder, scanning the screen of his phone. "Mmmm, no. Even if corporate news was my beat, which it's not, *Beverage Business Quarterly* is not a Johnson Media property. Nice try."

"Then who ratted us out?" Mr. Pike asked the room at large. "It had to be someone with insider knowledge."

Smithson made a show of starting to say something before

cutting himself off with a shake of the head, wiping a hand over his mouth like he needed to physically contain the words.

"What is it?" Mr. Pike asked.

"I'm just thinking, maybe it was Chuck."

Charlie pointed at himself, certain he'd misheard.

"Your dad told me how you're always trying to bail on the business." Smithson shrugged, as if it were a casual remark instead of a devastating accusation. "Don't really have a head for the game."

"That is not what I said," Mr. Pike protested.

"Charlie would never—" Jean and Mugsy spoke at the same time, breaking off to look at each other like two cats grudgingly accepting the other's existence while reserving the right to brawl later.

"All I know is, I put a lot of sweat equity into making this weekend happen," Smithson said, folding a boast into a complaint. "I did not sign on to have my name associated with a public disaster."

"But it's not *your* name, is it, Captain Narcissism?" Jean scowled at him. "And why do you sound like that?"

"I have no idea what you're referring to."

"Like all of a sudden you're Little Lord Fauntleroy instead of Neanderthal bro."

Now that she mentioned it, Smithson's voice had changed. It was less booming bass and more crisp syllables, and he hadn't chortled at his own jokes in several minutes.

"For your information, I went to Wharton. Part of my job is meeting people where they are." Smithson gestured at the office, and Charlie's dad, in a way that did not feel complimentary.

"Code-switching," Emma said.

Jean was still studying Smithson like a specimen under glass. "What else were you pretending about, Little Smitty?"

Charlie tried to see what she was seeing. Was that not a natural tan?

The friend with the curls looked up from her phone. "Um, it looks like he's writing a book."

"Him?" Jean scoffed. "No way. That's so many words."

"I use the term 'write' loosely," her friend clarified. "I'm sure he's paying a ghostwriter."

"Uh, no," Smithson retorted. "And if I did, it would be because I'm too busy for that low-level shit. Let someone else run spell-check."

"Hold on," Jean's friend said. "Here's the description. *The Pabst Smear: How to Build Your Brand by Tearing Down Your Rivals. A Negative Marketing Case Study* by Smithson Oliver Barrett."

"The Pap Smear?" Mrs. Pike whispered.

"Pabst, like the beer," Mugsy corrected. "What do you mean by negative marketing?"

"Why are you asking me?" Smithson looked over both shoulders, like there might be someone standing behind him.

"Because your name is on it," Mugsy reminded him.

Smithson shook his head. "Sounds fake."

"Are you questioning my sources?" There was a dangerous glint in Hildy's eyes.

"Where did you find that? The deal hasn't even been announced." Smithson sounded more annoyed than contrite.

"I know someone who works for your publisher." She turned to Jean, mouthing, "Sorority sister," behind her hand.

"Okay, you want the truth?" Smithson acted like they'd badgered him into confessing, but it was evident even to Charlie that he was happy to spill. "This is my last consulting gig anyway, so whatevs. Yes, I'm going to be the next Tony Robbins. The book is just the first step."

"I don't understand." Mr. Pike still looked hopeful, as if he believed Smithson could spin the situation in a nondisastrous light.

"Listen." Smithson spread his hands in a *be reasonable* gesture.

"We're both entrepreneurs. Men of the world. We know how it goes. Sometimes you're up, and sometimes you're down. And Pike's was going down. Nothing to be done about it."

"Funny you didn't mention that in your pitch. The one explaining why I should pay you a small fortune to help us rebrand." Charlie's dad was gripping his fancy letter opener so tightly, Mrs. Pike tugged it out of his hand.

"At least this way you go out with a bang," Smithson said. "Beer is about celebrating the good times."

"A party planner would have been cheaper," Mrs. Pike muttered.

"I tell you what. I'll mention you in my acknowledgments." Smithson winked at Charlie's dad, like he was doing him a favor.

"So you came here and pretended to help but you were really working against us." Charlie waited for someone to tell him he'd gotten it wrong, but no one pushed back—except Smithson.

"That's a very simplistic analysis." His smile was pure condescension. "In my book, I describe it as a fusion of political strategy and marketing innovation. Think about it. Everyone talks about building buzz, but where does that energy come from? It's not like there's an unlimited supply. When resources are scarce, you have to take what you need."

"By running a smear campaign," Jean said. "Like leaking that story about their business being in trouble. And then what, people buy Barrett's Best instead?"

Charlie spared a moment to admire her quick thinking. Sharp as a tack, his Jean.

"I don't expect you to understand. Mr. K here knows what I'm talking about."

"We have nothing in common," Philip Koenig replied, with devastating coolness.

"Dishonorable is as dishonorable does," Sergeant Cowboy said.

"Papa is a man of honor," Emma informed them. She gave her father a significant look. "He keeps his promises."

"You are correct as always, my darling." Mr. Koenig lowered his head. "I intended to wait until tomorrow to make the announcement, but I feel I should tell you now. I am stepping down."

Charlie's dad looked like he'd just learned the truth about Santa Claus. "What do you mean, Phil?"

"We're breaking up the Koenig empire."

Emma made a tsking sound.

"Corporation, not empire. And I am merely a man." He half bowed to Mr. Pike. "I realize this is not what you wished to hear."

A shriek pierced the air. Charlie's first thought was that his father had lost it and was going to start sobbing into his commemorative pint glass. Then he noticed Smithson jumping onto the nearest chair.

"Snake!" Smithson balanced precariously on the seat, pointing at the floor. "It touched my shoe!"

Charlie crouched to retrieve his poor harmless pet. "There you are, Emma!" he crooned. "You had quite an adventure, didn't you?"

"What is wrong with you?" Smithson made a gagging noise.

Mr. Pike stood. "How dare you speak to my son that way? Charlie is a good man."

Was that how his father saw him, even though Charlie had no interest in making or selling beer? The thought was almost as startling as the pitch of Smithson's screams.

"See how far that gets you in life." Smithson hopped down from the chair, patting his head like a bird settling its feathers. If birds used hair gel.

Charlie raised Snake Emma so she was at eye level with Smithson. Her tongue flicked as she hissed.

"I'll send you my bill," Smithson yelped, before fleeing into the night.

"What a turd," Sergeant Cowboy said.

"My sentiments exactly," Mr. Koenig agreed. Even Charlie's father looked disgusted.

It seemed like a happy ending—bad guy vanquished, snake found, his beloved by his side—but as usual, Charlie hadn't taken the business implications into account.

"What now?" His father leaned his elbows on the desk, cradling his head in both hands. "How am I supposed to face this crowd? I can't pretend everything's hunky-dory after we've been publicly humiliated."

Charlie switched Snake Emma to his opposite hand so he could pat his father on the back. It wasn't the bruising between-the-shoulder-blades pounding his dad favored; Charlie's style was more of a *there, there*. And that was okay. He didn't have to be the same as anyone else, because Jean liked him the way he was.

"Maybe you shouldn't pretend anymore, Dad."

Chapter 35

Jean had worked in enough bars to recognize the early stages of a grown-man meltdown.

"I can't go out there and admit I failed you and your mother. And all the other Pikes." Charlie's father kissed the tips of two fingers before pointing them at one of the framed black-and-white photos on the wall. "You too, Mugsy. And everyone else who works for us. The distributors. Warehouse employees. Truck drivers. Mailroom staff. The whole town—"

Jean tuned out the rest of the self-pity spiral. When Mr. Pike paused to draw in a shuddering breath, she tried to pump the brakes. "Maybe it's not the end of the world. Sometimes a shitty turn of events can open new possibilities."

"Like a breakup leading you to an amazing physical and spiritual connection you can't get out of your head," Adriana suggested.

"Or realizing you only think you want to murder someone because you're actually obsessed with them," Jean said. Charlie's whole body jerked when he realized she was talking about him.

"And getting a chance to tell someone that you never meant you were settling for them because they're *first* best. Not second. The *most* best person ever, as far as you're concerned." Charlie hoped that that was enough superlatives to get his point across to Jean.

"And I will finally have time to enjoy my yacht," Mr. Koenig volunteered.

"Do you hear that, dear?" Mrs. Pike cupped a hand to her ear. "He's going sailing! I've always wanted to take a river cruise."

"Have you ever seen moonlight on the Danube?" Euro Daddy

replied. All he needed was a rose between his teeth to complete the effect.

"I haven't." Mrs. Pike gave a girlish giggle. "How big is your yacht?"

That got her husband's attention. "Sandy!"

"What? I'm sure he has room for both of us."

Mr. Pike sagged in his chair. "We can't just walk away."

"I'm tired. You're tired. Charlie wants to go to grad school." His wife shrugged. "We had a great run."

Mr. Pike's mouth fell open. "But who am I if there's no Pike's?"

One of the random tidbits Jean remembered from her college Intro to Psych class was that babies were easy to mess with because as soon as you moved a toy out of sight, they assumed it no longer existed. Maybe that was how men thought about their jobs. Or at least men like Charlie's father.

"Think of it more like shedding a skin," Charlie said, stroking Snake Emma. "Maybe Pike's isn't ending so much as taking on a new form. Instead of beer, we could make herbal elixirs."

"Are you talking about pot, son?" Mr. Pike looked aghast.

"No, Dad. Mugsy's teas." He gestured at Mugsy, who had been startled out of her resting Don't Try Me face. "Maybe it's our turn to support her. We have the equipment, the network . . . all that stuff."

Mugsy shook her head. "I'm not ready, Charlie."

"You won't know until you try."

Jean could tell from his tone that Charlie was parroting back advice his former babysitter had given him, probably more than once.

"I'll invest in you," he assured her, excitement giving way to a frown. "Most of my money is tied up in company stock, but I could transfer my shares to you!"

Her scowl returned in full force. "I'm not taking your inheritance, Charlie."

"Consider it a loan. Or a rental. How much money do you have on you?"

"About ten bucks," she said, like that settled it.

"Great." Charlie looked around the room. "Anyone have change for a ten?"

"Do you take Venmo?" Adriana asked Mugsy. "I'd love to invest in your company."

Human Emma cleared her throat. "Perhaps you'd prefer a partner with industry experience?"

Charlie glanced between them, clearly not wanting to get in the middle. (Unlike Jean, who hoped the soap opera would play on.) "My advisor thinks I can get a fellowship. For grad school. Tuition and a stipend. I don't need much more than that."

"Because you're a superstar," Jean told him, enjoying the resulting blush.

"An *intellectual* superstar," Emma Koenig pointed out. "Which is the preferable kind."

Meow, Jean thought.

"We can be regular people together." Charlie turned to Jean with a question in his eyes. "But not *normal,*" he added, like that might be a sticking point.

"Better to have realistic goals," she agreed.

Mr. Pike still looked lost. "This is a lot of change."

It occurred to Jean that he might be more like his son than either of them realized.

"Not really." Charlie's voice was gentle. "It'll still be a family business. Does it matter whose name is on a bottle or a building?"

Jean's eyes felt suspiciously damp. Maybe there was hope for privileged white men after all—or at least this one.

"To everything, there is a season," Mrs. Pike agreed, finger-brushing her husband's hair back to a semblance of order. "And for us, this is the season of letting go of the past . . . and going on a European cruise."

Adriana looked at the older couple with a trace of wistfulness before sneaking a glance at Mugsy. "Should I tell my crew to pack it in, or do you want us to stay?"

It was evident to everyone (with the possible exception of Charlie's dad) that she was talking about more than the concert. *Silent Storm,* Jean thought. *Bringing all the girls to the yard.*

Mr. Pike stood, accepting his wife's outstretched hand. "Let's go out there with our heads held high. Make it a going away party."

While the rest of the group headed for the patio doors, Jean pulled Charlie deeper into the house. In the dark and deserted hallway, she pinned him against the wall.

"Other people's lives are so messy," she said, kissing his collarbone.

"Yes," he agreed, pulling her closer.

"They freak out and fly off the handle at the first sign of trouble."

Charlie made a wordless noise of assent as her fingers crept under his shirt and stroked up his sides, not skipping any of the ticklish spots.

There were a million things Jean wanted to ask him, about grad school and where they were going and how much he loved her, but first she had a more pressing question.

"Are you going to introduce me to your snake?"

He was close enough for her to feel him swallow. "I'd love to."

There was a very Charlie pause. Jean was pretty sure she could hear the wheels in his wonderful brain whirring, before he asked, "Which one?"

Epilogue

"I am a freaking pioneer," Jean said as she fished a six-pack out of the creek behind Charlie's house. "Out here in nature, making it work." She pictured herself chopping wood for an imaginary stove and then cooking up biscuits. Maybe pulling a few turnips out of the ground. "Call me Calamity Jean."

She'd never actually eaten a turnip before, but it sounded like something a rugged frontierswoman would grow in her windswept patch of dirt. Definitely the most punk rock root vegetable.

"Do you still miss the wagon?" Charlie asked, interrupting this fantasy sequence. He was sprawled on a blanket in the shade, next to their turnip-free picnic lunch. With his long legs crossed at the ankle and his dark hair tousled by the breeze, he looked like a poet or a pianist—someone who should be wearing a ruffled shirt. As opposed to a budding snakeologist.

"We had some good times in that wagon." She gave him the Groucho Marx eyebrows, even though he was already blushing. Jean suspected she'd still be able to fluster Charlie when he was an old man. Her mouth seemed to know exactly which of his buttons to push, in more ways than one. "But you know I love our yurt."

It was fun to say the word and living there felt like sleepaway camp for grown-ups. Charlie's parents had offered to build a cabin on their property to give the two of them privacy, but that would have felt too permanent. This way they had their own space without being tied down.

After the dust from the centennial settled, they'd packed their bags and flown back to Hawaii so Jean could finally introduce Charlie to her friends. A highlight of the trip was running into Pauline in the checkout line at Foodland, where she first asked Charlie to autograph the back of her receipt and then serenaded him with her favorite Adriana tracks, lending them her own unique lyrical stylings—which didn't stop half a dozen other shoppers from joining in.

From there, Charlie had returned to Australia to spend another month at the research station, before they reunited in California so he could start grad school that fall.

All that travel and relocation would have been outside Jean's budget if she hadn't scored a major art commission last summer. She still remembered the electric thrill of opening the email and reading the words: *Adriana wondered if you could sketch a few concepts for her new album cover, in the style of your tattoo? She'd love you to include some native plants, if possible.*

Fuck yeah, Jean could do that. She didn't care if it was part of Adriana's ongoing campaign to woo Mugsy; she'd taken the opportunity and run with it. Where Adriana led, others followed, which meant enough freelance work for Jean to pay her share of the rent and buy all the art supplies she needed.

And now Charlie was a year closer to being Dr. Pike and they were back in his old stomping grounds. It felt surprisingly good to return to this patch of land at the edge of the Black Hills, with the red and ocher ridges rising like castle walls around the green valley. The word "home" danced at the edge of her consciousness, but Jean wasn't quite ready to admit that. What she could say was that it was a great place to paint. She was trying something new, a series of large landscapes that had already attracted interest from a gallery in Santa Fe, though they didn't like her suggestion for an exhibition title. That was fine—they were still Big Ass Canvases in Jean's heart.

The other client she'd picked up this past year was Mugsy, who was busy getting her tea business off the ground. Over time, and some killer graphic design work, including a bespoke logo and hand-lettered labels, their grudging mutual acceptance (as copresidents of the Charlie Fan Club) had grown into respect, and then friendship. That gave Jean a lot more leeway when it came to teasing Mugsy about the mysterious benefactors who'd pushed the Mugsy's Brewhaha Kickstarter past its fundraising goal in under thirty-six hours. Jean wondered if one (or more!) of them might show up for the official launch party tomorrow night. Her money was on Emma Koenig. It was the quiet ones who took you by surprise. Then again, she hadn't written Mugsy another hit song. (The sultry single "Bruja's Brew" wasn't quite as ubiquitous as "The Lost Weekend" but it had a respectable run up the charts.) Or shared pictures of herself sipping one of Mugsy's Mixers with her thirty-seven million followers.

Fortunately, this shindig was a more low-key affair than last summer's centennial. The guest list was mostly family and friends. Charlie's parents were flying back, fresh from a cruise around the British Isles. In fact, their flight should be landing soon, which meant the clock was ticking. Jean liked the elder Pikes, but not to the point where she felt comfortable getting caught cavorting with their son in broad daylight.

She collapsed on the blanket next to him, reaching for the top button of her shirt. His gaze locked onto her fingers.

"Charlie," she said.

"Oh, sorry." He unfastened his watch and set it aside before stripping off his T-shirt.

That wasn't what she'd been getting at, but his instincts were on point. Someone had trained him well.

"Are we painting?" he asked as he unbuckled his belt. "Skinny-dipping?"

That was her Charlie all over: game for anything.

"Do you know what I love?" she asked.

"Me," he said at once.

If she achieved nothing else in this lifetime, Jean could at least point to Charlie Pike's absolute certainty that he was adored as a signature accomplishment.

"And?" she prompted, accepting the wedge of cheese he handed her.

"Art?" His voice trailed off as she unhooked her bra. "Um, nakedness? Dirty jokes? Not using an alarm clock? Surprises?"

He really did see to the depths of her soul. "I was talking about this," she said, pulling down her shorts. Jean's free hand framed the juicy red apple inked on her hip. It lined up perfectly with his snake—an inside joke, just for the two of them.

"It looks good enough to eat." Charlie pressed the tip of one finger to the circle of red, eyes lighting with mischief. "*Eve.*"

"You want to role-play?" She lunged at him, wrestling him onto the grass. As always, he gave new meaning to the term "pushover," going limp so she could pin his arms above his head. Well, parts of him were limp. "Is there a serpent in this garden or are you happy to see me?"

"I'm always happy to see you. Like a snake that feels less stressed when it recognizes its own kind, because social buffering helps it relax."

"I'll buffer you anytime. Not that I want you to get *too* relaxed, if you know what I mean."

"Jean." His ridiculously long lashes fanned as he tried not to laugh.

"I'm putting out signals. Let's make a mating ball, baby." There were very few bits of snake trivia Jean couldn't bend to her own purposes, which generally fell under one of two umbrellas: making Charlie laugh or seducing him. Ideally, she was accomplishing both at once—like right now.

"We can take a dip in the creek after. If you want."

"Oh yeah? And then what, we run around naked until we dry off?"

Charlie shook his head. "I brought towels."

It was an established fact that towels were their love language.

"I might have to keep you," Jean said, as if the thought had just occurred to her. She squeezed his wrists, pressing the pads of her thumbs to the center of his palms.

"Oh no," he said mildly. "Help." He shifted his arms slightly, making no effort to break her hold. "Looks like you caught me."

Jean bent low enough to whisper in his ear. "We'll call it a win-win."

Acknowledgments

I don't want to jinx myself, but I think I may have finally cracked the code to writing shorter acknowledgments, on this, my fourth book: I'm leaving for the airport in twenty minutes!

Since I am currently looking out the window at a classic Black Hills vista of towering pines and blue sky, I'll start by thanking all the friends from this chapter of my life, especially Lettie and Jim Mortimer, whose beautiful home inspired the setting for several scenes in this book. Thanks also for sharing the Henry Fonda anecdote that cemented my decision to set the latter half of the story here.

Additional thanks to the town of Council Grove and Flint Hills Books, where I spent a delightful writing retreat dreaming up the cowboy poetry scene.

And to my friend and fellow writer Miranda Asebedo, surprise! I named a character after you to commemorate a milestone birthday.

Speaking of writer friends, I could never have written this book without the constant support and keen artistic insights of my cherished compatriot Megan Bannen.

For the particular and intense joy that comes from receiving blurbs from writers I admire with my whole heart, epic helpings of gratitude to Abbi Waxman, Megan Bannen, Katie Cotugno, KJ Micciche, Katie Shepard, Jacqueline Firkins, Julian Winters, and Jen Comfort. If I knew how to make those heart emoticons, I would put two dozen here.

On the publishing side, I am indebted to the hardworking and supportive team at St. Martin's Press that includes: publishing director Anne Marie Tallberg; designers Meryl Levavi and Olga Grlic; managing editor Chrisinda Lynch; Laurie Henderson and Janna Dokos in production; mechanical designer Soleil Paz; the marketing genius of Brant Janeway and Kejana Ayala; indefatigable publicist Zoe Miller; proofreader Courtney Littler; snake-savvy cold reader Susan Barnett; and Lesley Allen, a copy editor with a subtle and elegant touch.

I have to give a special shout-out to my editor, Kelly Stone, who treated this inherited book with the utmost care, intelligence, and enthusiasm. From the minute I opened your first edit letter, I knew I was in excellent hands, for *The Odds of Getting Even* and beyond!

Thank you also to Lisa Bonvissuto for early feedback, and your excitement about this story and these characters.

Sincerest gratitude to cover artist Vi-An Nguyen, who once again combined a beautiful landscape and silly creatures, this time in a sunset-hued western delight, and to the Raven Book Store for years of invaluable support and enthusiasm.

Finally, to my family, who help me every day in ways large and small, from going along on crucial research trips to discussing the ins and outs of the beer business to forcing their book clubs to read everything I write: you know who you are. And I love you all very much.

About the Author

Amanda Sellet is a former journalist and the author of rom-coms for teens and adults, including *By the Book,* which *Booklist* described in a starred review as "impossible to read without laughing out loud." She loves old movies, baked goods, and embarrassing her teen daughter.